C000246882

UNEASY

GEORGE NASH

UNEASY
QUEST

Published in 2020 by

Bizpace Publishing

www.bizpace.ie

ISBN (paperback) 978-1-8380920-0-9

ISBN (ebook) 978-1-8380920-1-6

Cover Design and Interior Layout by designforwriters.com

Dedicated to Bernadette Murphy Nash –
my partner in everything

Contents

GUIDE TO PRONUNCIATION OF IRISH/GAELIC NAMES

Bridín: ....'Bree-deen'
Donal:..'Doh-nahl'
O'Brien:...'O-Bry-n'
O'Muinacháin: ....'Oh-mween-ah-kawn'
Diarmaid: .... 'Deer-mad'
MacMurrough:.. 'Mack-mur-o'
Maurice: .... 'Mor-iss'
Tadhg:.............................. 'Tige - Tiger – without the r'
MacCarthy or McCarthy:....................'Mack-cart-thee'
Caolach:... 'Kway-lock'
Turlough:..'Tur-lock'
Déise:..'Day-sha'

†

THE WELSH NAMES:
Huw:............................. As in the English/Irish 'Hugh'
Daiwin:..'Die-win'

AUTHOR'S NOTE

UNEASY QUEST IS SET during the first two years of the Norman arrival in Ireland (1169-1171). Even though I have generally kept to the historical timeline, some early forays such as the expedition to Limerick where Bridín and Huw meet are fictionalised. Any errors of historical facts and dates are entirely my own.

George Nash.

CHAPTER 1

PEMBROKESHIRE, WALES
MAY 1169

Huw Ashe dragged his father from underneath the bloody body of Arnel de Bourg. De Bourg's body twitched, his dagger still tightly gripped in his left hand. Instinctively, Huw stepped back, out of range of any strike. He picked up de Bourg's sword and rammed it into the dying man's neck, holding it there until the body lay still. His father groaned as he rolled onto his side and was violently sick. On his knees, Huw stared at the bloody bodies of the two men, his heart pounding wildly. At least his father was alive. He looked towards the tree line where de Bourg's two bodyguards lay. His shocked mind began to come back into focus and he remembered the two bodyguards charging towards his father and his own instinctive reaction with his long bow. Two arrows in quick succession, and both men fell. He remembered the woman turning her horse and galloping away. It wouldn't take long for her to alert de Bourg's castle garrison. They had to get away quickly. His father was conscious and he half-dragged, half-carried him to their horses.

'Sir, you have to mount! We have to get away!' Huw had never shouted at his father before. Despite the large blood stains on his chain mail and tunic, Huw could not see any major wounds on his father's body.

'Sir Giles! Mount your horse!' Huw pushed him towards the horse. Still dazed from the ferocity of de Bourg's sword blows, Giles made an instinctive effort to mount. Huw pushed him upwards as the animal stood relatively still. When his father was safely in the saddle, Huw turned to look at the scene. Giles's sword was still stuck deep in de Bourg's underarm. He ran to the body and pulled the sword. After wiping the bloody blade on de Bourg's tunic, he mounted and they rode quickly away. They rode westward for two hours without stopping. Huw kept his mount upsides with the other horse. He feared that Giles might lose consciousness. Even though he got no response, Huw kept talking to his father and made sure he held tight to the horse's back.

'Sir, let us pull in and take some water.' Huw eventually felt safe enough to stop. He had kept to the hilly scrubland, away from the valleys and settlements, knowing that de Bourg's brothers would send search parties. He also knew there would be no court if they were caught. Sir Giles was a landed baron, but the land disputes had escalated and now the de Bourg family enjoyed King Henry's favour. Even if Huw and his father did get to court, they faced a death sentence.

'Huw! We cannot go home.' Giles had drunk the water and a little wine. He reached up from where he sat on the damp ground and grabbed his son's arm. 'We cannot go home!' he repeated, raising his voice when Huw did not respond.

'I know, sir. We are headed west along the coast, towards Sir Robert's castle.'

It was the only avenue of escape Huw could think of. He knew their own castle and holdings would be attacked and searched. There was silence for a few moments as they drank.

'We will have to leave Wales. The de Bourgs are not people to be appeased.' Giles looked across to where his son sat. 'Huw, I am sorry to have dragged you into this.'

'Sir, you tried everything with de Bourg – discussion, intermediaries, law. He was not for listening. Neither was the King.'

'I did not wish to fight him. I did not want to kill him.' Giles's voice trailed off as his throat dried.

'I know, sir. I know.'

†

Robert fitz William greeted his brother and nephew warmly. He was shocked at their fatal encounter with de Bourg, and the sight of Giles's bloodied body. They helped Giles to the infirmary and Robert sent for a healer.

As Giles was being treated, Robert and Huw sat by the fire in the great hall and drank warm wine.

'Huw, I did not think to see you again so soon. And in these circumstances… this is a bad business, Huw.' Robert always spoke what was in his mind. 'Your shoulders have filled out this last year. How old are you now, seventeen?'

'Just eighteen, sir.'

'Your cousins are away in the valleys. Can't keep track of them. Your hair has grown long!'

Huw laughed. His uncle's quick-fire speech was infectious. It had always made him laugh during his eight years living in the household.

'How is your Latin, Huw? Have you kept it up, and the longbow?'

'I still practice bow and sword every day, sir. Just as you taught me. Maybe not so much Latin.' Huw smiled in response to his uncle.

'Your mother and brother?'

'They were happy when I left them last week to go to Sir Giles. Daiwin is sixteen, grown as tall as I am.' Huw paused. Both men were silent for a moment.

'Bad business. I will arrange to get news to them when it's safe.' Robert took another drink. 'Your mother is a strong woman. Daiwin will want to join you.'

'Indeed, sir.' Huw pictured his hot-headed half-brother gathering his bow and sword, and riding to protect them. He trusted his mother to use her guile to keep him occupied in the village.

'They dare not attack me, and if they do, we will defend!' Robert fitz William's anger grew as he reflected on what had happened.

'Brother, Huw and I thank you, but we cannot stay.' Giles glanced at Huw. It was as if he was declining an invitation to a feast. 'We know you would keep us and defend us, but this matter has gone too far. There will be death sentences. The de Bourgs will have the law. The King will find it easy to condemn us, and anyone who helps. You must not become involved; I will need you to stay safe and see after my family while I am away.'

'Away?' Robert looked puzzled.

Huw also looked at his father. He had recovered his senses. Once he had washed and changed into fresh clothes, his injuries seemed less severe, and he had walked unaided from the infirmary. But they had not spoken about any escape plan.

'Huw and I will go to Ireland!'

'Ireland, sir?' Huw could not hide his surprise.

'With de Clare?' Robert spoke as he stood up from the table.

'De Clare?' Huw looked at his father and uncle in turn.

'Richard de Clare is raising an army to help an Irish lord regain his lands. Our cousin, Robert fitz Stephen, is to lead the vanguard. I'm sure he will take us on.' Giles paused for a moment and looked at Huw. 'Our land and livelihood here is forfeited. Strongbow's expedition may give us a chance of a new life. At worst, we will escape the certain death that awaits us here.'

'Strongbow?' Huw's confusion continued.

'De Clare is known to some as Strongbow,' Giles smiled briefly.

'It might work, if we can keep you hidden until fitz Stephen sails.' Robert had been silent as Giles explained matters to Huw.

'I believe fitz Stephen's departure is imminent. We must not stay here more than a day.'

'A day! No time to lose. I will send a rider to Milford to alert fitz Stephen. You shall have armour and horses, and any coin I have at hand.' Robert fitz William paced the floor as he planned. 'Huw, what do you need?'

Giles exchanged a brief smile with his son. His brother was always action first. 'Robert, we are in your debt again. Maybe one day, we can return and repay you.'

Robert waved his hand in dismissal as he opened the door and roared for his steward to attend.

CHAPTER 2

WEXFORD, IRELAND
MARCH 1170

HUW WAITED PATIENTLY AND listened as Maurice Regan spoke about supplies and the weather and the latest political intrigues. He knew that Regan would eventually arrive at what he really wanted to discuss.

'On another matter, Huw, my master's son-in-law, Donal O'Brien, King of Thomond, wishes to break from under the thumb of the High King. It is likely that O'Connor will attack O'Brien and force him into submission. He has asked King Diarmaid for help.' Regan paused to take a draft of wine. 'My Lord wishes to request our Norman allies to go to O'Brien's assistance to defend Limerick against the High King.'

'You have mentioned Limerick before, sir; where is this place?'

'My Lord calls it the arse-hole of Ireland,' Regan laughed. 'It is way west of here, at the mouth of a large river. Getting there requires a long trek across some wild Irish land, but a strengthened alliance with O'Brien could prove valuable to us all,' Regan hinted that rewards would be forthcoming for the Normans' assistance.

'I will inform my lords of your request. I'm sure they will want to help Lord MacMurrough's son-in-law,' Huw replied.

'Thank you, Huw. My King and his nobles have great respect for you.' Regan paused and looked at Huw. 'Your language skills and diplomacy have helped our alliance greatly.'

'Your teaching has helped, sir. This is a complex country with many Kings, though I only know of some.'

'Indeed,' Regan laughed. 'There are some I chose not to mention, but you should get on well with O'Brien and the Munster men.'

'Munster?'

'A warlike province to the south west. Two kingdoms now, with O'Brien in the north and the MacCarthy to the south. Often at war with each other.'

'A bit like Leinster then?'

'Some would say more savage and clever,' Regan laughed again. 'We try to leave them to themselves, except when the High King takes an interest.'

'As now?'

'Yes, as now. Lord MacMurrough does not wish O'Connor's influence to grow.'

'Will O'Connor start a war in Munster?' Huw was keen to know what might face his comrades in Limerick.

'He will threaten and rattle his spears but a show of power will send him home. More so if our Norman allies display their strength.'

'I will explain this to Sir Robert. When would you wish us to travel to Limerick?'

'The minute you are ready. Our spies in Connacht tell us that O'Connor is gathering an army to march south.'

'Connacht?'

'O'Connor's kingdom to the west.' Regan was enjoying Huw's confusion.

'So many kingdoms for a small country.'

'We would rid ourselves of a few with your help.'

'I'm sure we will agree to assist Lord MacMurrough's son-in-law in Limerick.'

†

The expedition to Limerick was the first time since coming to Ireland that Huw and his father had been separated. They had fought together on many of MacMurrough's raids, as the dispossessed King re-asserted control in Leinster. Now, Robert fitz Stephen had required Sir Giles to stay in Wexford as the main Norman forces departed under Sir Robert's command. Huw was concerned they would be away for months, and he would not be there to protect his father. He smiled as he considered the irony of this role reversal: the child worrying about the wellbeing of the father.

'Huw, is there no end to these bloody boggy pathways?' John Daws lilted in his Welsh accent. 'My boots and clothes are all sodden wet. I think this whole country will drown someday.'

'What makes it so different to south Wales, John Daws?' Huw spoke what most within earshot had been thinking. 'It never rained over your village, I suppose.'

They had been on the march for four days. The Irish scouts had said it would take four or five days to reach Limerick, but progress had been slow. The 300-strong Welsh archers were lightly clad and could move quickly even on the myriad of pathways that meandered through the heavily-forested and boggy terrain of central Ireland. The hundred or so men-at-arms and the fifty heavily-armoured mounted knights moved at a much slower pace, and so the archer band constantly had to wait for their Norman comrades. Their food supplies were running low, and they would have to forage if they did not reach Limerick soon. *No shortage of water at least*, Huw thought, and smiled to himself.

'I don't think there's much to smile about, Huw boy,' John Daws drawled on. 'What if we run out of food, then? We'll have to go looking in some of them villages we saw.'

'No one will let you go near any villages, John Daws. Not with those Irish women around, anyway.' Huw poked Daws in the back with his bow stave and made him jump.

'Right you are, Huw boy, he can't be trusted with sheep, never mind women,' Will Hen squeaked with laughter.

Huw laughed as they marched on. Daws and Hen. The big and the small. Huw was tall but Daws towered over him. Broad-shouldered, he could shoot an arrow farther than anyone in the troop. Will Hen was small and slight and spoke with a strange, squeaky, north Wales accent. He was deadly with a knife at close quarters. They had arrived in Wexford with Sir Robert fitz Stephen's Norman army nearly a year ago. Daws and Hen were part of the archer twenty-five under Huw's command.

'You there, hold up!' a knight called, as he approached from the rear on horseback. 'Where is Huw Ashe?'

Huw stepped out from his comrades in front of the Norman knight's horse. The animal reared up and nearly unshipped his rider.

'I am Huw Ashe,' Huw spoke calmly, as he reached out and held the horse's rein.

'Sir Robert fitz Stephen wants to talk to you at the rear of the column,' the rider eyed Huw.

'Tell Sir Robert I will be there shortly.' Huw let go of the horse's rein.

'See that you do, archer,' the knight replied, as he turned his horse away.

'You're in trouble now Huw, boy,' John Daws guffawed, punching Huw in the arm.

'Keep following the scouts, and don't let Daws be prattling

on about food all the time.' Huw turned and followed the knight back along the sodden pathway.

'Huw Ashe, how are you enjoying your trip across this fine land?' Fitz Stephen welcomed Huw warmly. Meiler fitz Henry slapped Huw on the back in greeting as the group of knights dismounted.

'Let us talk as we walk,' Fitz Stephen smiled as the party trudged along the soggy ground. 'Huw, you are to interpret when we meet with the Munster King. MacMurrough tells me that O'Brien only speaks a rough form of Gaelic. He has a close counsellor called Munchin or Munichain.' Fitz Stephen had difficulty with the Irish names. 'I want you to talk to this counsellor and find out as much as you can about the situation and what we might be facing.'

'Yes, sir,' Huw responded. 'Do we know anything about this Limerick town?'

'A bog hole, was it, that MacMurrough called it?' Meiler fitz Henry's voice carried loud through the morning air.

'Worse than that!' one of the other knights answered.

†

Two days later, the mist gave way to driving rain as they continued to trudge through heavy bog land. At least Limerick was visible up ahead, or so the scouts told Huw, as they trotted back along the column to inform the commanders.

'Can't see a thing in this rain,' John Daws continued in his complaining tone to no one in particular. 'Do you think they cook their food in Limerick?'

'We'll soon find out. There's a welcoming party up ahead on that ridge.' Huw could make out about a dozen horsemen on a raised piece of ground in the middle of what was mainly flat terrain.

'I hope we don't have to fight them, Huw, before we get our dinner,' John Daws's voice was a bit edgier than it had been while giving a running commentary on their surroundings as they marched across Ireland.

The archer troop slowed to standstill as they saw the mounted warriors ahead. Shortly, fitz Stephen and two mounted knights rode up from the back. One of them towed an un-mounted horse.

'Mount up, Huw Ashe, and come with us,' fitz Stephen called to Huw as his horse walked by. Fitz Stephen, Huw and the two knights trotted forward towards the men on the ridge. Four riders left the group and advanced slowly to meet them.

When the two groups met, a small, flabby man in an ornate purple cloak addressed the Norman group in Latin.

'I am O'Muinacháin, counsellor to Donal O'Brien, King of Munster. My master, the King, requests that you accompany us to his camp, where food will be provided before he holds council,' O'Muinacháin spoke formally and slowly in a high-pitched nasal voice.

Huw translated into Norman French, even though fitz Stephen and the others probably understood the Latin. Fitz Stephen gave his assent, sending the knights back to inform fitz Henry to organise the men to follow.

O'Brien's camp looked like a small wooden town, surrounded by a large number of rough fabric tents. The camp was close to a wide fast-flowing river, with a walled town and a busy port on the opposite bank. As Huw rode towards the camp he could see in the distance that the river broadened into what looked like an estuary. They must have travelled across Ireland and reached the western coast. He gazed at the walled town of Limerick with some wonderment. Protected by the waters of the large river, it was far from the 'bog-hole' that MacMurrough had described. Conversation on the journey to the camp had been muted, with O'Muinacháin reluctant to engage in discussion. Huw listened as O'Muinacháin and the other Irish officers spoke to each other in Gaelic. He understood enough to know that they were scathing of Huw and his rank. O'Muinacháin resented having to ride in Huw's company. He also seemed suspicious and apprehensive about the presence of the Normans. On the only occasion that O'Muinacháin addressed him directly, it was to try to find out the overall strength of the Normans in Ireland, and if additional forces would follow from England. Huw was polite but evasive with his answers.

When the soldiers and archers had pitched their tents, and hot pottage with bread and ale had been distributed, the Norman leaders were summoned to the great hall. King Donal O'Brien was seated on a raised chair with O'Muinacháin and his nobles standing around. All were well dressed in ornate robes and seemed prepared for a formal occasion. Huw was immediately aware of the rough state of his own clothes and those of the Normans, after their long march across the country. O'Brien rose and spoke in Gaelic. Huw understood much of what he said and recognised that he was issuing a formal welcome to the Norman lords and army. O'Muinacháin immediately translated O'Brien's words into Latin. Huw did not translate into Norman French and did not reveal he had understood O'Brien's Gaelic. Fitz Stephen made a formal response, and O'Brien began to introduce his nobles, who stepped forward and nodded as their names were called.

O'Brien called forward his wife Orla and introduced her two lady-attendants as his cousins. Huw heard only one name, Bridín O'Brien, as the ladies bowed to their King and his guests. He stared at Bridín as she bowed. Her long dark red hair was plaited and, as she rose, his eyes met hers for a moment. He thought he saw a brief flicker of a smile on her face before she and her companion melted back into the group standing around the King. Was that a smile of greeting, he wondered, or was she just smirking at the state of his clothes and the dirt in his hair?

The guests were invited to sit at the banquet tables and the smell of roast meat made Huw realise how hungry he was. He hoped John Daws, Will Hen and the boys were well fed. Throughout the meal, Huw felt that Bridín O'Brien's eyes occasionally glanced in his direction, but anytime he looked she was busily eating or talking with the Irish nobles. O'Muinacháin sat close to Bridín. The King's small fat counsel attacked his food gluttonously, but also kept a wary eye on Bridín. As the drink flowed and the talk became louder, Huw was able to cast longer glances at Bridín and O'Muinacháin, without being observed. O'Muinacháin slobbered over the table as he stuffed enormous quantities of meat into his mouth. Huw saw that he passed some of the choicest meat on to Bridín's plate. She smiled at O'Muinacháin but at the same time paid him little attention. O'Muinacháin's eyes had become glazed and his face redder as he downed more and more of the strong drink being served from earthen jugs. His eyes darted fleetingly from his food to Bridín and then to whatever man she was talking to. Huw noticed that Bridín stopped short of flirting with O'Muinacháin and the other men around her, and yet seemed to be attentive to all.

His thoughts of Bridín were interrupted as someone at the King's table began to sing. The conversation and laughter died down as the man's strong voice carried across the room. The King and his nobles seemed transfixed by the song. Huw understood enough of the Gaelic to know that the song was about the O'Brien kingdom in Munster and the losing of a fateful battle. As the song went on, tears welled in the eyes of the King and some of his nobles. The Normans at Huw's table were silent, knowing that what was happening was important to their Irish hosts, even if they didn't understand the words. Huw observed a quizzical look on fitz Stephen's face and nodded to him. He would explain the words later. Meiler fitz Henry drank deep from his cup, trying to drown a stifled laugh.

When the man finally finished singing, the room erupted with loud cheers and applause. Swords appeared and were banged loudly on the wooden tables. O'Brien left his seat and approached the Normans. He spoke so loudly and incoherently in Gaelic that Huw could barely make out a word or two. It sounded like some sort of a threat to slaughter people and take back their lands. The Norman knights looked alarmed at the King's approach and their hands edged towards their swords. In a brief pause before they had time to react further, Huw grabbed his cup and quickly got to his feet. He bowed, then looked O'Brien in the eye, raised the cup above his head and called loudly in his best Latin:

'Victory to the O'Briens!'

There was silence in the room. The King stood there staring at Huw and the Normans. From the corner of his eye, Huw saw Bridín O'Brien step forward towards the centre of the room. She raised her cup and exclaimed:

'Victory to the O'Briens, the true Kings of all Munster!'

In an instant the Irish nobles were on their feet, shouting and banging their swords on the tables. The Normans quickly followed suit and toasted their Irish hosts. The King roared with laughter and went around slapping his Norman guests on the back and muttering incomprehensible words to them in Gaelic.

Huw glanced across the room at Bridín. She raised her tankard and smiled warmly at him. Huw raised his cup in return, and they toasted each other.

CHAPTER 3

LIMERICK
APRIL 1170

BRIDÍN O'BRIEN SAT IN an alcove of the great hall and waited patiently. King Donal was holding court, his voice booming loudly through the building as he gave his judgements. He had summoned Bridín earlier to come and read to him.

'No!' the King roared. 'Enough, enough! Land, cattle, is that all you people think about?'

Bridín knew the King was angry and tired. His voice always gave him away. She waited for the final explosion of words.

'Get out. Get out now! Talk. Negotiate. You are all of the same blood. Same family. Come back to my court when you have a solution.' O'Brien paused and his voice became a little calmer. 'A peaceful solution,' he added. 'I will come and deal with you in the field if there is any bloodshed. O'Muinacháin will help you if needed. Now go!' There was silence in the great hall except for the shuffling of feet as people left. 'Bridín! Are you there?'

'Yes sir, I am here.' Bridín bowed as she entered the main hall.

'Ah, my young cousin. Let us go and take some wine. You will read to me?'

'As you wish sir.'

†

'Cousin, what do you make of our Norman visitors?' They sat at the table in King Donal's private rooms.

'I don't know, sir.' Bridín was surprised at the seriousness of the King's tone.

He looked at her as she drank from her cup. 'Come now, we are family and I know you have opinions about everything. You often let me know!' He paused. 'You have been at our council meetings. Translated their Latin words better than O'Muinacháin. Do you trust them?'

'I think they are formidable, sir. They are heavily armed and seem capable. We do not fully understand if they intend to stay in Ireland.' Bridín paused and looked at her King.

'Go on, cousin Bridín, tell me what you think.'

'They may be trustworthy, but I do not think we should trust them. They will help with your quest against the High King as they promised Lord MacMurrough. But they will also serve their own interests. Whatever they might be.'

'And your fellow translator, the Welshman?'

'Huw Ashe?' Again Bridín was taken by surprise at the King's question. She felt herself blush. 'He is different. Speaks Latin and French. I think he also understands Gaelic.'

'Gaelic?' This time it was the King's turn to express surprise. 'He has made an enemy in O'Muinacháin. He wants me to ban him from our councils.'

'Will you sir?'

'My counsellor sees conspiracies everywhere. It's his job.' The King laughed. 'Perhaps you can find out more about our Welsh translator and keep us informed?'

'Yes, sir, as you wish.'

'Now, read to me our holy Latin texts and tell me what they mean. After, you might ask my Queen to attend me.'

'Of course sir.'

'Bridín, one other matter. You have been in our household for some years now and are of our royal blood. How old are you?'

'Seventeen, my Lord.'

'Seventeen. Are you happy as my Queen's lady?'

'Happy indeed, sir. I am very well treated by the Royal household. You have educated me like no other woman. I could not ask for more.'

✝

Later that evening Bridín sat alone in her quarters and pondered the King's questions. She was indeed happy. Why would she not be? She had a life that many would envy. She was related to the King and of royal blood, but her father was distant in line, third cousins at best, and not wealthy. She had been surprised when she was sent to the King's court; surprised even more when the King insisted that she should be educated. This was usually reserved for the male bloodline. She had never questioned the King. He was her master and treated her respectfully. Sometimes she acted as the King's Latin translator when O'Muinacháin was not present. Other times, as today, she was also an unofficial counsellor. Could O'Muinacháin be jealous of her? She had never thought of it before. And why was the King's counsellor wary of Huw Ashe?

✝

Weeks passed, and the Normans waited in Limerick with no action. Each day seemed to bring different news about the movement of Rory O'Connor's forces. The High King had a large army on the move towards Limerick, but the scouts brought conflicting information of the army's actual location and strength. The Norman leadership grew restless.

'So many councils to discuss useless information,' Fitz Stephen complained to Huw. 'Many want to return to Wexford.'

The Welsh archers were glad to have the time to recover after their long march across the country. Huw used the time to get more information about the nature of the conflict and the strategic forces at play between the different kingdoms in this part of Ireland. He relayed any information he got to fitz Stephen.

On a cold April evening, Huw left the Normans and the Irish nobles as they feasted and drank after another council meeting. He wanted to take a closer look at the walled town on the other side of the river. He was standing amongst some tall reeds looking across the water when he sensed someone close behind him. His hand instinctively drew his dagger. He kept perfectly still and waited for his attacker to make the first move.

'Don't worry, if I wanted to kill you I would have done it before now.' Bridín's voice was soft and calm. Huw turned, expecting to see her with a couple of armed bodyguards. She was alone. 'I think, Welsh Huw Ashe, that you understand much more of our Gaelic language than you reveal to us.'

Huw knew by her tone that she was teasing him. *But part of her is trying to find out how much of the language I really understand*, he thought. *Perhaps she is a spy for O'Muinacháin.* That thought left him as quickly as it had entered his mind. He decided to be honest.

'I understand much of what is said, but I do not have enough words to speak well.' Huw stumbled over some of the Gaelic words, and he noticed a fleeting smirk on Bridín's lips.

'Well enough spoken, that I can understand. You could put your dagger away, if you feel safe with me,' she laughed.

'Lady, I would like to learn more about Limerick and the people here. Would you be willing to tell me?'

'You do not need to call me lady. My name is Bridín, and I'm happy to tell you anything you wish to know,' Bridín replied slowly, allowing her words to be easily understood. 'Let us walk along the riverbank and we can talk.'

It was cold on the riverbank and they wrapped their cloaks around them as they walked. Huw learned that Bridín was Donal O'Brien's cousin and had joined the Queen's service when Orla had married the King.

'King Donal insisted that the monks teach me Latin. He sometimes gets me to read and translate for him.'

'We are two translators, then. I was sent to my uncle's household to be educated.'

'You also speak French?' Bridín asked.

'I have a Norman father. My mother, Gwen, is Welsh.'

'Is there a Welsh language also?' She looked mildly curious.

'Yes, my Welsh is the best!' Huw laughed. He told Bridín about his life and family in Wales and his close relationship with his Norman father. 'Sir Giles and my mother…' Huw paused, struggling for words. 'They could not marry. His marriage was already arranged.'

'And you?' Bridín stopped and looked at him.

'Where did I come from?' Huw laughed. 'I was born in my mother's village. My father made sure we had everything. He never denied me.' He paused and looked away.

'You don't have to speak of it more.' Bridín touched his arm.

'It's not something I have spoken much about. It seems strange now.'

They walked on closer to the river.

'My father's wife died in childbirth some years ago. He has two younger children and I have a half-brother about as old as you.' Huw stopped and half laughed, realising the family puzzle he had described.

'A complex family! What is your brother's name? Is he here too?'

'Daiwin is at home in Wales with our mother. We have had no news of them for a year.'

'That is sad. It must be difficult. Will you return home?' Bridín held her breath fearing she may have asked too much.

Huw did not answer immediately.

'My duty is here with my father. I do not know what will happen.'

Huw wanted to tell Bridín about their land dispute with de Bourg and the fatal outcome. He wanted to explain that he and his father came to Ireland as fugitives, not invaders. 'My father and I joined this expedition more by accident than design. We got caught up in the adventure of it.' He knew his explanation was vague and only partially true. 'Are there other things you wish to know about us Welsh and Normans?'

Bridín had many questions about the Normans, and their reasons for being in Ireland; whether more would come, and if they would travel to Limerick. Huw suspected there was concern amongst the O'Briens about having a heavily armed army of foreigners in their midst, even if they were currently allies. He related the story of how Diarmaid MacMurrough had gone to Wales to enlist Strongbow's help to win back his kingdom in Leinster.

'I am not sure, but Strongbow may come with more forces.' Huw stopped, unsure if he should continue. 'My father may wish to bring our complex family to Ireland and settle here.' Bridín stopped to look at him and he saw the surprise and puzzlement in her face. 'My father quarrelled with a neighbouring lord over land. There was conflict, a fight…' His voice faltered and he struggled with his emotions as he recalled the fatal encounter with Arnel de Bourg and their forced exile from Wales. 'We did not have the favour of King Henry. We had to leave our home and escape to Ireland.' Huw fell silent for a moment; he had told Bridín more than he wanted. 'Now it's your turn to tell me something. What was that song about, at the first banquet?'

'Ah, the MacCarthy and the O'Brien!' Bridín smiled.

Huw learned that the O'Briens and MacCarthys were bitter enemies. The MacCarthy Mór was now King of the eastern side of Munster: land that had been ruled by the O'Briens when Munster was united as one kingdom. He began to understand the fierce emotion he had seen in the eyes of the King and his nobles that night.

They stopped close to a gap in the riverbank. Bridín mentioned, to his surprise, that it was possible to ford the river at that point. Huw looked across the dark expanse of fast-flowing water to where the walled town stood.

'What do you call it?'

'The Shannon River.'

'The Shannon River,' Huw repeated the name to pronounce it correctly. Bridín smirked at his Welsh inflection of the name. 'Does King Donal rule the town?'

Bridín considered her answer. 'Yes and no,' she replied eventually. 'The Northmen control the town and the shipping trade. They pay homage and give some service to the King when required. In return, he leaves them in peace and guards them from attack across the river.'

The daylight was fading rapidly and the wind from the river felt icy. Bridín shivered, and Huw instinctively put his arm around her to protect her from the cold. She did not draw away as he put his large cloak around them.

'Just for a moment until I warm up.' She smiled an impish smile and Huw tried to determine if she was serious or not.

'Yes, I need to get warm too. Perhaps we should return to camp.' Bridín took a half step closer, as if to stand in his way. 'Lady, are you trying keep me prisoner here?'

'You've learnt a lot of useful Gaelic words in the last few minutes.'

Neither could contain their laughter as they huddled close to keep warm.

✝

Huw and Bridín were so engrossed with each other that neither noticed the two men who had followed them. O'Muinacháin and his bodyguard were now crouched behind a thicket of bushes on a raised bank about a hundred paces away. O'Muinacháin strained to hear what they were saying, but the noise of the wind and the river prevented him from making out the words. He was torn between thoughts of getting Bridín away from Huw and wanting to know what they were saying. When he saw them move close together, O'Muinacháin's jealousy took over and he stepped out from his hiding place.

'Lady Bridín, your King needs you to attend him,' he called loudly across the reeds.

Bridín and Huw tensed at the sound of the unexpected voice and stepped away from each other.

'The King commands you to his presence,' O'Muinacháin repeated, as he walked towards them. 'You must go to him now!' His eyes flitted back and forth from Bridín to Huw who saw anger—and something else—in O'Muinacháin's eyes and face. What was it? Scorn? Hatred?

'Yes, Counsel, I will attend the King immediately,' Bridín replied. She nodded to Huw as she left him on the riverbank as darkness descended.

Later, Huw would learn that, in return for his service, King Donal O'Brien had promised O'Muinacháin a wife of higher rank from amongst the O'Brien family. O'Muinacháin had his eyes and heart set on Bridín.

CHAPTER 4

BANKS OF THE SHANNON RIVER
APRIL 1170.

FITZ STEPHEN WAS HAPPY when the news came that Rory O'Connor had crossed the Shannon north of Lough Derg and entered the kingdom of Thomond.

'Action at last! We were all growing restless,' he whispered to Huw at the council meeting when O'Brien relayed the news.

'Yes indee,d sir. Our archers will be glad to move. Too much practice time.'

Huw would be happy to stay in Limerick, but fitz Stephen was right about the restlessness. Many thought they had come all this way for no reason; Huw had found a reason.

He was disappointed when Bridín was not present at the council meeting. He had not seen her since their encounter on the banks of the river. O'Muinacháin and his camp spies now watched him closely. He wondered if Bridín was also being watched, and if she thought about him. Maybe he was just a source of information. Had O'Muinacháin sent her that night at the river? He wished he could get to meet and talk to her again before the army departed. But even if he could leave his duties, how would he contact her? The King's guard would hardly just let him walk into the royal compound and knock on her door. He knew that a friendship between a noble-born Irish lady and a lowly foreigner would not be approved by the

King of Thomond. O'Muinacháin would have told the King of their meeting by the river. His spies would know if they ever met again; it could be dangerous for her. Maybe the King has already sent her away? Huw's thoughts were troubled as the combined Thomond and Norman army left Limerick and marched north along the Shannon River.

†

The army had been on the move for two weeks. There had been a number of encounters with the High King's forces, but no open field battle. O'Connor's army outnumbered O'Brien's, but the High King was reluctant to engage in full scale warfare. The presence of the Norman forces seemed to act as a deterrent and most of the encounters were little more than skirmishes. Huw's Welsh archers were at the forefront of a number of encounters. Rory O'Connor's light cavalry was vulnerable to the deadly fire of the Welsh archers, with many of his mounted warriors dying from arrow fire as they probed in the open field. O'Connor's officers eventually recognised the threat posed by the archers and withdrew whenever a major encounter threatened. The Norman knights and men-at-arms presented a formidable barrier at the centre of O'Brien's army. They advanced as O'Connor's men retreated from the archer fire.

O'Connor's army was eventually pushed back to their original crossing point on the Shannon. They formed strong defensive positions, while the bulk of the army crossed the wooden bridge. Donal O'Brien, happy to see the High King retreat, did not seek to push home his advantage by pursuing O'Connor into Connacht and when the last of the surviving rear guard crossed the river, they burned the wooden bridge. Huw and the Norman leaders watched as Donal O'Brien rode up to the river bank. Across the water, Rory O'Connor, the

High King of Ireland, rode forward from amongst his officers. The two Kings waved to each other and O'Connor shouted something in Gaelic. Huw was unsure, but he thought that O'Connor said that he would be back. O'Brien roared what sounded like a taunting challenge and then laughed and turned away.

The Thomond army camped on the banks of the Shannon for a number of days, while their scouts crossed the river and reported back on the movements of the High King's forces. When O'Brien was satisfied that the High King's army had dispersed and returned to their lands in Connacht, he left a garrison at the river crossing and brought his army back to Limerick.

†

During the week of feasting and celebrations that followed their successful campaign, Donal O'Brien and his nobles paid homage to their Norman allies for their part in the successful defence of Thomond. Fitz Stephen and his knights were happy to enjoy the hospitality, even though messengers had arrived from MacMurrough seeking their immediate return to Wexford.

'Two days rest, and then we travel,' fitz Stephen told Huw. 'You will be happy to return to your father?'

'Yes, sir, glad indeed.' Huw did not disclose his mixed feelings about leaving Limerick. He had not seen Bridín since they returned. He had expected that she would be at the banquets celebrating the King's victory, but although Queen Orla and other noble ladies were present, Bridín was not. Huw became resigned to leaving Limerick and never seeing her again.

†

On the eve of their departure from Limerick, Huw left the feast in the King's hall to return to his Welsh comrades. The drink was flowing freely, and his departure was hardly noticed. As the evening was calm, Huw walked towards the river before returning to his quarters. His thoughts were of Bridín as he sat on a bank close to the water. What might he say to her if they met again? Did she even like him? Would he leave, and never see her again?

The birds calling in the reeds and the loud noise of the river intermingled with his thoughts of Bridín. Lost in the noise and his thoughts, he did not notice the two men approaching from behind and they quickly dragged him to the ground. His thoughts disappeared totally when a third attacker stunned him with a blow to the head. He was then gagged and his hands tied securely behind his back. Lifted to his feet, Huw's world went black as a sack was pulled over his head. Half senseless and unable to see, he was marched away through the reeds with a man on either side holding him by the elbows. After a short while he was bundled face down into a cart which trundled quickly away. Prone on the floor of the cart, Huw felt helpless and his head throbbed. When his senses partly returned and he tried to get up, he was trodden on by the men on either side and pushed back down.

†

'My toes are so itchy, wish I could scratch them,' Huw spoke softly to himself.

There was little hope of scratching anything from where he hung upside down, tied to the branch of a tree by his ankles; anytime he moved, he swayed from side to side. The sack was still tied over his head so he could not see, but he could hear a number of men talking close by. He guessed he had been in the cart for about two hours. He could not be sure, as his full senses had only returned after he had stopped struggling and lain quietly on the cart floor. He had tried to listen for sounds as the cart rolled noisily over rough terrain, and on a couple of occasions he had thought he heard water. Perhaps they were just passing close to a small stream. When they eventually stopped, he had been dragged a short distance and strung up by the ankles. He had hung in this position for nearly an hour and his feet and legs were numb. Thinking about his feet made the itching worse.

Huw tried to listen to the men talking but he couldn't make out any clear sentence. Just a word or a sniggered laugh here and there. He wondered what they were waiting for. Were they just going to let him hang there to die? It did not make any sense, as they could have killed him anytime they wanted. He would not even see the dagger or sword thrust coming. When he relaxed and allowed his body to swing easily, the pain and numbness subsided a little. His mind also became sharper and he realised that his captors must be waiting for someone to arrive. Why else was he still alive?

He didn't have to wait long to find out.

The voices of the men died down as at least two horses approached. The sounds of hooves stopped close by and he could hear the horses blowing heavily. Huw recognised the high-pitched voice of one of the newcomers. Like the horses, O'Muinacháin seemed out of breath as he spoke to the guards. Huw's heart began to race as he heard footsteps approaching. He took a deep breath and waited.

CHAPTER 5

WEST TIPPERARY
MAY 1170

Bridín muttered under her breath as she helped Queen Orla undress. The Queen had drunk freely in the banquet hall and lingered much longer than usual. When she finally left and got to her chambers she wanted to talk. Drowsy from too much wine, she was unable to help as Bridín struggled with her robes, as if she were a sleepy child.

'Ah, Bridín, I'm sorry you're stuck here. You'd've enjoyed it,' the Queen slurred. 'I'll talk to the King again. A young woman shouldn't be a prisoner.'

'Yes, my Lady, thank you.'

The King had ordered her to be confined to the Queen's quarters after her meeting with Huw. She had not met the King that night, and there was no explanation; O'Muinacháin must have told him of their meeting. At least she had not been sent back to her family.

'The King likes you, m'dear. You are one of his favourites. I'll ask him at the right time.'

'Yes, my Lady, thank you.'

'We mustn't let that slobbering fool have his way.'

'Fool, my Lady?'

'The O'Muinacháin fool.'

Eventually, with the help of the two maids, she got the

Queen into bed, where she fell asleep almost immediately. Bridín wondered what she had meant about O'Muinacháin. She would try to find out, but for now she just wanted to escape for a few hours. Leaving the sleeping Queen in the care of the maids, she slipped out of her chambers, hoping not to be seen. Being known to the guards, she passed through the outer gates without difficulty. The night was bright and she wanted to think. Careful not to be followed, she walked along the pathway through the reeds to the river, towards the spot where she had met Huw Ashe. She half hoped that he might be there again. Hearing voices ahead, she instinctively crouched down amongst the reeds and listened as the footsteps of a number of people passed by no more than twenty paces away. She followed them, creeping through the reeds. After a short distance they came to a clearing. She watched as three men bundled another man into a cart and drove away westwards along the path close to river. The captive had a sack over his head but Bridín recognised the clothes of a Welsh archer. She knew the man was Huw.

Bridín stared in disbelief as the cart creaked quickly away. Her mind was blank and she seemed frozen to the spot where she crouched. A bird screeched loudly in the reeds and Bridín jumped. Her senses returned as she realised Huw was in great danger. She had to do something. But what? It was useless for her to follow the cart. Alone, she could do little. She had to get help. Quickly she went through her options. The men who had taken Huw were Irish warriors, probably from the King's army. Could her cousin Donal O'Brien have taken Huw captive? For what purpose? She couldn't go to the King in case he or some of his nobles were involved. Bridín thought about going to Huw's archer comrades in the camp. They would certainly want to help, but how could she tell them what had happened? She didn't speak their language, and they didn't understand Gaelic.

She would have to seek help from the Norman commanders. Bridín ran back towards the camp. As she left the reed bank, she almost crashed into Meiler fitz Henry adjusting his tunic. Fitz Henry was startled but quickly recovered his composure.

'My lady, what are you doing running about in the reeds?'

Bridín did not understand his Norman French words, but she was reassured by fitz Henry's manner. She quickly blurted out in Latin what had happened. Fitz Henry struggled to understand, but eventually recognised enough of the words to know that Huw Ashe had been taken and his military brain immediately took over. He would get two or three of Huw's comrades, and some horses from the camp. Bridín was to get warm clothing and return to this spot to wait for them. Fitz Henry was reluctant to take her, but Bridín insisted.

'I know the path the cart took, and you will need a Gaelic translator.'

✝

Fitz Henry had difficulty again with language when he located the men he needed. They had just a few words of Norman French, but they understood quickly that Huw was in danger. Fitz Henry insisted that a small group on horseback would travel quicker than a mini army, and would be more likely to surprise Huw's captors. It was quickly agreed that John Daws and Will Hen would go with fitz Henry. In less than an hour, fitz Henry, the two Welsh archers and Bridín were mounted and on the pathway along the Shannon banks where the cart had headed. The wine fitz Henry had consumed at the banquet was beginning to clear from his mind. He knew they would have to catch up quickly, before Huw was taken inland where he might never be found. *That is, if he is still alive,* fitz Henry thought grimly to himself. He calculated, from what Bridín had told him, that the cart had over two hours start on them, but they would travel much quicker than the cart while the moon stayed bright in the night sky. With luck, maybe Huw's captors would stop for food when they felt safe.

†

Huw kept still as the sack was removed from his head. His eyes struggled to focus in the fading light as his body swung to and fro. For the first time he realised that he was hanging some way above the ground. He had imagined that his head was just above the grass as he hung by the ankles. Being higher than he had thought, he felt more vulnerable. O'Muinacháin put his face close to his.

'So, Welshman, how does Ireland look when it's upside down?' O'Muinacháin spoke in Gaelic, and his soldiers sniggered.

Huw counted five men in the light of the campfire that blazed in the centre of the clearing, with probably one or two more on sentry duty. 'Your breath stinks, O'Muinacháin. Could you move away a bit?' Huw replied, in perfect Latin.

'We'll see if you're so clever when your eyes are looking up at you from the ground.' O'Muinacháin's voice quivered with rage as he grabbed Huw by the hair. Huw looked at him, and O'Muinacháin noted the confusion in his eyes. 'Ah, I see you're not familiar with how we deal with hostages who have lost their usefulness.' His voice calmed somewhat as he drew his dagger from his belt. Holding Huw's hair with one hand, he raised the dagger towards his head, stopping just before the point touched the eyeball. Huw remained perfectly still. 'When a hostage is no longer a bargaining tool, or needed as security, we may allow him to live, but we take out his eyes before he is sent back to his people. It acts as a reminder for future bargaining.' O'Muinacháin was smiling and enjoying the threatening power he held in his hands. Huw said nothing. 'So you see, Welshman, the best that can happen is that you will lose your eyes. The worst, if you do not answer my questions and agree to do what I tell you, is that you will lose your life, very, very, slowly.'

O'Muinacháin dragged out the last words in Gaelic, so that all the men in the camp understood. Then, with a quick flick of his wrist, O'Muinacháin slashed his dagger across Huw's forehead, cutting the skin through to the skull all along the hairline. Huw clinched his mouth tight to prevent a scream. The pain was instant and blood dripped through his hair onto the grass.

'You hang there for a while to think about what I said.' O'Muinacháin spat and walked away toward the fire. 'Food and drink, before we butcher our Welsh meat!' he laughed towards the men around the campfire. Their laughter was stilted and nervous in return.

†

Fitz Henry, Bridín, and the two Welshmen followed the path as it meandered northwards, close to the banks of the Shannon. Bridín led the way and kept up a steady pace. She was not willing to slow down. At a bend in the river the pathway turned sharply inland and they paused to consider whether to follow the path or the river. They could see no signs that the cart had left the path, so they turned inland, away from the river. The pathway became rougher, with patches of boggy turf that forced them to slow to a walk. The muddy ground had marks made recently by a cartwheel. The landscape around quickly changed from wet reed land to heather and bush. Looking ahead through the moonlight, fitz Henry noticed some dark clumps, indicating the beginning of a forest.

'Let us dismount and leave the pathway. We should circle around and approach the point where the path meets the trees from the side. Walk slowly, and be as quiet as possible.' Fitz Henry spoke quietly in Latin, gesturing all the while. Everybody understood quickly and they set off in a broad arc across the scrubby heather. Fitz Henry thought it likely that the cart men might make camp for the night. If so, they would also post a sentry where the path entered the forest. They had circled out about four hundred paces when John Daws motioned them to stop.

'One of us needs to creep forward to deal with the sentry, and scout a bit in the forest. If there is a sentry, he will surely hear the horses before we get near,' he drawled in Welsh to Will Hen.

'I'll go, Daws, you're too big and clumsy. I'll have a dagger in his neck before you could catch your breath,' Will Hen's squeaky voice made fitz Henry smirk.

John Daws grinned and nodded. He knew that Hen was best with the dagger. Daws motioned to the others what was intended and they nodded their agreement. Will Hen was already away through the heather, low to the ground and deadly quiet.

†

They settled down to wait for Will Hen's return. Bridín quickly became impatient and began to walk around. John Daws produced some bread and cheese from his satchel and offered it around, settling down to enjoy his dry supper when it was clear that no one was interested. After a while they all became impatient and began to peer through the darkness toward the trees. Fitz Henry was about to suggest he should go and find out what was happening when Will Hen reappeared as silently as he had left them.

'One sentry by the pathway.' He sliced his fingers across his throat to indicate what had happened. 'About two hundred paces into the forest, six men around a campfire, Huw strung up by the ankles from a tree.' Will Hen was breathless as he quickly blurted out what he had seen in his sing-song Welsh, while signing the numbers with his hands. On a dry piece of ground he marked out the camp details with his finger. 'Huw looks hurt, but he's alive.' Hen looked around as he spoke, holding up both thumbs as a sign.

'We need to go now before the sentry is missed.' Fitz Henry gestured towards the trees with his fist, knowing the others didn't understand his Norman-French. Fitz Henry knew that the others didn't understand his Norman-French.

He started to check his weapons and went and tied his horse securely. The others followed suit. Fitz Henry thought that the archers' long bows would be useless in the darkness, unless they got close and had light from the fire. He looked at the Welsh men and pointed to their daggers and swords. They nodded their understanding, but they also strung their long bows.

'Lady, you stay here and mind the horses,' Fitz Henry motioned to Bridín.

He was met by a fierce stare as Bridín drew a dagger from somewhere under her robe.

'I'm coming with you.' Bridín's language and intent was understood by all. Fitz Henry shrugged. The two Welshmen knew better than to argue with a fiery woman holding a dagger.

CHAPTER 6

WEXFORD
MAY 1170

HUW'S HEAD ACHED. THE combination of being hung upside down for some hours and the knife wound in his forehead made his head feel painfully tight. It was like something was tightening, trying to crush his skull. Occasionally one of the men passed by and gave him a push or a twirl, so that his body was almost constantly in motion. They thought it funny, but Huw began to feel the familiar nauseous feeling he had when he was seasick. He fought the feeling of wanting to throw up. He tried to relax his breathing and tried to think of Bridín, of his mother, of Wales, of anything but getting sick.

'Now, let us do our business, Welshman,' O'Muineacháin spat out as he approached Huw. 'Hold him steady!' he shouted at two of his men. The men held Huw by his shoulders as O'Muineacháin moved closer and spoke clearly in Latin to Huw's upside down face. 'In return for your sightless life, you are to give up all contact with the Lady Bridín. When you consider it, I'm sure you will not want to burden her with a blind man. Also, I want to know about the strength of the Norman forces in Ireland. What are their intentions for this country? Is the English King to come here? Will they seek lands in Thomond?' O'Muineacháin paused. 'If you give me this information, and I believe you, your life will be spared.'

Huw felt the spittle from O'Muinacháin's mouth hit his face as he spat out the words. He stared blankly into the darkness. *If I could convince him to cut me down, at least I could make a fight of it*, he thought.

'Well, what is your answer?' O'Muinacháin rasped impatiently.

'I'll tell you what I know.' Huw made his voice hoarse and he slurred the words out slowly. 'But it's difficult to talk in this position.'

'You'll stay where you are until I'm finished with you!' O'Muinacháin grabbed Huw by the hair, while the two men held his shoulders firmly. He drew his dagger and pushed the point into the skin between the bridge of Huw's nose and his left eye. A loud scream broke the night air and echoed through the forest. Huw had closed his eyes tight but he recognised the sound of the arrow as it buried into the soft neck tissue of one of the men holding him. Hot blood spattered onto Huw's face. He knew that the blood wasn't his. O'Muinacháin froze wild-eyed as a second arrow smashed into the eye socket of the second man. This one did not scream as the force of the shaft knocked him sharply backwards. Huw swirled gently. The first man continued to scream, as he writhed in pain on the ground while grappling with the arrow in his neck.

'Huw Ashe! I tried to tell those mad Welsh friends of yours not to shoot arrows in the dark. Lucky they missed you.' Huw recognised the Norman-French voice before he saw Meiler fitz Henry standing about ten paces away from where he hung. His vision was blurred as blood seeped from the cuts on his face. *At least I still have both eyes*, he thought. 'Your friends are killing those men by the fire and I don't have a long bow. So I won't be able to save your life, as that little fat man will probably cut your throat before I get to him.' Fitz Henry spoke slowly in Latin so that O'Muinacháin might understand him. 'However, I will tell your father that you died well, and I promise that the little fat man will have a very slow, painful death.'

Huw heard O'Muinacháin whimper as he sucked in his breath and dropped the dagger to the ground. He remained fixed to the to the spot where he stood, his frightened eyes darting from Huw to fitz Henry and then to his men who were dying near the fire.

In three quick steps fitz Henry was beside them. With the point of his sword he forced the shivering O'Muinacháin to the ground and kicked him until he was turned face-down in the dirt.

'Move, and you will lose your head,' Fitz Henry growled at O'Muinacháin.

Huw felt strong arms around his shoulders and waist as fitz Henry cut the rope.

'Bloody hell, Huw boy, what have they done to your pretty face?' John Daws grinned broadly as he eased Huw to the ground.

Huw wanted to laugh and tell John Daws what he thought of him, but the nausea took over and he began to throw up. As he passed out, he felt the softness of Bridín's hands as she wiped the blood and muck from his face.

†

Huw's head was sore when he awoke to see Bridín's smiling face looking at him. She had a wet cloth and was wiping the congealed blood from his hair.

'Luckily that thick Welsh hair of yours will cover the scar on your forehead,' Bridín spoke softly in Gaelic and Huw though it was the sweetest sound he ever heard. He looked at her, glad that he still had his eyes.

'Huw, I think we should skewer that fat bastard!'

Fitz Henry's loud voice interrupted Huw's thoughts of Bridín. He gestured towards O'Muinacháin, who was gagged and bound to a nearby tree. Huw sat up and looked across to where O'Muinacháin was slumped and shivering in the cold morning air.

'Sir, I don't like the man much, but perhaps it would be better if he stayed alive. King Donal would never let the disappearance of his counsellor pass without retribution. The Lady Bridín, and all of us, will be missed from camp.' Huw spoke quietly so only the three of them could hear. He paused to collect his thoughts. Looking at Bridín, he saw agreement in her eyes as she nodded. 'We will have to return to Wexford soon, Sir Meiler,' Huw paused to glance again at Bridín. She was looking at him intently. 'The Lady Bridín has placed herself in great danger by helping me. I will have to ensure her safety before we leave. Maybe I can use O'Muinacháin to bring that about.'

'A little Welsh blackmail, eh, Huw? But perhaps you will not be returning to Wexford with us?' Fitz Henry had an amused look in his eye as he looked at Huw and Bridín in turn. Huw thought he noticed a slight blush on Bridín's face before she turned away.

'I must return to Wexford to fulfil my duty to my father and our Norman comrades,' Huw said, slowly and deliberately. 'But I will return to Limerick, as I'm destined to do.'

Fitz Henry and Bridín were aware of Huw's seriousness and intensity. Neither said anything.

'I will speak to O'Muinacháin and offer him the choice of dying now, if he does not agree to my proposal, or later, if he ever breaks his promise to remain silent and not to harm Lady Bridín.'

Bridín and fitz Henry nodded their assent. Neither felt the need to speak.

O'Muinacháin shook as Huw approached him with his sword drawn.

'Counsellor, your eyes and your life are forfeited.' Huw pointed the sword close to O'Muinacháin's face. 'We have all agreed that I should take out your eyes before killing you. That seems just, as it is what you intended for me.'

'Please, I would not have harmed you!' O'Muinacháin shut his eyes tight and turned his head away.

'Shut up!' Huw put his sword under O'Muinacháin's chin, forcing him to turn his head back. 'Open your eyes and listen well. You would already be dead, except for the Lady Bridín. She pleaded and you have her to thank for your life.' O'Muinacháin opened his eyes and looked at Huw. 'I may not kill you… if I get your word that you will not reveal anything of this. You must not tell King Donal, and you must protect Lady Bridín.' Huw paused to let his words sink in. 'Your King and Sir Robert fitz Stephen have made a pact and will exchange messengers. I *will* know if any harm comes to Lady Bridín. Do you agree to protect her?' O'Muinacháin still shook as he stared at Huw. 'Well? What is your answer?'

'I will do as you say. The King shall not know. The Lady Bridín will be safe.' O'Muinacháin spoke in short bursts, struggling for breath.

'Swear it! Swear it on my sword and your own blood.'

O'Muinacháin flinched as Huw's sword grazed the underside of his chin. 'I swear it. I swear.'

Huw knew O'Muinacháin could not be trusted, and his promises would not hold long in his absence. He would have to find a way to return to Limerick.

†

On their ride back to camp Huw developed a chill that began to turn into a fever. Blood still seeped from the wound on his forehead.

'Huw Ashe, you can not walk back across Ireland in this state.' Bridín rode alongside him, a little behind the others.

Huw did not reply. He had difficulty keeping his senses and staying on his horse.

'Stay in Limerick until you are well enough to travel.' Bridín nudged her horse closer to his, thinking he was going to fall. 'I could look after you. The King would allow it, I'm sure,' she added quickly.

'My Lady, I don't think I'll have to walk to Wexford. Sir Robert promised me a horse.' Huw forced the words and a brief smile.

'You seem to have difficulty staying on a horse.'

Huw laughed through his pain as he held tight to the horse's mane.

'Lady, I wish to thank you for what you have done. Sir Meiler told me. If it wasn't for you…' Huw's coughing forced him to break off. 'You have put yourself in great danger. O'Muin-acháin—' Huw's words were interrupted again as he coughed violently.

Bridín reached across to grab Huw's reins. She brought both horses to a stop and helped him dismount. 'Huw, you are ill. You need care.' She gave him some water, from the water bag John Daws had given her. Fitz Henry had ridden on towards Limerick with O'Muinacháin.

'Lady, it will pass quickly.' Huw sat at the edge of the pathway. 'Better, now that we're not moving.' He smiled briefly. 'I have to return to Wexford. My father… my duty.' Huw looked at Bridín. 'I wish I could stay, Lady, to make sure you are safe.'

'You can call me Bridín. I've told you before.'

'Lady Bridín.'

'I am not Lady to you, but I would be your friend.' Bridín poured water on her hands and reached out to wash the blood from Huw's face.

'Can we be friends, Lady Bridín? You are Irish, noble-born; I am a Welsh archer.'

'Yes, we can, if we want to be... and isn't your father a landed Norman baron?' Bridín smiled.

'Yes, I suppose I'm a half-bred Norman.' Huw laughed, then coughed. 'You mustn't make me laugh. It hurts.'

'A non-laughing, half-bred Norman Welsh archer. I've always wanted a friend like that.'

Huw coughed long and loud as he tried to hold his laughter.

†

As Bridín and Huw approached Limerick, they dismounted again. They could see that preparations were already underway for the Norman departure to Wexford. John Daws had ridden ahead.

'Will we go to the riverbank?' Huw asked as they walked the horses.

'A dangerous place for Welshmen. Should you not go and get your wounds attended?'

'Talking with you is a cure itself.' Huw paused, fearful he had said too much.

'Your Gaelic improves daily. We should talk some more then.'

They tied the horses amongst the reeds and walked to the riverbank. Huw shivered and Bridín put her cloak over his shoulders and her arm around his waist.

'Just making sure you don't collapse.'

'Thank you, Lady. This seems familiar; I hope O'Muinacháin doesn't appear.'

'Maybe you *should* have killed him back there.' It was Bridín's turn to shiver and she drew Huw closer.

'Coming here with you, I thought the same. Will you be safe?'

'There was something Queen Orla said about O'Muinacháin. I think she will help me if needed.'

'I wish I could stay. I will find a way to return.'

'I would like that, Huw Ashe.'

'When my father and family are safe, I will come back, Bridín.'

'What did you say?'

'When my father and…'

'Not that, the other word.'

'Bridín.'

'Say it again.'

'Bridín.'

As Bridín kissed him, he felt his dutiful resolve to return to Wexford waver. The kiss was quickly interrupted as Huw's fever forced him to break away and cough repeatedly.

'Are you trying to kill me, Lady?'

'You and your duty will do that well enough without my help.' Bridín chided as she gave him water to ease the cough.

CHAPTER 7

SLANEY RIVER BANKS
JUNE 1170

GILES FELT APPREHENSIVE WHEN Huw departed for Limerick with fitz Stephen. He had wanted to go with the expedition, but fitz Stephen asked him to stay in Wexford to oversee the construction of a major fortification, a request he could not turn down. It would provide valuable experience, and give bargaining power with fitz Stephen and Strongbow when he sought lands to settle his family. He missed Huw and his language skills. Communicating with his Irish workers was difficult. After a year in Ireland, he also missed his Welsh home and longed for news of his family. His hopes for settlement were quickly shattered and news from Wales came unexpectedly.

Word had reached Wexford of another Norman force, led by Raymond fitz William, landing on the coast. Rumour was rife that this small force was the precursor to a larger army led by Strongbow himself. Giles looked forward to meeting his cousin Raymond and getting news of Wales and Strongbow.

He watched closely as a crew of men worked on the roof of the main building. From his vantage point on a building platform, he saw a small group of riders approaching from the south while they were still some way distant. The riders' mail and helmets glinted in the early evening sun. Giles hurried to his tent to wash and put on a clean tunic to be ready to meet the new arrivals, giving orders to prepare food and wine.

'Raymond! Welcome to the first Norman castle in Ireland!' Giles called out, recognising the leading figure as the riders approached.

Raymond dismounted and approached, looking intently at the figure greeting him.

'Giles fitz William! I did not recognise you at first.' He beamed and embraced Giles in a bear-hug. He was a low-sized, heavy set man. Younger than Giles, he had a rough beard and his armour was spattered with mud and grime.

'We have food and wine prepared for when you are rested. There are tents with hot water for you and your comrades to wash.' Giles beckoned towards the small group of men on horseback. If he had looked closer he would have seen the scowling faces of Henry and William de Bourg. They had hung to the back of the group when they recognised the man greeting them.

†

Giles waited in the mess tent for his guests to join him. He was looking forward to getting all the news from Wales and the recent landings. He turned as two knights entered the large tent. Giles stepped forward to greet the men but stopped abruptly, recognising Arnel de Bourg's brothers. For a moment no one spoke. Giles was keenly aware of being without armour or sword. The de Bourgs did not have armour, but their swords and daggers were on their belts. One small food dagger against two broad swords; Giles calculated the odds of surviving.

The taller of the two brothers eyed Giles coldly and spoke with a rasping nasal voice.

'Fitz William, you murdered our brother in cold blood, and we have come to avenge his death.' Giles listened, preparing his mind for combat as Henry de Bourg continued. 'Tonight, we have to eat with you, as our loyalty to Sir Raymond demands. Tomorrow, we will come for you and kill you like the common dog you are.' De Bourg paused and Giles's body relaxed slightly even though his mind remained tense and alert. 'Know this, fitz William, when we have cut up your body and thrown it to the dogs, we will have our revenge on your family.' De Bourg spoke slowly and deliberately. 'Your children and bastards will follow you to hell, as will your Welsh whore, when we are finished with her. We swear this on the blood of our dead brother.'

Henry de Bourg's voice trembled with rage and his lips quivered as he spat out the final oath. Giles made no reply but his mind raced. He would have to protect his family at all costs.

Just then, the tent flap flew open and Raymond fitz William barged in, followed by the other knights.

'Giles, I see you know Henry and William de Bourg!' Raymond quickly introduced the other knights to Giles. 'Now, I'm starved, where's this food and drink you promised us?' Raymond laughed as he clapped Giles on the back with his broad hand.

†

Giles urged his horse forward, as the morning sun began to burn away the fog that clung over the bogs and heather. He had crept quietly out of the camp in the middle of the night and was now riding as fast as he could towards Ferns. All through the meal with Raymond and his knights, his mind had been in turmoil. He had drunk very little wine and while the others were sleeping after hours of feasting and drinking, he had returned to his quarters and thought about his situation. He did not like running away, and felt a deep sense of loyalty to Robert fitz Stephen. However, the fortification was almost built and his fellow knights could be trusted to complete the work. If he stayed and fought the de Bourgs he would probably be killed; his family would not be alerted, and they might all suffer the same fate.

Giles realised he would have to go to Huw to warn him, and then to Wales to protect Gwen and his children. After writing a quick message for one of his officer knights, asking him to complete the building work, he donned his sword and armour, saddled his best horse and walked quietly out of the camp. He headed for Ferns intending to ask MacMurrough to provide him with scouts to take him to Limerick. He knew there were dangers in revealing himself and his plans, but he had to take the risk; travelling alone across Ireland was unthinkable. He had never been far west of Wexford Town, but MacMurrough might have news of fitz Stephen and the forces in Limerick. Giles went over his plans as he galloped across the heather towards Ferns. With luck he would get there before nightfall.

†

By the time Giles reached Ferns, a small advance party of scouts from fitz Stephen's force had already arrived. The news that Huw would soon return cheered Giles somewhat, even though the de Bourg threat played on his mind. It was a relief that he did not have to reveal his situation to MacMurrough. Giles was never sure of how MacMurrough would react and whose side he would support in any conflict. It was possible, too, that the law in Ireland would side with the de Bourgs. King Henry would certainly side with them, if the killing of Arnel de Bourg was brought to his court.

The following morning, Giles's spirits were uplifted by a visitor to his quarters.

'Sir Giles! Sir Giles!'

Giles rose quickly from his table to grab his sword scabbard. He just had time to unsheathe and face the tall Welsh archer who entered.

'Sir Giles! It's me, Daiwin!'

'Daiwin Ashe! You are here… from Wales? How did you get here? You are welcome!' Giles blurted out random words in his surprise. He dropped his sword and stepped forward to embrace the young man. 'But why are you here? Your mother… is she—?' Giles didn't get to complete the question.

'Mother is safe, sir, for now. She sent me to find news of Huw, and you. Well, I wanted to come, sort of insisted.'

'Did my brother Robert come and tell you what happened?'

'Yes sir, he came. Wanted to protect us, bring us to his castle. But we stayed in the village.' Daiwin paused for breath. 'Other men came too, watching us. But they stopped coming and things were normal. A few months back, it was.'

'De Bourg men?'

'I think so, sir, but they never did anything. Just watched.'

'Waiting for me and Huw to show up.'

'That's what we thought, sir.'

'And now, Gwen, your mother, she is still in the village?'

'Yes. Brothers and cousins all around. She is safe,' Daiwin insisted.

'Safe for now, I hope.' Giles decided not to tell Daiwin just yet of his recent encounter with the de Bourg brothers. 'Come and sit, and eat. Let us talk of Wales and I will tell you something of Ireland.'

'What of Huw, sir?'

'Good news, good news. Word is that they return from Limerick soon.' Giles smiled, noticing Daiwin's puzzled look. 'Sit and eat. I will tell you all.'

†

The main Norman force from Limerick arrived in Ferns two days later. Giles was taken aback when he saw the wounds on Huw's face, as his comrades helped him from his horse.

'You look like you have been through a battle or two.' Giles and Huw smiled as they clasped hands and embraced.

'It probably looks worse than it is, sir.' Huw's pale face forced a grin as he tried to reassure his father. He couldn't disguise that he was weak and unsteady on his feet, and pale and gaunt looking. The fever had weakened his body further during the long journey back to Wexford, despite fitz Stephen having assigned John Daws and Will Hen to look after him. Giles knew he needed rest and time to rebuild his strength.

'Huw, I know you need food and rest, but I have to talk to you and Daiwin.'

'Daiwin?'

'Ah, did I not mention? Daiwin is come from Wales!'

'Daiwin is here in Ferns?'

'Indeed.' Giles smiled at Huw's disbelief. 'We need to talk. It is urgent and cannot wait. I will send for him.'

†

Once the three of them were gathered in his quarters, Giles told them about his encounter with the de Bourgs and their revenge oath.

'It is not just the three of us. Your mother and my other children in Wales are also in danger.' Giles's voice wavered.

There was silence for a while as they all took in the heightened danger their family now faced. It was Daiwin who broke the silence.

'Sir, let me go and bring my mother and your children to Ireland. If they are here, at least we can protect them. If you go, it will seem as though you are running away and the de

48

Bourgs will follow you.' Daiwin hesitated and the others looked at him with surprise. 'Huw is sick and needs to recover. The sea journey would just add to his sickness and he would be a hindrance.' Daiwin smiled and Giles nodded. They knew of Huw's propensity towards seasickness. 'If you can get us leave to go, I could take a couple of men and be in Wales in a day or two.'

His father and half-brother were impressed with the logic and simplicity of Daiwin's plan. They knew that a couple of Welsh archers would not be missed and the de Bourgs would not be aware that anything was amiss.

Giles pondered the idea and considered Daiwin. How old was he now? Seventeen? He had grown a lot in the last year and was strong and sturdy. He could obviously think for himself. Huw was not well enough to travel and if Giles asked to return to Wales, fitz Stephen would want to know the reason. It was best that fitz Stephen and the other Norman commanders did not know that he had killed Arnel de Bourg. The law would be on the side of the de Bourgs.

Huw had difficulty thinking clearly. His head throbbed and the fever made him shiver and sweat at the same time. He wanted to protest that Daiwin was too young for such a task, but the calm logic that his half-brother displayed said otherwise. When he recovered he could follow Daiwin to Wales, if needed.

'You must take John Daws and Will Hen with you.' Huw spoke with authority even though his voice was hoarse and weak. 'Sir, you will need to give them letters of safe passage and letters for your brother,' Huw said to Giles, who nodded his agreement.

'That's settled then. I will go and get ready.' Daiwin was up and out of the tent before they had time to say another word.

CHAPTER 8

THE WELSH COAST
JULY 1170

'Let's get something proper to eat and drink before we head inland, Dai.' John Daws's demand made the others think of food. They had just stepped on to the quay in Milford Haven.

'You might be right, John, I'm hungry after that sea air. But not too much to drink. We have a journey ahead, and a job to do.' Daiwin's reminder was as much to himself as it was to his two companions.

While they ate, Daiwin briefed Daws and Will Hen on the main details of their task. He omitted the killing of Arnel de Bourg, instead hinting that that Giles and the de Bourgs were in dispute over land. Daws and Will Hen did not question him too closely. It was enough for them to know that Huw and his family were in danger.

†

Giles had decided it was best if Daiwin went to his home village to collect Gwen before travelling on to his brother's castle, where his two young children were being fostered. Gwen would be well known to Sir Robert.

It was late on their second day in Wales when they reached the village. Daiwin was shocked to see the remains of his family home. Only some of the mud walls remained; most of the house was gone. Burned remains of the thatch roof littered the ground. Inside the ruin, the few remaining pieces of furniture smelled strongly of smoke.

'Daiwin! Is that you?' Dai turned quickly and reached for his sword. Will Hen and John Daws did likewise.

'Uncle Thomas!' Dai relaxed as he recognised his mother's brother. 'What's happened? Where is my mother?'

Thomas quickly told them how the de Bourg soldiers had come and terrorised the village.

'They beat my two boys and threatened to hang them.' Thomas shook and his voice quivered when he mentioned his sons. 'They tied us up and gagged us and warned everyone in the village not to interfere. Then they took Gwen and burned your cottage.'

'They took my mother! Where?' Daiwin asked.

'I don't know, Dai, all I know is that they tied her hands and put her on a horse and rode off. At least when she left here, she was still alive.' Thomas spoke the last words slowly as though they gave him some comfort. 'I'm sorry, Dai, there was nothing we could do,' he pleaded softly.

Daiwin's mind was working furiously and he barely heard his uncle speak. Assuming his mother was alive, the de Bourgs would have taken her to their castle and would hold her as hostage until they were sure of having their full revenge. It was unlikely they would kill her until they had news from Ireland.

'What happened was not your fault.' Daiwin put his hand on his uncle's shoulder. 'You might have some food for us before we set off for the de Bourg lands.'

†

Riding quickly, Daiwin, Daws and Hen stopped only once, at a small village inn for food. They easily passed as young men on the road seeking service as soldiers with the barons and landowners. The innkeeper was happy to tell them about the local barons and John Daws chatted with the innkeeper about the de Bourgs and their castle. When they left the inn they knew the castle's location, the access roads, and the typical people who came and went.

'We should probably keep pretending to be looking for service as soldiers,' John Daws said, as the three of them sat in the warm sunshine on a hill overlooking the road. The de Bourg castle and surrounding town were visible in the distance. It was early afternoon and the town was busy, with people working in the fields and carts entering and leaving the castle. 'It looks like people can come and go as they please. Should be easy enough to get in.'

'There will be guards checking people they don't know,' Will Hen chirped.

'We'll find a way of getting in, but getting out with my mother might be a bit harder.' Daiwin's tone was rueful.

After talking for a while, it was clear to Daiwin that it would be best if he entered the castle alone. If anything happened to him, one of the others could attempt the rescue, with one kept in reserve to return to Ireland if needed, but if the three of them were killed or captured, Huw and Giles might never know what happened. He would approach the castle alone, seeking enlistment as an archer. John and Will would split up and seek work in the town. They agreed that if Dai gained access and had not returned in three days, one of the others would attempt to get in. If nothing happened within a further three days, the third man would return to Ireland to inform Huw and Giles. Daiwin knew the plan was shaky and many things could go wrong, but it was the best they could come up with.

†

After a restless and hungry night in the open, Daiwin approached the guard house at the main castle gate. The gate was not yet opened for the day and the two guards barely looked up as Dai drew near. There was little greeting as Dai quickly explained that he was an archer seeking service. One of the guards looked him over and, noticing the broad shoulders and the bow stave, told him to wait while he called the sergeant. After half an hour, the sergeant arrived.

'So, you want to join my lord's army,' the sergeant sneered. 'Are you able to use that long bow of yours?'

'I can use it when I need to.' The words emerged as defiant, and Dai was angry for letting himself get caught by the sergeant's attempt to ruffle him. Just then the castle gates swung open. A number of horsemen trotted over the timber drawbridge.

'Sergeant, get over here!' The lead horseman called, as he reined his horse to a halt. The sergeant quickly adjusted his tunic, brushed Dai aside and hurried over to the horsemen. Dai could not hear what was said but saw the sergeant gesture in his direction. After a further exchange of words the sergeant beckoned Dai over.

'I'm told you are seeking service in my brother's army. Show what you can do with that longbow,' Vere de Bourg said in heavily accented Welsh as he gazed down at Dai from his mount. 'Let's see you hit that tree stump, on the far side of the moat.' De Bourg pointed to where a small tree stump was sticking out of the far bank, over the dirty water.

'Yes, sir.' Dai strung his longbow quickly without further words or question. Maybe a hundred paces, he thought as he put an arrow in the grove. Letting fly, he knew immediately that the shaft would fall short. He had another arrow ready before the first splashed into the murky water. *Ten paces short*, Dai thought. What did Huw always say? *Eye on the target, see it hitting deep in your mind, and let it go.* When the first arrow flew, the horse turned and before de Bourg could speak, Dai had loosed the second shaft. This one was straight and true and buried deep into the soft rotting wood.

'You're quick enough, Welshman, to do what's not asked of you. Two out of three so.' He motioned towards the tree stump as his horse stomped the ground.

Dai's third arrow was in the air and smashing into the stump, almost before the horse had time to settle after de Bourg's gesturing.

De Bourg could not help giving a snorty laugh as he saw that Dai had another arrow in the groove, ready for a new target. This time, he did not let fly, but waited for de Bourg's command.

'Alright, I believe you can shoot, Welshman. What's your name?'

'Daiwin James, sir.'

'Right, Daiwin James, we will give you a trial. Sergeant, take this man to the kitchens and give him some food. Then bring him to the sergeant-at-arms for instruction. Now, you fool!' De Bourg shouted, as the guard sergeant hesitated. 'I will check on your progress, Daiwin James,' De Bourg called, already trotting away with his troop before Dai could thank him.

Dai saw Gwen almost as soon as he and the sergeant entered through the delivery door to the kitchens. She was crouched over a large vessel, washing and peeling dirty vegetables. Dai had to compose himself quickly to stop calling out to her.

'Sit there, while I go and get us some food.' The sergeant motioned Dai to a long rough table near the door. Dai sat in a far corner with his back towards Gwen, as his mind raced.

After the young serving girl brought their food, Dai and the Sergeant ate quickly. Dai smiled and thanked the young woman when she returned with jugs of small ale. He glanced towards Gwen, fearing that she might have heard his voice

The sergeant guffawed as he saw Dai and the girl exchange glances.

'So, you like Alice then, do you?' the sergeant said, with his mouth full. 'She's not been with a man yet, have you, Alice?'

Alice held Dai's stare as she put down the jugs and walked away.

'Sergeant, can I have a minute to try my luck with that girl?' Dai smirked at the sergeant as they finished the food.

The sergeant hesitated for a moment. 'I must go across the yard to the privy anyway, so you be outside the door when I'm finished.'

When he had gone, Dai turned and walked quickly over to where Alice and his mother were working. Gwen was still bent over the vegetables and didn't look up as he approached.

'Alice, this is my mother.' Dai spoke in an even tone and looked at Alice as he put his hand over Gwen's mouth and held her tightly with his other arm.

After her initial shock and struggle, Gwen recognised the voice talking to Alice. She turned and saw her son's smiling eyes. Mother and son hugged where they stood on the stone kitchen floor.

Dai knew that he would have to trust Alice and he told them about their rescue plan for Gwen.

'I have to find a way of getting you out,' Dai finished his story quickly. 'I must go with the sergeant now, but I will find a way of returning to the kitchen this evening.'

'I'll be here.' His mother replied with a flicker of a smile.

'I'll help you, if I can,' Alice blurted out, as Dai headed for the door before the sergeant came looking for him.

✝

Dai's first and last day in the service of the de Bourgs passed quickly. He almost enjoyed it, particularly when archery and sword practice began in the afternoon. Their dinner in the middle of the day was eaten at the training ground barracks. There was no sign of Gwen or Alice when the food was brought from the kitchens. All day, his mind was full of thoughts and half-plans of how to get Gwen from the castle without having to fight his way out. He knew that on his own, he could not possibly escape by using force. He cursed when he realised he had no way of communicating with John and Will. *We should have organised some way of exchanging messages. Huw would have been better prepared*, he thought.

After the training sessions finished in the late afternoon, Dai had to report back to the guard sergeant to register for pay and to be allocated a bed in the barracks. The sergeant dealt with Dai quickly.

'I suppose you will be calling on Alice later,' the sergeant sneered as he dismissed Dai.

'I might do that, if I have time, sergeant.'

✝

When Dai approached the kitchen delivery door, Alice was there.

'I've been waiting for you,' Alice blushed as Dai smiled easily at her. 'I mean, Gwen and I, we talked about you.' She hesitated, as Dai looked around and motioned her away from the door.

Dai stood close to Alice and put his arm around her waist. She did not try to push him away.

'It will look better if anyone should pass and see us,' Dai reassured her.

'Yes,' Alice smiled at him and Dai saw a touch of devilment in her eyes. 'I have a plan to help you escape, but I will have to come with you.' She paused as Dai began to say something. He stopped and nodded at her to go on. 'I am well known to the gate-keepers and in the town. I sometimes go there to get farmers to deliver corn and vegetables to the castle. Tomorrow after breakfast, I could go out and take Gwen with me. The gate-keepers may not know who she is.'

'You mean, just walk out the castle gate, simple as that?' Dai asked. 'Surely the guards know my mother is being held prisoner?'

'She is not locked up, just made to slave in the kitchens. Most ordinary people here do not know or care who she is. So long as we're not seen by any of the lord's family or his officers—' Alice broke off in mid-sentence as she felt Dai's hold increase around her waist. He stared at her intently.

'Alice, why would you do this? You know it's not a game. You could be in great danger.' Dai's voice was quiet but intense. The ridiculous simplicity of what Alice suggested brought with it the realisation that it might work. Alice and his mother would walk out the castle gates tomorrow, and he could just leave whenever the opportunity arose.

'I like Gwen. She's a kind person, and she seems to like you.' Alice smiled with a hint of something in her voice that Dai did not quite understand. 'And maybe I don't want to spend my life in these kitchens, trying to fend off those soldiers, and the lords, if they begin to notice me. If we do this, you have to promise to take me with you to Ireland.

Gwen told me about that,' she added quickly, as Dai looked at her with surprise.

†

Dai slept little that night, twisting and turning in his cot as he listened to the snoring of the other men and thought about Alice and his mother. So many things could go wrong. What if the guards knew his mother, and Alice was held and forced to reveal all? How would they make contact with John Daws and Will Hen?

When Dai was woken by the shouts of the night guards banging their swords on the open door posts, it felt like he had only been asleep for minutes.

'Get up, you beauties, and greet the day, if you're still alive!'

'Muster in the great courtyard at dawn, or you'll feel my boot!' The sergeant's shrill voice made everyone jump. Dai was up and fully dressed in a moment. The day was breaking as muster call finished, and the men headed to the mess hall for a hot breakfast. Dai ate quickly and was ready to go before his companions finished eating.

'Easy there, boy,' the sergeant growled a Dai. 'We have a long day ahead, but we're not being attacked.'

Some of the other men sniggered at the sergeant's sarcasm. Dai smiled and sat down again, internally cursing himself for appearing too eager.

†

In the kitchens, Alice and Gwen worked methodically to complete their morning duties. As she had hoped, the steward assigned Alice to go into the town for vegetables and flour and she did not mention that Gwen would accompany her. The

58

morning was a busy period in the castle life, and she hoped they might slip away without being noticed.

After allowing all to quieten down after breakfast, Alice and Gwen walked across the courtyard to the main castle gate. One of the two guards on duty was almost asleep. Alice approached the other with her best smile.

'Where are you two off to, Alice, my love?' The guard's familiarity made Gwen stop and look up from the ground. 'And who's your friend then, Alice?'

'This is Gwen, sir, she's new in the kitchens. The steward has sent us to buy vegetables and flour, so that you and your friends don't starve.'

The guard laughed and turned his attention away from Gwen.

'If I let you through, would you make a special dinner for me, Alice? And maybe we can have some fun afterwards?' the guard asked as Alice brushed past him, firmly holding on to Gwen's arm.

'I will surely, sir,' Alice called over her shoulder while both women stepped quickly across the wooden drawbridge.

†

John Daws was up early, as hunger made his belly rumble. He had got some work the previous day in a tavern, hefting ale barrels and cleaning the kitchen. He had helped the landlord deal with some troublesome customers, and had been fed and allowed to sleep in the store sheds. Now, as morning activity began in the town, he needed food to get his huge frame provisioned for the day ahead.

Daws and Will Hen had split up, with Daws remaining in the town and Hen heading back to the hill overlooking the castle. Hen was to keep watch, while Daws scouted for horses, carts, and other means of escape, should they be needed.

On his way into the kitchen, Daws met the landlord and scrounged some bread and cold mutton in return for agreeing to work again in the tavern when needed. The landlord promised a meal and a jug of ale in the afternoon and Daws grinned broadly. He would be able to watch the road from the castle without attracting attention, *and* get fed. Even better, the tavern stables would also have horses and carts should they need to leave quickly.

Gwen was still shaking, afraid to look back as she and Alice walked down the dusty road away from the castle gates. The early sun was warm and smells from the bustling town began to reach them as they approached. As she realised she had escaped, panic set in. She didn't want to go back, and the thought that they might be captured at any time made her worry. Now that she had her freedom, she didn't want to lose it.

'Don't be frightened, we're out and we're not going back.' Alice spoke softly but with such fierce conviction that Gwen relaxed a little. 'How are we going to find Daiwin's two friends? We don't know what they look like and they don't know you.'

'They don't even know there is another woman in the plot,' Gwen laughed slightly, as she thought about their situation. 'They don't know that there is a clever Alice helping us!'

'We'll find them somehow,' Alice said with her youthful conviction.

†

Will Hen had slept on a fern bed on the hillside until the morning sunshine woke him. After some fresh stream water and bread, he was wide awake. He settled down to watch the castle gates and the road. After a few hours, he noticed the two women walking down from the castle. At first he took little notice; then, realising they were the only people travelling from the castle towards the town, something made him pay closer attention. The women huddled together as they walked. Leaving his vantage point, he crept down the hill through the ferns and bushes for a closer look. At a turn in the road, he laid low to allow a noisy cart pass by. He was no more than twenty paces from the road as the two women came towards him.

Just as they passed his hiding place, he called out, 'Gwen, is that you?'

Gwen and Alice stood still for an instant in the middle of the road. Then Gwen started to run.

'Gwen, I'm a friend of Daiwin,' Hen blurted out loudly. Alice was about to run after Gwen when she heard Daiwin's name. 'I'm Will, a friend of Daiwin,' Hen called again as Alice stopped, a few paces behind Gwen who had also heard her son's name. Both women turned as Will Hen emerged from the bushes.

'Don't be frightened,' he called. 'We are here to bring Gwen to Ireland.'

†

Hen decided it was best if Gwen and Alice stayed hidden while he went into the town to find John Daws. He led the women up the hillside to his overnight hiding place. 'You keep watch on the road and castle gates, while I go to get Daws. I just have to find the right tavern.' Hen smirked at his own words. 'Stay here, and keep well hidden. I should be back before noon,' he said, looking up at the burning sun; then he was off.

He found Daws cleaning out the first tavern on the road to the castle. Hen related the story of the two women, and waited while Daws stole some food. They then hurried back up the hillside.

'One of us should take the women and start the journey back to Milford,' Daws said as they made their way through the ferns.

'Sometimes you talk sense, John Daws,' Hen agreed. 'You take the women and I'll wait and get into the castle tomorrow if Dai doesn't get out today.'

When they reached the hiding place, they explained the plan to Gwen and Alice. Both were initially reluctant to leave without Dai, but Hen and Daws insisted that Dai would want them to be safe.

After sharing out their coin, Daws took most of the food he had scavenged, leaving Hen with some stale bread and cheese.

'You have lots of lovely fresh water from the stream, boy, and your little body doesn't need much food,' Daws drawled, as he slapped Hen on the back.

'You take care of the women, and we'll meet in that quay tavern in Milford,' Hen snorted in return. 'Keep your wits, and no drinking. If we're not there within two days, take passage on the first ship to the south Irish coast.' Hen noticed the women listening anxiously. 'We'll follow soon and meet you at Ferns.'

'All right, boy, don't you worry,' John Daws returned as they set off on their journey.

†

Dai spent the day practising fighting drills with his squad. Vere De Bourg and other officers came and watched during the day. There was no possibility of escaping while they were exercising. They were too closely watched, and he wouldn't get far.

In the evening, while the men ate their meal, Dai was relieved to not see Alice and his mother. The gates were closed and the drawbridge hauled in the early evening, and he resigned himself to spending another night in the castle. Somehow, he would have to make a break before tomorrow evening.

His planning thoughts were interrupted by de Bourg entering the soldiers' mess hall. De Bourg beckoned Dai's sergeant, and everyone watched as they engaged in animated discussion.

The sergeant's face was red when he returned to the table.

'No sleep for you tonight, me lads,' he sneered. 'Get your weapons from the armoury and report to me at the main gate. Now!'

Dai and his squad of twenty were fully armed and at the main gate before Vere de Bourg and two officers got there on horseback.

'We are to search the town for two women who have escaped from the castle,' the sergeant bellowed. 'Taverns, houses, barns, all to be searched. The women are not to be harmed!'

With that the gates opened and the drawbridge clattered down. The men followed the three men on horseback across the timber bridge and headed toward the town in the early evening sunshine.

CHAPTER 9

FERNS, CO. WEXFORD.
JULY 1170

Huw woke abruptly from the dream. Once again, the woman slipped by in the water before he could see her face. Was it Bridín? Their hands almost touched but the woman's head was turned away and he couldn't be sure it was her. It was always the same. How many times had he had a similar dream?

The noise of men shouting outside the tent brought him back to reality. His body was wet with night sweat and his head throbbed. Ferns, he remembered; the noisy sound of soldiers assembling. He needed to get up to see what was happening. *I must go and find my father*, he thought. The shivering began as he reached for his tunic, and he grabbed the tent pole to keep himself upright. Huw cursed himself as he fought the light-headedness. In the weeks since returning from Limerick his wounds had healed well enough. The fever had lingered, and the Irish weather had not helped. Some days it was cold and rained incessantly. Other days, the sun shone. His body seemed to mirror the weather: cold and wet with sweat one minute, then hot and bursting with energy at other times.

Giles entered the tent just as Huw struggled into his tunic. 'Hot pottage and bread, Huw. Are you well enough to be up?'

Huw felt nauseous as he smelled the food but he sat on the cot and smiled as he took the bowl.

'I'm feeling much better and ready for action.' Huw motioned to the activity outside the tent.

'Maybe not today, Huw. There's water everywhere, and you can't swim. You'll find it hard in this land,' Giles chuckled to himself, as the rain pelted down on the tent.

Huw forced himself to eat. The taste made him feel a little sick, as the smell had, but the warmth of the food was comforting. 'No news of Daiwin?' He knew the answer but asked anyway.

Giles shook his head. Dai had been gone for three weeks. *Too soon to start to worry*, Giles thought. Yet the waiting without any news played on his mind. Should he have gone himself? Was Daiwin too young and inexperienced? What if the de Bourgs had been watching Gwen's house, or if they had already come for her? *I must not convey my fears to Huw*, Giles thought. *He is still not fully recovered and needs more rest.*

Giles's thoughts were interrupted sharply by a soldier shouting outside the tent flap. 'Sir Giles, Sir Giles, you need to come immediately.' The noise of the rain made the man shout louder.

'What is it?' Giles demanded, as he pulled back the tent flap.

'Sorry, sir, but Lord MacMurrough insists that you attend him immediately,' the man answered.

Huw got up from his cot to go with Giles, but his father put his hand on his shoulder. 'Finish your food, Huw, and stay in from this rain.'

Huw gulped down the remaining food and put on his heavy cloak. 'I can't stay in this tent forever, and you may need me to translate,' he insisted.

Giles made to argue, but he knew the determined look on his son's face.

'Don't worry, I am safe while under the protection of fitz Stephen and MacMurrough.' Giles did not feel as confident as he sounded.

MacMurrough's great hall was crowded when Huw and Giles entered. MacMurrough and Sir Robert fitz Stephen were seated at the great table, with the de Bourg brothers standing in front. Giles stood tensely, and his hand instinctively felt for his sword. Huw touched his father's sword arm briefly.

'Let us see what they want.' Huw's voice was calm and steady.

As they walked through the crowd towards the great table, Huw felt for his own sword scabbard to reassure himself that it was within easy reach.

'Sir Giles, these lords have made serious accusations against you,' MacMurrough spoke formally and slowly in Latin. The noise from the other people in the hall died to a murmur, as everyone turned and looked towards the great table. Huw noticed Maurice Regan standing to one side of the table and they exchanged nods. 'They claim that you murdered their brother, Sir Arnel de Bourg, in a cowardly attack, and that you should be handed over to them as prisoner, so that they may have justice done in the name of King Henry of England.'

The elder de Bourg brother stepped forward and started to speak, but MacMurrough raised his hand to silence him. 'Sir Giles, what do you have to say to this charge?' MacMurrough continued.

'My family and the de Bourgs have been in dispute over lands. The de Bourgs had been breaching my boundaries and stealing livestock.' Giles spoke evenly in Latin and held MacMurrough with a steady gaze. 'Arnel de Bourg and I did indeed engage in combat, and I did kill him. But it was at his instigation. The fight was fair, and he died well.' Giles added the last bit, as it was how he now remembered the fight and de Bourg's death. 'I regret what happened, but it was his life or mine. He gave me no choice.'

There was silence in the room, as all present realised the seriousness of what was unfolding.

'Do you have more to say?' MacMurrough turned to the de Bourgs.

Henry de Bourg stepped forward towards MacMurrough. Huw could see that he was trying to control his anger.

'My Lord, a lady from our household saw the attack by Giles fitz William on my brother. She swears that fitz William waited in ambush for them, and that he attacked and killed my brother without warning or provocation. She is a witness to the events and she will testify at King Henry's court.' De Bourg's measured words were taken in by all in the hall.

Huw felt that the words were well practised and carried conviction. He glanced at the two people sitting across the table and thought he saw a worried look on Sir Robert fitz Stephen's face.

'These are serious matters between lords of King Henry's realm.' MacMurrough spoke after a few moments of silence. 'It seems that this affair is not of my court, but should be judged by King Henry. Maybe Sir Giles would return to England to make his case at court.' MacMurrough hesitated, as Sir Robert fitz Stephen rose from his chair.

Henry de Bourg turned towards Giles with his hand on his sword.

'My Lord, we will take fitz William to King Henry's court for judgement.' De Bourg sensed that MacMurrough would side with him.

'Hold!' Fitz Stephen bellowed. 'Step back, Sir Henry. As the representative of Sir Richard de Clare, and leader of this expedition, I would hold counsel with Lord MacMurrough.'

Fitz Stephen's authoritative voice made MacMurrough shift on his chair.

'Yes, we will hold counsel with Sir Robert,' MacMurrough conceded quickly.

Henry de Bourg began to protest but MacMurrough stopped him.

'We will meet again in the great hall before our evening meal. Sir Robert and I will give our judgement.' MacMurrough spoke with as much formality as he could muster.

†

John Daws, Gwen and Alice landed in Wexford two days after setting out from Milford Haven on a small costal trader. The passage had been smooth, but the captain had made two stops on the Welsh coast which delayed their arrival. Daws had some coin left, and he bargained with a farmer who had just sold his crops to take them to Ferns in his empty cart. Daws wasn't sure if the farmer understood where they wanted to go, so he drew him a rough map in the dirt. When he mentioned King Diarmaid MacMurrough, the farmer nodded and seemed to understand.

'I think we're going the right way,' Daws said in Welsh to Alice and Gwen. The two women huddled together in the back of the cart. The sounds and smells were different in Ireland and they couldn't understand the strange language they heard in Wexford town. They were apprehensive, but felt relatively safe in the protection of John Daws. 'Sir Giles and Huw will be waiting for us in Ferns,' Daws assured them.

They had waited in Milford Haven for four days, without any news of Dai or Will Hen. Daws got some work in a tavern near the quay and also bargained to get a room for the women – his mother and sister, he told the landlord. Daws laughed at his own ingenuity, and seemed to like calling Gwen his mother. He kept watch on the quay during the day and met sailors in the tavern who kept him informed of ships coming and going. It was easy enough to persuade the coaster captain to take them on board for the trip to Ireland.

'Giles should appoint you as his negotiator when we get to Ireland,' Gwen told him.

'I'd have to learn the language, like Huw boy,' Daws replied. 'Very strange, it is.'

†

The cart with Daws, Gwen and Alice arrived at Ferns on the afternoon of the day Giles and Huw had attended MacMurrough's court in the great hall. Daws used his new-found negotiating skills with the Irish guards on the main gate to gain entry to the camp. He convinced them he was from the Welsh archer troop and that the ladies were here at the pleasure of Sir Robert fitz Stephen. The cart driver conversed in Gaelic with the guards and seemed to reassure them.

'Didn't think they would let us in. I'll really have to get Huw teach me some words of this Ireland language,' Daws told the two women.

The rain had stopped and Huw and Giles were talking outside the tent when the cart creaked up along the sodden pathway. Huw recognised the huge frame of John Daws walking alongside the cart.

'John Daws!' he shouted. 'There's no one else in Ireland with that awkward Welsh walk.'

†

Daws and Gwen had just finished relating their stories when a messenger from fitz Stephen arrived for Giles.

'Sir Robert wants to meet us immediately. We have to go for a while.' He turned to Gwen and Alice. 'John Daws will stay here with you until we get back. No one will bother you.' Giles looked at Daws, who nodded in reply.

Giles and Huw walked quickly to fitz Stephen's quarters. Sir Robert met them alone in his tent.

'Giles, Huw,' fitz Stephen began, 'I've spoken at length with MacMurrough. He insists that this is not his affair. He wants to hand Giles over to the de Bourgs, and for you to return to Wales. Giles, I do not trust the de Bourgs, and will offer you my protection here. However, my protection may not be enough.' Fitz Stephen broke off in mid-sentence to let Giles speak.

'Robert, this affair is of my doing, and I am sorry for getting you involved. The de Bourgs have sworn an oath to kill me and all my family. I cannot return to Wales with them.' Giles spoke quietly to his friend and commander. 'If you will allow us some time, we will leave Ferns at once and try to make a life for ourselves in some other part of this land.' Giles surprised himself at how clearly the words came. It was as though this plan had been formulated for a long time and was now ready to be put into action.

'For now, that seems the best course for you,' Fitz Stephen replied after some moments of silence. 'I will have letters prepared confirming your status and my protection. Maybe in the future these will be of some help.' He smiled. 'I will give you as much coin as I can muster, and you should take horses, arms and provisions.' After a pause, he continued, 'You and Huw have contributed greatly to our campaign here. It isn't clear how this Irish expedition will progress, but I will ensure that de Clare knows how much you both assisted me.' He looked at Huw. 'We must find some way of communicating, when you are settled somewhere.'

'Yes, sir,' Huw immediately began forming a plan. 'We have many friends amongst the archer troop.'

Fitz Stephen looked quizzical at first, but then nodded in approval. 'See to it, Huw. I will recognise and listen to any man using the name Huw Ashe.' He smiled at his own suggestion.

'Ashe is the word, sir, and Ashe will be the man.' Huw grinned in return.

Giles looked a bit bemused at the rapid exchange between his son and fitz Stephen, but he knew that they would have an ally at a high level in the Norman leadership.

'Thank you, Robert, your help and support is greatly appreciated.' Giles smiled and held out his hand.

†

'Letters of support, and a bag of coin. Should be more than enough to start a new life in Ireland,' Giles laughed as they walked briskly back to their tent.

'Indeed, sir. If we could scrounge a cart, we would be rich men. Maybe Daws could buy the cart from his Irish driver.' Huw began to plan.

'I'm not sure if we can ask John Daws to come with us, Huw. This trouble is ours and what we are planning is dangerous and risky.'

Huw immediately realised his father was right. This was their family's battle, and they were about to leave the relative security and protection of the Norman and MacMurrough alliance. They would have to face this task on their own.

'What of Daiwin, Hen and your children? We have no knowledge of them in Wales,' Huw asked as the wider difficulty of their family's situation became clearer to both men.

'We will have to form a more effective plan, Huw. But for now, we need to escape from Ferns.'

†

Will Hen watched from his vantage point on the hillside as the squad of fighting men left the castle and headed down the road towards the town. He decided to get closer to the road.

Hen followed the path he had travelled when he met the two women, arriving just before the troop arrived. He could not get too close for fear of being seen by the horsemen, so he lay low in the scrub and listened. The soldier troop trotted by, maybe four abreast. Hen could hear the muted Welsh voices as the men chatted to each other and wondered for a moment if Daiwin was among them. He couldn't risk having a look. He heard some of the men talking about a search, and he definitely heard them mention women. Hen circled away from the road towards the town. He could pass for a local in the village, and maybe find out what the men were looking for. He hid his bow stave and arrows in a thicket, and circled to the far end of the town. He went into the first small tavern he came across, and ordered ale and cheese. The ten or so people in the tavern looked up at the newcomer, but didn't take too much notice. Hen set about his food and waited.

Daiwin and three other soldiers were sent to search the outhouses and stables behind the row of mud and timber buildings along one side of the main road. After nearly an hour searching they had found nothing; anyone they met shook their heads when asked about two women. He could hear noise and shouting from the other searchers, but nothing to indicate that they had found anything.

Dai and one of his companions entered the tavern from the stable yard at the rear. They started to ask if anyone had seen two women from the castle and Dai did not immediately see his friend until Hen got up and called on the landlord to bring more ale. Dai quickly hid his surprise, as his fellow soldier quizzed Hen about the women.

'Two women – let me know when you find them, lad,' Hen smirked and made a rough gesture to the young soldier. 'Hold that ale 'til I get back from the privy,' he called loudly to the landlord.

There was no one except Hen in the outside privy, when Dai entered.

'Will, good to see you!' Dai whispered urgently. 'What happened?'

In less than a minute Hen told Dai about Gwen, Alice and Daws heading to Milford Haven.

'If no one else has seen them, it will take de Bourg some time to find out that they are on their way to Ireland.' Dai spoke quietly. 'But he may think they will make for Robert fitz William's castle for safe keeping.'

'Sir Giles's children will be in great danger. We need to get to the castle quickly, and take the children before de Bourg gets there.' Dai spoke his thoughts out loud, and Hen nodded in understanding. 'I will slip away from the rest of the soldiers when it gets dark.'

CHAPTER 10

SHANNON ESTUARY
AUGUST 1170

BRIDÍN AND HER PARTY had followed the banks of the large river for three days until it was no longer a river, as the wide expanse of water expanded towards the sea. She had never travelled this far west from Limerick before. She was on horseback, with her two maids chatting continuously inside the cover of the small horse-drawn wagon. One guard rode twenty paces ahead, with another a short distance behind the cart. The other two soldiers on horseback were Bridín's personal bodyguards and they stayed close by her side. The four soldiers in the party got increasingly nervous, the farther they travelled from Limerick.

It was late August and the days were still mild enough to be pleasant as the party moved slowly along the rough track. Bridín reflected on how her life had been turned on its head following Huw's departure for Wexford. Thinking of Huw brought a brief smile to her face.

O'Muinacháin had not held long to his oath, after Huw and the Normans departed. Bridín wasn't sure how O'Muinacháin had explained his injuries and the loss of his soldiers to the King. For the first week he had avoided Bridín, barely acknowledging her at O'Brien's court. Then, whatever had passed between himself and the King, O'Muinacháin became much more attentive and assertive in his dealings with Bridín. He insisted on sitting beside her in the banquet hall and sometimes followed her to her quarters to talk to her. One evening, flushed and full with food and drink, he confronted Bridín as she retired to her chamber.

'Bridín, I have kept my word. I have not told the King about you and the Welsh man.' O'Muinacháin held Bridín's arm as he prevented her passing by in the dark corridor. 'But the King has many spies. He knows of your indiscretion and is not pleased with you.' O'Muinacháin's breath smelled of drink, and Bridín could feel his spittle on her face as he pushed closer to her. 'I have asked the King for your hand in marriage and he has promised you to me. You are to be mine, Bridín. The King commands it.'

'You're drunk sir, let me pass.' Bridín tried to sound assertive.

O'Muinacháin stood where he was and tightened his grip on her arm. He drew her closer and slipped his other arm around Bridín's body. For the first time ever, Bridín felt afraid of him. She struggled, but he held her tighter. Bridín noticed his eyes were glazed and his face damp with sweat. She smelled his foul breath. Her heart was pounding and she felt pain from the tightness of his grip.

'You are mine,' O'Muinacháin repeated. 'The King says so. There is nothing you can do.'

He pushed Bridín roughly against the wall of the dark corridor. She could hear muffled voices coming from the great hall across the courtyard, but it was quiet in the ladies sleeping chambers. The Queen had already gone to bed and would be sleeping soundly after drinking freely with her evening meal. These thoughts flicked quickly through her mind, as O'Muinacháin forced his knee between her legs. His breathing became heavier and the hand holding her by the waist dropped down and began to lift up her gown. When

Bridín felt O'Muinacháin's sweaty hand on her body inside her gown she suddenly relaxed and stopped struggling. O'Muinacháin seemed surprised and in turn relaxed his grip, and looked into her eyes.

She had difficulty remembering the details of what happened next. She recalled thinking that it was a long time before O'Muinacháin reacted. At first he gave a short stifled grunt as he reached behind his back and tried to turn his head to see what had happened. Then Bridín saw his eyes rolling as he slipped quietly to the floor and turned onto his side. The knife was stuck in his lower back and there was a growing dark, wet patch on his tunic. Bridín looked at her hands. There was blood on her palms and fingers, and her gown was bloody where she had wiped them. She felt a certain calmness as she stood there looking at O'Muinacháin's body. She remembered taking the knife from his belt but she had no memory of stabbing it downwards into his back.

Bridín left O'Muinacháin's body where it lay and walked quickly to her bed chamber. The other two ladies-in-waiting were asleep. They too would have drunk freely with the Queen before they left the great hall. Bridín washed her hands in the basin with some cold water and then quietly opened the door to the Queen's chamber.

Bridín had been surprised by the reaction of Queen Orla. The Queen had always been friendly enough towards Bridín, without being familiar or confiding in her. Bridín thought Queen Orla was somewhat unhappy with her situation in life. She had been given by MacMurrough to Donal O'Brien in marriage, to form a better alliance between Thomond and the King of Leinster. It often seemed that O'Brien cared little about the alliance, even though he was careful not to offend his queen. For her part, Orla seemed resigned to her lot, never showing too much enthusiasm for the activities of the court. Bridín always thought that the Queen liked her food and wine a bit too much. After the evening banquets, she usually slept deep and late. The King never came to her sleeping chamber.

Bridín had difficulty waking Queen Orla that night she crept into her chamber. She put her candle on the bedside table and called gently. She had to touch the Queen's shoulder a number of times before Orla opened her eyes.

'What is it, girl, are we being attacked?' the queen asked in her disinterested way.

'No, my Lady, nothing like that,' Bridín whispered. Something in Bridín's face made the Queen sit up.

Bridín quickly told Queen Orla what had happened with O'Muinacháin. She got up and dressed herself as Bridín was coming to the end of her story. She had never seen the Queen move so quickly or with so much purpose.

'You have done us all a service by striking down that bastard.' Bridín was shocked by the Queen's words. 'But you are in great danger, if not from my husband the King, then from some of the nobles at court. O'Muinacháin spied for many of them and they will not take kindly to him being murdered by a woman. We will have to get you away from here quickly.' Queen Orla paused and looked at Bridín. She was shaking and just nodded in return. The Queen poured a tankard of warm wine and handed it to Bridín. 'I will arrange for a small troop from my personal guard to accompany you, but where can they take you that is safe?' the Queen asked, talking to herself more than Bridín.

'I could go east to my father near the MacCarthy border.' Bridín's mind was clearing as she realised that her situation was not hopeless and that the Queen would help her; she had not had a plan when she approached the Queen, other than to ask her to intercede with the King.

While the Queen woke Lady Cait and sent her to bring her steward, Bridín changed her clothes and packed some things in a leather satchel.

'Take my heavy cloak and wear this ring.' Queen Orla gave Bridín one of the rings from her fingers. 'This is from my father, King Diarmaid. It may help you.'

'My Lady, you are so kind, but the ring is too much. Are you leaving yourself exposed to attack at court?'

Queen Orla waved her hand and then reached out to hold Bridín's hands.

'You take my ring and get as far away from here as you can tonight. Keep going and don't look back until you find your father. I will be safe. My husband will not want any dispute with Diarmaid MacMurrough.'

In less than two hours, Queen Orla's steward had quietly organised four members of her guard and a covered cart with food and drink. These were now waiting in the darkness close to the main gate. The steward would accompany the party to the gate and ensure they were allowed to pass through. Lady Cait had woken two of the ladies' maids who would accompany Bridín. Queen Orla spoke to the maids to reassure them and gave them each more coins than they had ever seen.

Just as they were ready to leave, Bridín knelt before Queen Orla to thank her. The Queen lifted Bridín gently by the elbow and hugged her. She placed a large pouch of coins in Bridín's hands.

'I will speak to my husband the King, when he is calmed. Perhaps you will return to us,' the Queen paused and smiled, 'in a year or two.' Bridín tried to smile in return. 'For now, you need to travel and hide yourself away. We will try to get messages to you, especially if your young Welshman should return.' Queen Orla smiled again.

'My lady, you knew?' Bridín looked at the Queen in surprise.

'I too have spies around court, Bridín,' she replied with mischief in her eyes.

King Donal O'Brien and his nobles slept soundly as Bridín and her party left as quietly as they could through the main gate and headed west along the southern bank of the Shannon.

Some hours after Bridín left, Queen Orla took her candle and walked along the corridor to where Bridín had left O'Muinacháin. The body was curled up like a baby on its side with a small pool of blood underneath where the dagger protruded. Orla had heard the rasp-like breathing when she entered the corridor and she knew that O'Muinacháin was still alive. Looking closer, she saw that the dagger had not penetrated deeply and was mainly embedded in his clothes. Orla sighed to herself and, standing over O'Muinacháin, looking at his pale miserable face in the candlelight, she thought it would be easy to finish him off. Just stab him a few more times, she thought with some glee. Who would know? She dismissed the thought as quickly as it had come. Pity he hadn't died, but maybe better for Bridín if he lives.

Queen Orla went back to her chamber and poured herself a large tankard of wine. Lady Cait had returned to bed and was sleeping soundly. The Queen finished her wine slowly and then called Lady Cait and bid her go and tell the King's guard that O'Muinacháin had been attacked and needed help.

†

'We'll keep going until the sun goes down,' Bridín said to her bodyguards. One of the soldiers went forward to tell the rider in front. Dusk was closing in and she thought they should leave the track and find a safe place to spend the night. She wasn't sure where the O'Brien kingdom ended, and wondered how she would make contact with her father. *Perhaps we should turn inland in the morning*, she thought.

Bridín spent the night in the covered wagon with her two maids. The wind howled throughout the night and she got little sleep. Not long after sunrise, after a breakfast of cold meat and bread, the lead soldier found a rough path heading inland. The terrain looked barren, with few trees. The ground was slightly raised and in the distance they could see smoke rising from a gathering of small dwellings. The pathway was barely wide enough to allow the wagon to pass, and progress was slow as they meandered downwards towards the small village.

The four riders appeared suddenly from around a bend in the pathway. The leading guard quickly galloped back to the cart. Bridín turned instinctively in her saddle to find an escape route. At least six more mounted men were blocking the path about a hundred paces behind. She realised it would be impossible to turn the wagon on the narrow pathway, even if the men were not blocking their way. Some of the mounted men had bows strung with arrows in the groove.

'Hold.' Bridín spoke firmly to her guards as they made to unsheathe their swords. 'We are outnumbered and there may be more of them that we can't see. I will talk with them.' Bridín nudged her horse forward towards the men ahead. She stopped about twenty paces from them. 'I am Bridín O'Brien, cousin to King Donal Mór O'Brien, and I am come to find my father Aon O'Brien.' Bridín tried to hold her voice steady.

There was a laugh from one of the group of riders but no one moved. Bridín held her ground. After some moments and a murmured discussion that Bridín could not hear, one of the riders came forward and stopped just to one side of Bridín.

'Lady, I am MacCarthy, son of the MacCarthy Mór. You must tell your guards to lay down their weapons. If they do not, we will kill them all where they stand. You shall have to submit as my prisoner.' MacCarthy stared directly at Bridín as he spoke. It seemed like he was having a quiet conversation, but his eyes and expression showed he was deadly serious.

Bridín did not reply, she sat motionless on her horse. Then she turned towards her party. 'We must surrender to these men,' she said loudly but calmly. 'You must throw down your swords and daggers, otherwise this man will kill me now.' Bridín added the last words as she turned back to look at MacCarthy. He raised his eyes slightly and nodded to her.

The guards hesitated and MacCarthy drew his sword.

'Do it now!' Bridín called again to her men. She hoped she had made the right decision, as the swords and daggers clattered to the ground.

'We will not kill them. You have my word.' MacCarthy looked closely at Bridín as two of his men went forward to collect the discarded weapons. 'I hope your maids can ride those horses, Lady, otherwise they will have to walk.' MacCarthy spoke in a slightly cheeky tone to Bridín as his men unhitched the wagon and pushed it off the pathway and down a small incline into some yellow-flowered bushes. 'The wagon would slow us down and we will not be keeping to the pathways,' he continued, as Bridín looked at him. 'You can take your clothes and as much else as your men can carry.'

When the goods from the wagon had been shared out and everyone was mounted, MacCarthy's men led them eastwards away from the path, avoiding the village that Bridín had seen. They climbed to higher ground until such time as the sea was visible again to their right and then travelled parallel with the shoreline, even though at times the sea disappeared from sight.

Bridín tried as best she could to note the direction they travelled and tried to form a mental picture of some landmarks that they passed. She wanted to ask MacCarthy where they were going, but he had ridden ahead to scout with two other men. She noticed that they circled widely to avoid any villages as they travelled. They stopped at mid-day to eat and to water the horses. Despite her fears, Bridín marvelled at the expanse of land and sea all around.

In the late afternoon, a large town came into view from their vantage point in the hills. The town nestled at the edge of a wide bay, with a mountain range stretching along the far shoreline. Bridín could see large sandy beaches all along the bay. Large boats were entering and leaving the town and Bridín was surprised that she did not know of this place.

After a quick stop for food and water, they mounted again and set off eastwards on a circular route that would avoid the town. It appeared that they were heading towards the foothills of the mountain range. After a while they slowed to walking pace as they began to climb. The horses were blowing hard as they approached the crest of a steep hill. Looking back, Bridín could still see the town on the edge of the bay. Ahead, the two MacCarthy forward scouts were waving their arms for the rest of the group to come forward. Reaching the two men on the crest of the hill, Bridín could see a huge valley on the other side of the mountain range, with a river meandering towards the sea. The river broadened out into an estuary, with mountains on either side as far as her eyes could see.

'A wonderful sight, Lady.' MacCarthy had reined in along-side Bridín. 'On the far side of the river is the MacCarthy kingdom.' He looked at Bridín, noticing her amazement at the sight before them. 'We will ford the river where it narrows near that village,' he said, pointing down to the flat land in the valley. 'You will have to come with us, Lady, but we will let your men go free when we reach the river. You can bring your two serving girls with you, or we will free them also, as you wish.'

'They will choose themselves if they wish to come with me.' Bridín was defiant. 'What is the name of that river?'

'We call it the Mang River, Lady.'

MacCarthy rode alongside Bridín on the way down the hillside towards the Mang River. He told her that they were on a scouting mission when they spotted her small group on that remote track.

'We thought you might have something of value in your wagon,' MacCarthy laughed easily as he spoke. 'If you hadn't told us who you were we might just have taken your coin and let you go.' He looked at Bridín with mirth in his eyes.

'You can still let me go now,' Bridín answered with a little venom in her voice.

'Why were you travelling in the wild lands so far away from O'Brien's court?' MacCarthy asked her directly.

Bridín was silent for a while. She wanted to tell MacCarthy some story that might be believable, but nothing came to mind. Instead she told him the truth about her encounter with O'Muinacháin and her flight from the court.

'You killed that O'Muinacháin bastard!' MacCarthy laughed out loud. 'My father may reward you well, Lady.'

'You know O'Muinacháin?'

'Only saw him once, but my father spoke with him at truce talks. You know that we dispute with your people over territory and lordship?' MacCarthy paused to look at Bridín. 'My father didn't like O'Muinacháin's shifty eyes and pompous talk.'

†

When they reached the Mang River, MacCarthy kept his word and allowed Bridín's guards to leave. He gave them their swords and daggers but not the bows. Bridín's maids decided to go with her. The river was low as the tide was out and they quickly reached the far bank.

'Welcome to our kingdom, Lady,' MacCarthy smiled at Bridín as they looked back across the river and valley. Bridín

could see that the hill they had crossed was at the edge of a
mountain range that stretched south west along the sea inlet.
A thick mist was coming in from the sea so she couldn't see
how far the mountains extended. Turning eastwards, a higher
mountain range circled all around in the distance.

'You do not have to call me lady. My name is Bridín,' she
called to MacCarthy as they turned their horses towards the
easterly mountains. 'What is your name?'

'I am Tadhg, Lady, son of the MacCarthy Mór, or so he
tells me anyway.' MacCarthy nudged his horse to trot forward.

Bridín recalled a similar introduction some months ago on
the banks of the Shannon. She wondered where Huw was
now, as her horse followed Tadhg MacCarthy away from the
southern bank of the Mang River.

CHAPTER 11

WATERFORD COAST
AUGUST 1170

HUW SAT STILL ON his horse and gazed at the huge expanse of coastline. Sandy beaches glistened in the August sunshine. He had regained his strength and health during the time they travelled after escaping from Ferns. The weather helped, with almost no rain for three weeks; a great country, when it was dry. He had gone ahead of the others to scout the hills that overlooked the sea. He loved looking at the sea and might nearly get to like it, from a distance. Looking eastwards to his left he could see the cart, with his father riding alongside. John Daws was maybe fifty paces behind, guarding the rear.

They had headed south-west after leaving Ferns. Giles had decided that even though they had to avoid Wexford town, they should not travel too far away from the sea ports in case Daiwin returned from Wales. After a number of days, they had forded two large rivers and headed in a southerly direction towards the coast. They had passed close enough to be able to see the large port of Waterford, but did not enter the town for fear of being seen by de Bourg's spies. They needed food, so they planned for someone to go to Waterford to buy supplies and scout for news, once they were settled a safe distance away.

Daws had insisted on helping and going with them. He bought the cart from the farmer in Ferns and collected enough food from his Welsh comrades to supply them for the first few days.

'I'll have to come with you, Huw boy. You are sick and useless and your father will easily be spotted by spies. I'm nearly half-Irish now,' Daws claimed in his good-natured way. 'I'll be able to go back to Wexford to check for Dai's arrival.'

Huw knew that Daws was right and they would need him, at least until Dai returned and they could settle somewhere safe.

'You'll probably cause more trouble than you're worth,' Huw told him. Daws laughed as he set about loading the cart.

†

Sitting there in the warm sunshine, Huw wondered about Bridín. What would she be doing now in Limerick? He had thought of suggesting to his father that they go to Limerick, but that would take them farther away from Dai and Giles's children. He knew that getting back to Limerick would be more difficult now.

He noticed Giles waving, so he roused himself and urged his horse into a gallop down across the hillside towards the cart. Daws had joined them when Huw got there.

'Speaking to Gwen and Alice, they think this may be a nice place to camp for a while,' Giles waved his hand towards the sandy coastline. 'I'm inclined to agree. We don't want to get too far away from Wexford and there's been no sign of any of our countrymen on this side of that big river.' He looked at Huw as he spoke.

'Yes, sir, a good place. Maybe there would be some fish to be had, and I noticed lots of rabbits.' Huw winked at Daws, knowing that he'd be hungry.

'You seem to be getting your wits back,' Daws shot back at Huw. 'Took you long enough. We could go across to those sand dunes and scout for a good place.'

'Let's see if you can ride that horse,' Huw was already galloping towards the dunes as he goaded Daws into following him.

Giles shook his head as he watched the two raise a cloud of dust as they headed across the heather.

'It's good to see Huw in high spirits and getting his strength back.' Gwen echoed Giles's thoughts, as the three of them laughed at the antics of the two riders racing towards the sand dunes.

It had taken Gwen and Alice Evans some time to get accustomed to the new land. Giles and Huw tried to explain what had happened since they came to Ireland over a year ago, and what they knew about the Irish people and customs. Alice seemed frightened, and had spoken very little. Gwen made sure that she kept by her side and reassured her as best she could. Gwen told Giles that she thought Alice had just realised she was alone in a strange land, with people she hardly knew. They had no home to offer her and now they were on the run and constantly on the lookout for danger.

Giles and Gwen had little time together and it was almost impossible to be alone. They had exchanged looks and had kissed briefly when Gwen had arrived from Wales, but little else.

'I'm going to follow them to the dunes. I need to run to make sure my legs are working after being in the cart for so long.' Alice surprised Gwen and Giles, and she was out of the cart and running towards the dunes before they could reply.

'Maybe Alice is finally finding her feet,' Giles said, smiling at his own wit. He dismounted and held out his hand to help Gwen from the cart. 'We could walk some ourselves and maybe sit in the sunshine.' He took Gwen by the arm as they walked a small distance up the hillside overlooking the sea. They sat on a small bank in the heather and gazed at the sea and sand. The older couple could hear Huw and Daws calling to Alice as she ran towards them.

'This might not be such a bad land in which to live.' Giles put his arm around Gwen's waist.

'It has possibilities,' she replied. 'We just need a house, some land, and a small army to protect us.' She and Giles laughed.

'Indeed, not too much to hope for, but you forgot about the pardon from King Henry and a truce with the de Bourg family,' he added to the list.

'And the safe return of Daiwin and your children,' Gwen added softly as their laughter died down.

'Yes, indeed; with Daiwin and the children here, perhaps we could start work on the other things.'

✝

Giles, Huw and Daws worked for a day and a half to erect a fortified camp between two high sand dunes. The seaward dune would give the canvas tent some protection from the easterly winds from the sea. The dunes on the inland side prevented them being seen from the pathway or the hillside. Daws had trapped and hunted a dozen rabbits and Huw found a small fishing village when he scouted east along the coast. He risked going into the village to buy fish with small coins. Their grain supply was running low and they decided that Huw and Daws should take the cart to Waterford to buy as much as they could without attracting suspicion.

'Your accent is strange, Huw, but do you know enough of the language to buy food?' Giles asked. 'Perhaps if John doesn't speak at all, no one will take much notice.'

'I can be dumb enough, sir, when I want to be, my mother always said,' Daws chipped in.

'Our coin should speak well enough. We'll get as much as we can and be back in less than three days,' Huw said, calculating roughly how much time their trip would take. 'Maybe you should only light fires at night until we return.' Huw nodded to the smoke rising from the fire where Gwen and Alice were roasting rabbits.

'We'll try and make ourselves look like travellers enjoying the sunshine by the sea, if anyone should come looking,' Giles laughed.

'So long as you don't talk to them in Norman French, sir, maybe a bit of church Latin would be ok. They might think you a priest, trying to save two fallen women.' Huw reminded his father of his lack of knowledge of the Gaelic language.

'You will have to teach us all how to speak Gaelic, Huw, if we are to survive here.' Giles knew they would have to learn many things to survive in Ireland.

'We'll start when I get back. I'll speak only Gaelic to Daws on the way.'

†

The next morning as the sun rose in the east, Huw and John Daws set off for Waterford town.

Huw decided to track eastwards along the coastline, wanting to learn different routes. After nearly a day's travel they began to meet people walking towards them along the pathway. At first it was just one or two, but then larger groups of people passed by. Some of them seemed to be dazed, or ill. There were one or two carts carrying sick people. Huw wanted to ask them where they came from, but he was still not confident using the Gaelic language and he did not wish to attract attention.

'Something funny going on, Huw boy, those people don't look happy,' Daws called from his horse behind the cart. Huw had got the job of cart driver, with Daws claiming that he would be better as the horseback sentry.

'Do you think they're coming from Waterford town?' Huw had just got the words out when they saw and smelled the smoke rising over the next ridge on the cliff pathway.

When they reached the top of the ridge, the town of Waterford came in to view a short distance away along the coast. The smell of smoke was carried in the slight breeze that drifted from the town. Groups of people gathered outside the walls, and more were heading towards them along the path.

Huw worked up his courage and asked a few people what had happened. From the short replies, he quickly understood what had taken place.

'A large army of Norman soldiers took the town,' he told John Daws. 'MacMurrough and his people are there. Many were killed and others are leaving.' Huw gestured to the people passing by.

'What are we going to do for our grain now?' Daws was staring at the battered town as he spoke.

'I don't know about the supplies, but we can't risk going in there as we are. All the Norman lords and knights from Ferns would be there, including the de Bourgs. They must have got reinforcements to take a walled town like that.' Huw gaped at the walls as he talked. 'I'd like to talk to Sir Robert, though, to find out what's happening and if he has any news of Daiwin.'

'You can't just walk in, boy. There'll be mayhem in the streets and those de Bourg bastards will get you and string you. You'd be useless to us hung.'

Huw laughed as Daws made hand signs of him stretched at the end of a rope. 'Maybe the mayhem might help me to get in unnoticed. Once inside, I could blend in with the other Welsh men.'

'What's this "me" word you're using there, boy? Do you think I'd let you go in there on your own?'

For a few minutes neither of them spoke as they stood looking intently at the walls of the town. A pile of rubble to the left of a stone tower indicated where the walls must have been breached. Huw wondered how the wall was toppled.

'John, I think I might go in alone. If we both go and something happens to us, my father will come to find us. You need to stay free to return to Sir Giles and prevent him from coming to Waterford.' Huw looked at Daws. 'There'll be lots of drinking and celebrating and I should be able to slip in when it gets dark.' Daws nodded but said nothing. 'I'll try to make contact with Sir Robert or Maurice Regan. He knows me and I can trust him. A little,' Huw added, with a smile. 'Something big has happened here, and we need to find out what is going on.'

'Huw boy, you should be a counsel yourself. You're so sure of things I almost believe everything you say,' Daws lilted in his best sing-song accent. 'Worst is, you're probably right.'

†

Huw waited until dusk had fallen before setting off on foot towards the town. They had found some small tree and scrub cover inland where Daws would wait with the cart and horses. The high ground away from the trees would allow Daws to keep watch for any sign of trouble.

'I'll keep watch alright, boy, but what good will I be if you're captured and hung inside the town?' Daws protested. Huw assured him that it was the only way to find out what had happened.

'I should have time to buy some decent food that we can eat on the way home. Remember, John, if I'm not back by dusk tomorrow you must head back to my family.'

'Go on, go. Your father will probably string me up if I come back without you, though.' Daws whacked Huw on the back as he headed off.

Huw had little difficulty climbing over the rubble and entering the town through the breach in the wall. There were no sentries and nobody stopped him. He had brought his bow staff and sword, so he looked much like any other archer. There were campfires being lit outside the walls, with small groups of men drinking and laughing. Inside there were signs of battle; broken weapons, dirty clothing and blood lined the streets inside the wall breach, but he saw no bodies. The dead and dying had been cleared very quickly.

He decided his best option would be to trust Regan, as he would know MacMurrough's plans. But how to find him? The inner streets were full of men drinking and eating. The taverns were overflowing with people. Many were out on the streets in the warm evening air. Huw entered the first tavern where he heard lots of Welsh voices. A large jug of ale was pushed into his hands.

'Are we being attacked?' the man passing him the ale laughed, as he motioned to Huw's bow.

'Ha, no, just coming in from sentry duty,' Huw laughed and downed a big gulp of ale.

The man asked no more questions as he gestured to Huw to come and join his group in the corner of the tavern. Huw sat on the on the straw-lined floor with his back to the wall and listened as the men talked about the attack and the slaughter that followed. He did not recognise any one from his former troop. He learned that these were new men, only recently landed in Ireland as part of a much larger army. One name kept being repeated as the men spoke. Strongbow! The main army had finally arrived in Ireland!

Without asking too many questions, Huw found out where the Norman commanders were quartered. No one took much notice as he quietly slipped out of the tavern onto the street.

Huw kept to the shadows as he scouted the inner streets that led down to the river and the tower where Strongbow and MacMurrough were headquartered. There were sentries posted at the entrance to the tower and surrounding buildings. He knew that he couldn't risk trying to get inside; there would be a great hall in one of those buildings, and the lords would be feasting to celebrate the taking of the town. He would have to wait and bide his time. Maybe Regan would come out after the meal to go to his sleeping quarters, or to walk along the river. If not, he would try to make contact with him in the morning. Huw found a ruined outbuilding that allowed him a view of the entrance to the headquarters and settled down to wait.

†

Huw was woken from his half-sleep by loud voices as a number of Norman knights staggered out of the tower door. They were loud and laughing as they went to relieve themselves on the street. Huw was no more than fifty paces away and he could hear some of the drunken conversations. The night was bright, and as more knights and Irish nobles came out he recognised Meiler fitz Henry and some of the other knights, but most of the faces were new to him. If only he could get to talk to fitz Henry. Most of the men went back inside after a short while, leaving fitz Henry and two companions on the street.

'Sir Meiler!' Huw called as loudly as he dared, as he stepped out of his hiding place, staying in the shadows but allowing himself to be partly seen. 'Sir Meiler!' he called again.

Fitz Henry and his two comrades turned towards Huw.

'Who is that? What do you want?' fitz Henry shouted.

'Huw Ashe, sir!' Huw blurted his name out quickly before he could change his mind. If the other two recognised his name, he would have to run for it.

He saw fitz Henry draw his sword and mutter something—Huw couldn't hear what—to his comrades. The two knights also drew their swords, and the three of them walked towards him.

Huw grabbed his bow staff tightly but did not string it. Ten more paces, and he'd run. The three knights stopped in the middle of the street, hardly thirty paces away. Fitz Henry walked forward on his own.

'Huw Ashe, is that you?' Fitz Henry spoke quietly as he approached Huw.

'Yes, sir,' Huw whispered.

Fitz Henry sheathed his sword and walked back to his companions. He spoke to them, and they put their weapons away and returned to the tower.

'Devil's blood, Huw! You nearly got yourself killed. But then, you often do,' fitz Henry laughed. 'What of Giles, and how are you living?' Fitz Henry didn't wait for an answer. 'Let us walk down to the river. You know the de Bourgs are inside grovelling to de Clare and MacMurrough. Snivelling bastards, they are.'

Huw did not disagree as they walked towards the river.

Fitz Henry recounted how de Clare and a force of nearly two thousand men had landed east of Waterford town. Strongbow had finally fulfilled his promise to MacMurrough. Strongbow's forces had been joined by Robert fitz Stephen and Raymond fitz William and their armies and the combined Norman forces had laid siege to Waterford. The town had been well garrisoned, and the early attacks on the walls had failed. However, a determined attack on a weak point by Raymond's men led to a breach in the walls; the town had quickly fallen after that. Many of the town's defenders and citizens were slaughtered. MacMurrough and his family had arrived when the town was secure. As part of their agreement, MacMurrough's daughter Aoife had married Strongbow, with MacMurrough then naming Strongbow as his successor to the Kingdom of Leinster. At a council following the wedding, MacMurrough and Strongbow made plans to march north and take the town of Dublin.

Huw listened with amazement at how quickly it had all happened. And now it seemed that with their combined forces, Strongbow and MacMurrough would take and hold the key port of Dublin, as well as Waterford. Fitz Henry spoke excitedly as he told Huw about what was planned.

'There will be large tracts of land to be had. We are all promised large holdings if we fight well. What we take, we hold. You need to tell Giles, he has to have a part in this.'

Fitz Henry went on, enthused about what lay ahead. Huw tried to take it all in.

'I will relate this to my father, but he is still on the run after the Ferns court with MacMurrough and the de Bourgs.'

'Measly bastards they are, Huw, I might kill them myself if the chance presents.'

'We don't want you outlawed as well, Sir Meiler!'

'I think we're all half-outlaws now, Huw. It's rumoured that de Clare defied the King's ruling to come here with his army. We could all be hanged.' Fitz Henry laughed.

'Sir Meiler, I need to speak to Maurice Regan, MacMurrough's counsel, to see if we can find a way for my father to return. Could you ask him to meet me?'

'For sure, Huw, for sure. He's one of the few sober ones inside.' Fitz Henry gestured back towards the tower. 'Within the hour, at your hiding place?'

Before they took their leave, Fitz Henry promised that he would quietly tell fitz Stephen of their meeting. He gave Huw his pouch with whatever coin he had.

'I like the look of the land in Wexford, Huw. I'll be going back once the Dublin expedition is finished. Perhaps you and Giles could settle there too?'

'Perhaps, Sir Meiler, we may take up your kind offer.' They both laughed, and bid each other good fortune.

✝

Huw was surprised at the warmth of Maurice Regan's greeting when they met.

'Huw Ashe! We were worried about your family. My lord MacMurrough regrets what happened at his court. He doesn't fully understand Norman laws.' Regan was as diplomatic as always.

For half an hour, Huw and Regan discussed the conflict between Giles and the de Bourg family. Regan told Huw that MacMurrough was sympathetic towards Giles but wary of interfering between lords in King Henry's jurisdiction. Huw related the de Bourg threat to kill all of Giles's family.

'That would be contrary to our laws, and we would want to prevent that.' Regan assured him. He suggested that Giles and his family should stay in Wexford, if a little removed from MacMurrough's court and the main towns. 'Maybe somewhere near the south coast? We have kinsmen there, and we could arrange for them to help with shelter and food.'

'Thank you, sir, my family are very grateful for your help.' Again, Huw was surprised at the offer of assistance and wondered if there were other issues at play that he did not know about. Perhaps Sir Robert had interceded.

Regan and Huw quickly made arrangements for their relocation to South Wexford.

'It's rugged enough country, but the people will make you welcome. You should at least be able to winter there,' Regan assured him. 'We will communicate through one of my couriers and I'll try and visit. I'll be able to help if you wish to talk to Sir Robert.'

'Thank you again, sir, we are very grateful.' Huw asked no questions, but his suspicions that Sir Robert had played a part in the arrangements were Sir Robert had played a part in the arrangements.

As they were taking their leave, Regan handed Huw a large bag of coin. 'Sir Robert and Lord MacMurrough want to make sure that Sir Giles and your family are safe.' He clasped Huw firmly by the hand before leaving to return to the celebrations.

While Waterford town feasted and slept, Huw slipped quietly out through the broken walls and headed to wake John Daws. He didn't know that Daiwin and Will Hen were amongst those who slept that night in Waterford.

CHAPTER 12

SOUTH WEXFORD
AUTUMN 1170

IT WAS A MILD moonlit night when Dai and Will Hen met as arranged on the hillside near de Bourg's castle. They decided to set off immediately for Robert fitz William's estate in Pembroke. They would travel for a few hours and then get some rest, before heading on again at daybreak.

'De Bourg won't leave until dawn at the earliest.' Dai tried to put himself in de Bourg's place. 'We will have a good head start and we should be able to move faster than twenty men.'

'We'd be a lot quicker if we had a couple of horses,' Hen suggested.

Dai knew that Hen was right. 'Could we risk going back into the village? De Bourg and his officers had horses.'

'They might have only one or two sentries, if any. I could scout around and take a look?' Hen offered.

'We'll have a look and see if it's worth taking a chance. The tavern where we met had stables at the back.'

They circled back to the far end of the village. Dai strung his bow and kept watch while Hen cut the ties on the gates leading to the tavern yard.

'Try not to kill anyone on guard. Those soldiers are Welshmen,' Dai whispered to Hen as he slipped quietly inside and crouched while his eyes adjusted to the darkness of the yard. Without a word, Hen was away through the shadows to the stables. Dai stood in the half-opened gate with an arrow in the groove and waited. He thought he heard muffled sounds coming from the stables, before Hen emerged leading two ponies.

'No big Norman horses, Huw,' Hen squeaked. 'A couple of ponies will have to do.'

Huw closed the gate behind him and they walked the ponies quietly away from the tavern.

'Had to hit the sentry twice, Huw, but I didn't kill him,' Hen apologised, as they mounted the ponies and trotted into the night towards Pembroke.

†

It was dusk on the following day when they reached Robert fitz William's castle. Dai had the letters of recommendation from Giles and they were greeted warmly by Sir Robert who was eager for news of his brother and the happenings in Ireland.

'Giles's children are safe and well but they cannot travel with you to Ireland as they are already in Normandy.' Sir Robert spoke matter-of-factly. 'We had visits from de Bourg's men seeking Giles's whereabouts, so we thought it safest to send the children to our cousin in France. Giles will understand. He will know they are safe, and when these matters are settled he can travel there himself.' Sir Robert was pleased that he had put a good plan in place.

'Sir Giles will be happy to hear about the children's well-being.' Dai was surprised but felt that Sir Robert needed to be reassured. 'We will return to Ireland shortly. What about your own safety, Sir Robert?'

'Little enough to worry about here, everyone seems to be getting ready to go to Ireland. I'll be safe enough. I expect the de Bourgs will learn that Giles is in Ireland, and they'll travel there also.' Sir Robert told Dai and Hen about the large forces being mobilised and the preparations being made by Strongbow to take an army to Ireland. 'There are men being recruited all over South Wales and beyond. It is rumoured that de Clare will arrive in Pembroke harbour shortly and set sail. I'm nearly tempted to go myself with all these promises of land and wealth in Ireland. But someone must stay and look after the family, I suppose,' he added, with a hint of regret.

Sir Robert was a number of years older than Giles and Dai thought he heard a trace of envy in his voice.

'Ireland may prove difficult, sir, there are many kings and lords there, all with different claims on land and titles. Sir Giles thinks the success of the expedition cannot be taken for granted. I'm sure he is happy you are here, and looking after family interests.'

'Giles will do well if he has men like you and Huw with him, and your friend of course.' Sir Robert nodded towards Will Hen. 'Now we must feed you well before you continue on your travels.'

†

Dai and Hen ate and drank and rested well before they left the castle. Sir Robert insisted on giving Dai and Hen chain mail and armour from his armoury together with fresh horses. He pushed a bag of coin into Dai's hand before they left.

'Go with God, and look after my brother as best you can,' Sir Robert called as they took their leave.

Heading towards the coast on their horses with new armour and a bag of money, Dai and Hen felt like soldiers of fortune on their way to the next adventure.

'I never owned my own horse before, and I've never had this much money,' Will Hen chirped happily. Dai had shared out the money that Sir Robert had given them. 'Maybe I can buy a little farm in Ireland.'

'We'll find you a nice small Irish woman to keep you company. But first we have to get to Ireland and find Sir Giles and Huw. Perhaps we could join up with this army that's being raised. They might be happy to take on two well-armed soldiers with their own horses.'

'So long as we don't meet up with de Bourg and his men,' Will Hen added.

The port town of Pembroke was crowded with knights and soldiers and they had little difficulty signing on with the army. They were assigned to an archer twenty-five under Sir Miles de Barry's banner. Two days after Dai and Hen arrived in Pembroke, Strongbow's army sailed for Ireland.

†

Dai had little time to think about finding his family when Strongbow's army landed on the Waterford coast. Hearing they were to attack Waterford town, he knew that Ferns was not too far distant. When their army was joined by other forces, he quickly identified Sir Robert fitz Stephen's banner, but could not get close enough to check for Sir Giles and Huw. Dai hoped that the archer troops might join forces but command was strict and de Barry's troops were assigned guarding duties on the right flank of the army. The march to Waterford was brisk and the attack followed quickly once they reached the town.

De Barry's men were not in the vanguard of the main assault, being kept in a guarding role at the rear for fear of an ambush while the main force was attacking. From their positions at the rear, Dai had a good view of the breaching of the walls and the furious attack by the Normans once the walls had been damaged. He wondered if Huw and Giles were amongst the men pouring into the town, and he hoped they were safe.

When Dai's troop entered Waterford, the garrison had been defeated and the town had surrendered. There were dead and wounded everywhere. Dai was shocked to see soldiers and townspeople being killed even after the surrender. Squads of Norman soldiers were killing any of the wounded who could not run to escape. The screams of the dying were everywhere and Dai wondered why the commanders didn't stop the slaughter. Dai and Hen didn't speak about what they saw. If they had been in the vanguard of the assault they might now be doing the killing.

After some hours, orders came through that the bodies were to be cleared from the streets. The killing had finally stopped as the rampaging soldiers had turned their attention to drinking and women. Dai and Hen were part of a large group of archers and townspeople assigned the task of collecting the bodies and carting them outside the town walls for burial. Dusk was falling when the streets were cleared and they were finally relieved.

Dai and Hen quickly set about trying to find Huw. When they eventually located Sir Robert's troops, most were drunk and incoherent. From the snippets of conversation and answers to their questions, Dai began to understand that Huw and Sir Giles were not there.

'From what I can get, they seem to have left Ferns in a hurry some weeks ago,' Will Hen confirmed what Dai had heard from the men. 'John Daws, too, they say. What do you think happened?'

'Don't know, Will, but it must have been something big. One man here says they went missing overnight, another says they took a cart, food and horses, and had two women with them.'

'There's some story about a Norman lord getting a search party out to look for them.' Hen gestured to an archer drinking in the corner. 'He says they didn't find them.'

'At least, then, it seems that Daws got here safe with my mother and Alice,' Dai reassured himself. 'Maybe when things are calmer tomorrow we'll find out more.'

'We'll find them Dai. At least they're safe, and away from this hellhole.' Hen sounded hopeful as he put a hand on Dai's shoulder.

†

Huw headed into the small settlement alone. He had left the others to wait in a thickly-wooded area while he scouted forward on horseback. Regan had given him the name of the village head and assured him that they would be welcome. Huw was cautious and persuaded Giles that it was best for him to meet the local people first to make sure they were expected. He passed a large area of cultivated land with grain looking ripe and close to harvest. Beyond the grain fields, a rough timber palisade fence enclosed a number of small mud and timber houses with straw roofs. Smoke rose in a vertical line from some of the houses. It was a warm afternoon, with little wind to blow the smoke away. A number of men working in the fields stopped as Huw approached. The gate in the palisade fence was open and Huw could see a number of small children playing inside. *Not exactly a fortified castle*, Huw thought, as he walked his horse past the men and up towards the gate. As he approached the gate, the children saw him and scurried off into different houses. Huw reined in his horse at the entrance and waited.

After a short while, two men appeared from one of the houses and approached Huw. They were dressed in rough tunics and unarmed. Huw sat still on his horse as the men approached. He had already planned an escape route to his left, away from the grain fields.

'Are you the Welshman sent by Regan?' The taller of the two men spoke slowly in Gaelic.

'I am Huw Ashe, and Maurice Regan said to come here.' Huw concentrated to find the right Gaelic words.

'Regan said there were three men and two women. Have you lost the others?' the man asked.

Huw was not sure if that was meant to be serious or if the man was making fun of him.

'They're back there in a wood. I might be able to find them again.' Huw waved his hand back towards where he had come from, then smiled and dismounted.

The men nodded and smiled in return.

'I am Kinsella and this is Ogie. We'll help you find them.' The taller man held out his hand and Huw took the firm grip. Ogie smiled broadly as Huw shook his hand next.

'Your words are good, but the accent is strange.' Ogie blushed as he spoke and Huw realised that under the crop of longish ginger hair and dirty face, he was only a boy, of maybe sixteen.

'Your friend Regan taught me a lot of Gaelic words, but I haven't spoken them enough,' Huw explained.

'You'll have to speak them here, as we know no others,' Kinsella responded. 'If you are satisfied, go and bring your family. Ogie will go with you.'

†

'We can make a home here.' Gwen spoke to Giles through the open door as she took a break from cleaning around the hearth. He had been ill at ease since their arrival two weeks ago. 'It's small, but it will shelter us, and we can cook, if Huw can find us food,' she said with a smile towards her son.

Huw and Daws had gone hunting rabbits with Ogie, while some of the young women had taken Alice to collect wild berries and nuts.

'These people have truly welcomed us. I just hope I don't bring trouble to them.' Giles stopped chopping wood outside to come in to sit and look at Gwen. He felt out of place in the village even though Kinsella and his people had tried to make him welcome. Huw, Daws and Alice had found it easier to adapt and settle in. There were a number of young men and women in the village, and they had seemed fascinated with Huw and his ability to speak Gaelic. Daws and Alice were accepted quickly as Huw's friends, even though they didn't have the language to communicate. Huw spoke for them.

'I wish I had Huw's easy manner and patience,' Giles spoke fondly of their son. 'He could just as easily fit in at the King's court as this village.'

'He could indeed,' Gwen ventured. 'It helps that he can speak their language, but I think he has many talents in dealing with different people.'

'It's good that we have him with us. We would have had great difficulty understanding all of this.' Giles waved his hand towards the village and their surrounds. 'How would we have communicated with these people without him?'

Huw had acted as go-between and negotiator with Kinsella and the people of the village since they arrived. They had been given a house with a smaller outer building attached. Huw and Daws slept in the outer building, while Gwen, Giles and Alice slept in the house. The house had one area with a hearth for cooking and two curtained alcoves which served as sleeping quarters. Huw and Daws were happy to sleep in the stable, as they called it. The autumn weather was mild. The winter might be different, but for now it served them well.

'Better than the damp grass under the stars,' Daws had assured them in his cheery manner.

The village gave them a stock of grain, cheese and dried meat to keep them fed for the first few days. Someone came with milk every day and in return Huw promised their labour when the grain harvest started. Giles was looking forward to the harvest so he could repay some of the kindness shown to them by the village.

'At least I won't feel so awkward and useless when I can do some work for them,' he told Gwen. She could feel Giles's frustration as he idled around the house most days. She tried to find work for him helping her to make the house more liveable. She knew that he was used to larger and better living quarters, and to having estates to look after. As a baron and lord, village life was very strange to him.

'The harvest should be exciting, everyone is looking forward to it.' Gwen stopped her work to sit beside Giles. She slipped her arm around his waist.

'Are you checking my girth size, Lady? I know I have expanded a little these last few years,' Giles said as softly as he could in Welsh.

'We are all getting older, I suppose.' Gwen nestled closer. This was the first time they had been alone in each other's company for a long time. Their kiss lingered as they held each other gently. Giles was the first to break off from the embrace.

'Lady Gwen, do you think you would marry me?'

The question was unexpected and Gwen was startled. Then she laughed.

'Sir, your mind changes direction very quickly. I thought you were going to tell me about your prowess in harvesting grain.

Now you want a harvest wedding. Shouldn't we wait until the children are settled, at least?' Gwen's tone was teasing.

'Gwen... I do not mean to push. We are to live together here. With Alice, I know, but I thought—' Giles broke off in mid-sentence as Gwen laughed again and put her hand to his lips.

'Sir Giles, no more words are needed, you need not explain to me. I have waited for you long enough.' Gwen looked into Giles's eyes. 'I will marry you tomorrow if you wish.'

†

'I just want to make sure I heard your Gaelic right.' Kinsella asked Huw to repeat what he had said. 'You want a priest to do a marriage? Who are you marrying?'

'Not me, sir, my father wants to marry my mother.' Huw tried to choose his Gaelic words carefully.

'The monks might have difficulty with that arrangement.' Kinsella laughed loudly. 'We might not tell them all the details.'

Huw looked bemused and tried to explain his parents' situation. Kinsella listened for a moment before holding up his hand.

'Huw Ashe, too many words often confuse. There are many monks at the monastery. For certain, we can get one to come to do the marriage, but might we wait until the harvest is done?'

'Yes, indeed sir, after the harvest. We do not want to impose.' Kinsella stopped him again.

'You are our guests, and our friends, and with your help our harvesting will be quicker. Our friends at the monastery may also accept help with their harvest.' Kinsella raised his eyebrows in question. Huw nodded. 'A harvest wedding.' Kinsella laughed. 'My wife loves a good wedding.'

†

The harvest began two days later. The weather was fine and sunny and nearly everyone from the village was out in the fields, including the Welsh and Norman visitors. Some of the older women stayed behind to cook meals and bring food and drink to the workers. As the first day wore on, Huw noticed that other men began to arrive and join in the work.

'Friends and neighbours,' Kinsella told him. 'We will harvest in their village next.'

Huw was amazed at how his father took to the work. After a brief period while he learned the technique, he cut and carried as well as any man there. Daws, too, seemed to relish the hard work.

'Huw, I want a little farm of my own. Grow a few things, keep some pigs. I love pigs.' Daws prattled on, as he and Huw worked side by side. 'Maybe a few cattle as well.'

'Maybe one of Kinsella's daughters might look at you when she's a bit older. He might give you some land if you married one.' Huw spoke in quiet Welsh. 'Or he might stick a pike in your back.'

Daws laughed and began to sing a Welsh farming song.

'Ah, no, Daws, not singing, you don't have a note. You'll drive those men back to their villages if you don't shut up,' Huw pleaded in vain. All around people looked up from their work and called out to Daws. Some started to sing their own songs. 'Now look what you've done, Daws, the work will take forever.'

The harvesting took three days to complete. After all of the grain was separated and stored, most of the men, including Huw, Giles and Daws, travelled to the neighbours' village and started on their harvest. The village and fields were smaller than the Kinsella holdings, and in two days it was finished.

'Now for some drinking,' Kinsella called to Huw, as the last of the straw was stacked. 'We have to share their food and drink before we travel back.'

Huw looked at Kinsella with raised eyebrows.

'You have to learn our customs to survive in our land,'

Kinsella laughed. 'Make sure you and your friends get drunk, or the young Kinsellas won't be happy.'

'Young Kinsellas?' Huw asked.

'This is a Kinsella village also. The big man is known as Young Kinsella. He's my little brother.' Kinsella smiled and waved his hand in a circle. 'There are cousins in villages around as well. You can't go too far without meeting one of us.'

The drinking lasted well into the night, and Huw had to spill some of his drink as the session went on, to make sure that he was at least partly sober. Daws was unsteady on his feet as they helped Giles into the cart for the homeward journey.

'Please, Daws, no more singing,' Huw begged, as the cart rattled along the rough pathway in the moonlight. 'I don't feel too well and your songs make me want to throw up.'

Daws ignored him and sang even louder. Behind them on the pathway the other men began to laugh and sing. Huw looked at his father asleep in the back of the cart and laughed to himself before adding his Welsh voice to Daws's noise.

'Free Welsh men, free, free land to the sea.'

Neither of them knew all the words, but they quickly drowned out the Gaelic voices behind them.

†

It was late next morning when Huw was woken by Kinsella's knock on the door.

'So, Huw Ashe, what about this wedding? I'm not sure if your father could make it today,' he laughed, 'but if you are fit we could travel to the monastery to find a willing monk.'

'Yes indeed, sir, I'm fit.' Huw shook himself awake and out of his bed. 'Some bread and water, lots of water, and I'm with you.'

'I'm coming too,' Daws croaked from underneath his bedclothes.

CHAPTER 13

SOUTH WEXFORD
LATE AUTUMN 1170

Huw, Daws and Kinsella spent two days at the monastery helping the monks harvest their grain. Huw was beginning to get used to the back-breaking work and his hands had hardened once the blisters had worn off. Daws laughed at Huw in the evening when he found him bathing his hands in cold water.

'Afraid you won't be able to draw the bow string, Huw boy?' Daws asked in his best concerned voice. 'No battles this winter if we're lucky.'

'Don't you worry, John Daws, I'll be ready for whatever happens in the winter.' Huw's hands hurt, but he was happy to be back to full health and strength after his lingering illness. 'This Kinsella land seems peaceful enough. Maybe we'll be left alone here, for a while at least,' he said wistfully. 'Some peace at least for my father and mother to marry and settle.'

'We'll make sure of that, Huw boy, after a good wedding,' Daws echoed. 'What news of that?'

'Kinsella is gone to talk to a monk friend of his, to see what can be done.'

When he returned, Kinsella told them he had arranged for a monk to come to the village in two days.

'Father Ailbe is as good as his word, he'll be there. A few small coins will help him to remember,' Kinsella laughed as he told Huw of the arrangement. 'He likes weddings, Father Ailbe does, and mead too. He can do the service in Gaelic or Latin, whatever pleases you.'

'Sir Giles might prefer Latin. My mother will not care,' Huw responded with a smile.

'That's settled so,' Kinsella nodded. 'A little more of the good monks' mead and we might make it home by nightfall.'

A short time later, and more sober than after the last harvest, they headed homeward on foot through the early evening sunshine.

†

'Something's wrong here, Huw boy,' Daws spoke first as the three of them emerged from a wooded area on the brow of a small hill.

The light was fading but they could see the village in the distance. The smoke coming from some of the houses inside the palisade fence was thicker than normal. They could hear angry voices in the distance. Kinsella began to run, Huw and Daws following close behind. As they got a little closer, Huw could see the glint of armour and chain mail from the men gathered in front of the main palisade gate. Four on horseback in full Norman armour and maybe twenty more soldiers on foot. Huw counted quickly as he ran faster to catch up with Kinsella.

'No! Kinsella, hold,' Huw called to Kinsella to stop. 'We can't rush in there.' Kinsella ignored him and kept running towards the village. Huw gestured to Daws to come forward. Daws had edged a little to one side to get a better look at the village. As Huw gestured, Daws was already getting closer. He grabbed Kinsella around the shoulders and knocked him to the ground. Kinsella was up in a flash with his dagger drawn.

'Bastards,' he shouted. 'What are you doing to my family, Norman robbers! We took you in!'

Daws was on his feet but did not draw his sword. Huw stood still with his bow staff unstrung.

'Kinsella, look again at the village! The main gate is closed. Those soldiers are trying to get in. Giles and your family must be inside defending the gate.' Huw spoke evenly, looking Kinsella directly in the eye. 'Daws and I will help you, but we can't just rush those soldiers, we'll all be killed.'

Kinsella hesitated and looked from Daws to Huw. 'Who are those men, Huw Ashe, and why are they attacking us?' He turned his bewildered, fearful gaze towards his village.

'They are no friends of ours, Kinsella, but I know who they are and what they want.' Huw quickly told Kinsella about the conflict between Giles and the de Bourgs, and how they had sworn to kill all his family.

'They want to kill all of you?' Kinsella asked as he continued to stare at his home in the distance.

'Yes, sir, they do. Now you and your family are caught up in our fight. It was not our wish.' Huw immediately regretted coming to Kinsella's village and bringing this danger upon his people.

'It looks like they're discussing tactics before the next attack, Huw,' Daws gestured towards the source of the loud voices. 'If we could get a bit closer, we might hear what's going on.'

There was open land, where the corn had been cut, between them and the village. The only cover in front was a line of thick yellow-flowered bushes skirting the edge of the corn field.

'It looks like they beat off the first attack somehow.' Huw nodded his agreement as they both scoured the landscape to see how they might get closer without being seen.

'I can see about four crossbow men, and maybe a couple of longbows. They probably shot fire arrows into the roof thatch inside. We have to take the shooters first. John, what do you think?'

'Right enough, boy, they'll keep shooting into the village as long as arrows last. With them gone, our chances improve. We could track behind those bushes to get closer? Once we fire though, we're exposed,' Daws added.

'John, maybe you and Kinsella could circle around and get inside. He would want to be with his family.' Huw translated roughly into Gaelic for Kinsella to understand what they were thinking. 'They will have some men guarding the rear to catch people escaping – you two would have to deal with them.'

'Might not be as quick as Will Hen with a knife, but I can do that,' Daws nodded. 'Not too happy leaving you on your own, though.'

'Give me six of your arrows John, that'll make twenty I'll have. Might take two men at least, before they know where the fire is from. I'll run for the trees if they send horsemen.' Huw again explained to Kinsella what they were planning, and Kinsella nodded agreement.

'There's a small back gate, if we can get there I'll call to someone inside to open it,' Kinsella said.

'That's it so, John.' Huw explained about the gate to Daws. 'If I'm in trouble, I'll make for that gate too. I'll call out in Gaelic to open up.'

'All right, Huw boy. You'll have to teach me Gaelic words, one of these days.'

'If you're still alive I'll do that. Make you into a proper Irishman.'

'Make sure you keep your head, together with that mouth of yours,' Daws laughed as he spoke.

Their conversation lasted no more than two minutes before they parted, Daws and Kinsella circling away to the left, keeping out of sight of the village. Huw had to crawl a short distance before he reached the cover of the yellow bushes. Then he ran until he was about a hundred paces from the attackers. *Flimsy cover*, he thought, *but if I'm lucky they won't spot me for a while.* He could now hear the shouted French conversation between a mounted knight and someone behind the palisade fence. *Only Sir Giles in the village has that language*, Huw almost shouted out loud, realising his father was safe. The horseman was one of the de Bourg brothers.

'Last offer, fitz William, you come out now alone, your whore can live. If not, she and all your Irish dog friends will die. Women, children, all,' de Bourg roared.

There was no answer from inside. Huw felt that Giles might come out, even though he would know that de Bourg would slaughter everyone no matter what. *Can't give him that option*, Huw thought, *I need to start a fight.*

Huw quickly strung his long bow and stuck six arrows in the ground in front of him. He was not sure if he could pierce armour at that distance, so he singled out the crossbowmen. They were just standing around behind de Bourg, slightly closer to Huw. They were out of range of the small Irish bows of the villagers, so the crossbowmen were exposed, not expecting an attack. Huw stood upright, tall and firm with the first arrow in the groove. He knew he would be seen standing upright, but it was necessary to be upright to fully draw the bow. The first shaft fell five paces short and his target turned to look as he heard the arrow hit the ground. The second shaft was in the air as the man turned, and it crashed into his breast-bone, knocking him backwards. *One more before I move*, Huw thought. He picked the nearest man, held for an instant as he saw the arrow's target, then he loosed the cord. The second man was down and screaming with an arrow through his lower stomach before the rest of the attackers turned around and realised what was happening. Huw quickly loosed two more shafts but both missed as the men began to move and find cover. Huw crouched low and ran thirty paces behind the bush line. *I must get one more at least.* He stopped and stuck two arrows in the ground with another already in the groove. The crossbowmen were now lying on the ground shooting bolts at the bushes near where Huw had been. *Poor chance shooting at them now.* Instead, he picked the nearest mounted knight and aimed for one of his legs. *Him or the horse*, Huw thought, as he fired twice in quick succession. The man cursed and the horse screamed as both arrows struck home. Huw crouched and ran. The bushes quickly thinned and Huw saw that he was at the end of the cover. Two more arrows in the ground, he stood and looked over the last bush. Two mounted knights and maybe six men were heading in his direction. De Bourg held his ground and stood tall in his stirrups for looking for signs in the bushes. The other horseman was sitting on the ground beside his dying horse.

'To your right, fools,' de Bourg shouted at the advancing men, pointing at Huw. 'There's one there at the end.'

Huw picked one of the men on foot. He was running towards him, getting closer. Huw shot and the man toppled backwards with the shaft in his face. The other men on foot hesitated but the two horsemen gathered speed. They were now no more than fifty paces from Huw. The next arrow was away and embedded in the leading horse's chest, as Huw put the final arrow from the ground into the groove.

'Quickly, Huw, decide!' Huw spoke to himself: man or horse? The first knight was up on his feet after his fall and was heading towards him with his broadsword drawn. Huw didn't see the shafts as they crashed into the second horse's side. The knight roared as the heavy horse toppled to one side trapping his leg. The knight on foot stopped as an arrow glanced off his breast armour. Instantly Huw knew that it must be Daws. He glanced towards the village and saw the big man's unmistakable frame outside the village gate, with another arrow in the groove. Standing close to Daws, he recognised his father in his knight's armour with his broadsword drawn. Beside them stood Kinsella, and at least fifteen men with small Irish bows and spears.

'Our own little Irish, Welsh, Norman army!' Huw thought aloud again, then roared as he loosed an arrow at the knight on foot, 'The Kinsellas!' The shaft cracked into the man's body armour almost knocking him. Huw was out from his hiding place, another arrow in the groove. He walked quickly towards the knight who was now only ten paces away. 'Sir, you may not be so lucky with this shaft,' Huw said loudly to him, in Norman French. The man's visor was open and Huw could see the bewilderment in his face. 'Yield, sir, and you shall live,' Huw's voice was calmer now. The man turned to look towards de Bourg and the foot soldiers. They had retreated and were heading towards the woods beyond the corn fields. De Bourg was still standing high on his horse looking backwards towards the village.

The knight paused for a moment as he turned back towards Huw.

'I yield to you sir. Who are you?' The knight's voice was dry with shock.

'I am Huw Ashe, son of Sir Giles fitz William. And you?'

'Alun de Barry, and I am your prisoner. That is my brother David,' de Barry gestured to the knight trapped by the dying horse. 'Can I help him?'

Huw didn't hesitate. 'I will deal with the horse. You see if you can free him.'

Huw drew his knife and firmly holding the horse's mane he quickly cut the prone animal's windpipe. When the animal had stopped moving, Huw lifted the horse's back as much as he could while de Barry pulled his brother from underneath. The man groaned with pain and then passed out.

'Thank you, Huw Ashe.' De Barry looked up from his kneeling position beside his brother as Daws and Giles arrived with weapons drawn.

†

'Is it fair on these people that we should stay here? The de Bourgs will return.' Giles spoke his thoughts out loud.

They were all just finishing a morning meal prepared by Gwen and Alice. Huw and Daws had slept by the hearth that night, having put the de Barry knights in the outer stable. The younger de Barry, who had been trapped by his fallen horse, was unable to walk. They had put on rough timber splints where his leg had been crushed by the horse, but he was in pain and getting feverish. Alun de Barry had given his word not to try to escape.

'It will be trouble for Kinsella, us being here or not. Those bastards will not show mercy,' Daws replied as he finished his huge plate of food.

'John is right, sir.' Huw had been thinking the same as his father, but Daws's simple logic made sense. If they left, they would be leaving the village unprotected and they would not know if de Bourg returned and attacked the Kinsellas. 'We should at least stay and put up proper defences. The palisade fence gives little protection.'

'That is true. We can offer our help to Kinsella, but stay or leave, it is his decision to make. If they wish us to go, we will do so.' Giles looked at Gwen, who nodded agreement. 'Huw, talk to Kinsella, offer our help with fortifying the village, and tell him that we will leave when the work is done.'

†

'I have spoken to all the families in the village and they want you to stay, as do I,' Kinsella replied simply when Huw put their plan to him. 'We would welcome your help with making our village more secure. We have buried those dead men outside. Will the wounded man live?'

'His leg is broken, and he has a fever. He *should* live, but I'm not sure.'

'I will get my wife to come and help him. She is a healer.'

'You would do that for a man who attacked you, a man who would kill you?' Huw asked.

'We will do what we can to help him live, but the men are your prisoners. You must decide what to do with them,' Kinsella replied.

'My prisoners,' Huw echoed. 'We would not kill them, but we do not want them returning to de Bourg and giving knowledge of what is here. We will have to think about what to do.'

'Very good, Huw Ashe. Now, don't forget we have a wedding tomorrow,' Kinsella smiled.

'I *had* forgotten. I hope my father and mother remember.'

†

Father Ailbe arrived in the early afternoon on the following day. His cart was well stocked with two barrels of ale and mead in large earthenware jugs.

'Weddings can be thirsty work,' he winked, as Huw and Kinsella welcomed him.

'That's true, Father. We have some Kinsella ale that you might taste for us,' Kinsella responded.

'My father seems nervous today; maybe some of your drink might help him, Father,' Huw joined in the banter.

Giles and Gwen were married in the open air in the Kinsella village on that early September afternoon. The Kinsellas had decorated the village with wild plants and flowers. Village life and work stopped and everyone brought food and drink to fill the long tables lining the village centre. After Father Ailbe had done his work and the newly wedded couple had kissed, the feasting and drinking started. Singing too – lots of singing and storytelling.

Alice had arranged to spend some days living in the Kinsella house, to give Giles and Gwen some honeymoon time alone. Daws and Huw moved back in with the de Barry knights in the stable.

'A bit crowded, Huw, we'll have to build something,' Daws said to Huw as they drank Kinsella's ale.

'I'm not marrying you, Daws, you snore and have smelly feet.'

'Right you are, boy, you can sleep with those Norman boys, so.'

Giles had invited the de Barry knights to the wedding. 'It would be discourteous not to do so,' he had told Huw. Alun de Barry sat quietly at a table, looking out of place. His brother's fever still raged, but Kinsella's wife said that he would recover.

'Like you, Daws, he doesn't have a Gaelic word. We should go and talk to him.'

'Off you go, boy, I'll have a drink with Kinsella. And his daughter…' Daws said happily.

'You do that, Daws, she'll love a bit of Welsh singing. Try not to insult everyone.' Huw went and sat beside de Barry. He was drinking ale and seemed to be enjoying it as best he could. 'How did you come to be fighting for de Bourg?'

De Barry told Huw that he and his brother had just been in Ireland a few days when they met the de Bourgs after the sack of Waterford. They had come over in a small ship some days after Strongbow landed with his main army. They wanted to join their cousin Miles, who had a troop with Strongbow. Miles de Barry's troop was part of Strongbow's force, that had set out with MacMurrough to take Dublin. Alun and David had little money and did not know the land, so Henry de Bourg had offered them money and position if they joined the quest to find Giles fitz William. Somehow, de Bourg had found out that Giles and his family were in a Kinsella village in south Wexford; de Barry did not know how he had got the information. De Bourg had told him that Giles fitz William had murdered one of his brothers, and the de Bourgs wanted to bring him to King Henry's court for justice.

Huw told de Barry what had happened between Giles and the de Bourgs and how they had sworn an oath to kill all of Giles's family.

'I swear, Huw Ashe, we did not know this,' de Barry grabbed Huw by the arm. 'We would not have joined de Bourg if we had known. You and your father have shown us fairness in battle, and kindness afterwards, and so have these people here.' De Barry gestured towards the Kinsellas. 'We are in your debt, all of you.'

Huw realised that de Barry had drunk a lot of ale and mead, but he also sensed sincerity in his words. 'We will talk again tomorrow, sir, for now we must enjoy my parents' wedding.' Huw raised his tankard and they both drank deeply.

†

Huw rose early the next morning. He woke Alun de Barry and asked him to come with him to scout the land surrounding the village. De Barry was surprised but went willingly with Huw. The village was quiet as they left on foot by the main gate. Daws was still sleeping and Huw did not disturb his father.

'We have been invited by Kinsella to spend the winter here. In return we are going to help him fortify the village,' Huw paused as they reached the wooded area where they had last seen de Bourg. He looked de Barry in the eye. 'If you wish to leave now I will not stop you. You are released as my prisoner.' Huw spoke evenly and calmly to the startled de Barry. 'We will help care for your brother, and he can leave too, as he wishes, when he is recovered.'

De Barry looked back at the village from their vantage point. He did not speak for some moments.

'I do not wish to leave without my brother, Huw Ashe, and if you permit, I would stay and help with the village defences. David, too, will help, I'm sure – when he can.' De Barry was measured in his reply. 'We will not join again with de Bourg to fight against you, but we will fight with you, if your family will have us.'

'We cannot pay for your service and you will have to work for your food, but we will have you gladly.' Huw held out his hand and smiled. De Barry clasped it warmly.

CHAPTER 14

AN EARLY WEXFORD SETTLEMENT
LATE AUTUMN 1170

ALUN DE BARRY PROVED to be a strong and able worker in the months that followed the de Bourg attack. His brother recovered slowly, but he too contributed as he regained his health.

Most days, willing helpers came from other villages. Kinsella told Huw his many cousins were interested to learn about village fortifications. As part of the plan, Huw had Kinsella post sentries and engage in regular scouting forays into the surrounding countryside. In this way, they would be forewarned if another attack was on the way. David de Barry was put in charge of scouting and sentry operations. He still walked with some difficulty and had a limp, but he quickly regained his ability to ride a horse.

Giles designed a structure that integrated the existing village into a motte and bailey type fortification. It required the felling and trimming of a large amount of trees. They decided to cut from the front of the forests that were all around the village. This would afford less cover to anyone approaching, allowing them to be seen sooner. Kinsella thought they would have about three months until the weather got worse as winter arrived. These months were used to cut and transport the timber and to shape it to Giles's design. Large quantities of rocks and earth were carted into the village and used to form a foundation and mound for where the central structure would be erected. The existing palisade fence was reinforced with a second inner timber wall, almost twice the height of the fence. Four square tower platforms were erected at regular intervals around the wall. These were roofed and were big enough to comfortably hold six men with bows. The towers were lined by an inner platform that ran the length of the perimeter. A bridge tower was erected over the main gate.

The main gate provided the only area of contention between Giles and Kinsella. Giles wanted to dig out a deep ditch in front of the gate and to continue this about forty paces to each side. His plan was to extend the ditch all around the walls in time. Kinsella thought this would hinder access to the village and place restrictions on his people coming and going. The new drawbridge design for the gate would require it to be manned at all times.

'He does not understand what I want to do,' Giles complained to Huw. 'The gate is a weak area and needs strong defences. I think he pretends not to know that there will be a drawbridge to cross the ditch.' Giles looked to Huw for affirmation.

Huw was translator between Giles and Kinsella and he had begun to feel tension rising between the two men as the work intensified. He was not sure, but he thought he sensed some resentment in Kinsella. *Perhaps he feels we are taking over*, Huw thought, *and maybe we are.*

'I'll talk to Kinsella later today and try to find out his thinking.' Huw and Giles were sitting together having their noon meal. Huw nodded towards the dark clouds gathering in the east. 'It looks like rain is on the way.'

'A storm coming in from the sea, maybe.' Giles gazed away towards the darkening sky. 'We are lucky to have so much completed before the bad weather sets in.'

Giles had immersed himself in the construction work and Huw realised that he had taken little time for himself and his new wife over the last few months. Huw was very happy that his parents were now together, but he had not thought of how their new arrangement might be affecting them. They had lived separate lives for over twenty years. Huw felt that their new living arrangements must put a strain on their relationship, and his father was used to much larger and more comfortable accommodation. However, his mother seemed very happy and his father never spoke about any difficulties. Huw decided that it was not his place to intervene unless asked.

Alice had moved in with Kinsella and his wife. Niamh, Kinsella's oldest daughter, and Alice had become friends. Alice was beginning to learn some Gaelic words and she had settled well into village life. She often spoke to Huw about Daiwin and he told her about their family life in Wales as they grew up. He sometimes spoke to her in Gaelic and helped her to translate Welsh words.

Daws had taken advantage of the all the extra workers and building materials and had built another section onto the stable. He and Huw now used this as their living quarters, with the de Barry brothers billeted in the original outhouse. Daws too was learning some basic Gaelic words and phrases and he could converse in Gaelic about the weather.

'They talk a lot about the weather here, Huw boy, I have to know the words,' Daws explained, though Huw knew he was learning to talk about more than just the weather. Daws seemed to be friends with all the young men, and he had begun to teach them the skills of longbow shooting. 'Not strong enough to fully draw it yet, but they're getting more aim,' Daws said, giving Huw his views on Kinsella's men. 'Might be useful when those Bourg boys come again.'

'Indeed it might, John.' Huw realised then that everyone expected the de Bourgs to attack again. The only questions were when and how.

†

'I was thinking we should increase our scouting parties. Maybe go a little further and more often,' Huw had joined Kinsella on one of the towers. They were looking out over the woods towards the approaching rain. 'Our Norman friends might decide to visit again before the winter sets in.'

'If they are coming again, it will have to be soon, before the land gets boggy.' Kinsella had been having the same thoughts. 'We are better prepared, but they will bring more men, maybe?'

'They're not the kind of men to give up, and they will find others willing to fight for money.' Huw was honest with Kinsella. 'It would be better if we knew more of de Bourg's planning. Do you have people who could contact Maurice Regan?'

'That could be done, Huw Ashe. What do you want to know?'

'If we knew where de Bourg was based, we could do some scouting, and maybe Regan's people could find out what support he has gathered.'

'I will send someone to Ferns tomorrow. Is there anything else on your mind?'

Huw smiled at Kinsella's directness. 'What does your family call you, sir?'

'Fool, sometimes,' Kinsella laughed. 'But my friends call me Donal, and you can too.'

'I'll do that so,' Huw replied. 'My father is very grateful to you for allowing us to live here. He feels obliged and responsible to you and wants to return your kindness in the only way he knows.' He paused. 'Sometimes he can be over enthusiastic and single-minded. Stubborn, even, when his mind is made up. But he does not intend to take over your village and land. We will leave here in the springtime, or sooner if you wish.' Huw paused again, and looked out at the gathering darkness. 'He is worried that he may have offended you about the gate defences.'

'I am not offended, Huw Ashe, but maybe as stubborn as your father,' Kinsella replied slowly. 'Some people here are worried that our village may become a Norman stronghold, and they have told me their concerns. I have some of those fears, but maybe we need our homes to be better protected, and not just from foreigners.'

'Foreigners?' Huw had not heard the word used before.

'People are wary of the number of people coming across from Wales. More continue to arrive and King Diarmaid's army is now strong enough to take and hold Leinster. Our King is an ambitious man and maybe he is looking beyond Leinster. Ambition like that leads to wars between Kings.' Kinsella turned and looked directly at Huw, gesturing towards the village cornfields. 'New people need food and shelter, and land.'

The rain was beginning to arrive and Huw pondered on Kinsella's words. It was the first time he fully realised that the Norman expedition to Ireland might be the beginning of a much bigger invasion. Kinsella's concerns became much clearer to him. These people were worrying that their homes and land might be taken from them by force, and they felt under threat. Huw was shocked by this realisation.

'We have long had other enemies. The Northmen from the sea, ambitious Kings from the north, and the MacCarthys from Munster. To name but a few.' Kinsella smiled at Huw. 'So your father's plans are good. Tell him we'll dig the ditch and help him to build the gate bridge.'

'I will tell him, Donal Mór Kinsella, and we will dig and build it together.' Huw held out his hand and Kinsella clasped it. 'I have heard of these MacCarthys of Munster, are they part of a strong kingdom?' Huw remembered the song at Donal Mór O'Brien's feast, when he had first exchanged glances with Bridín.

'Strong enough to the west of us and along the coast. They've been known to come raiding when they're not farther west fighting the O'Briens. Tough people, and they had to be, to carve out a kingdom in Munster.' Kinsella gave grudging praise to a one-time enemy. 'We have some strong enemies in Ireland and maybe across the water who would have an eye for our land and our cattle, so we welcome your help with the fortifications. We can talk about you leaving whenever that time comes,' Donal Kinsella added cryptically, just before they ran to their houses to take shelter from the rain.

†

Huw briefed Giles on his conversation with Donal Kinsella, and in the rainy days that followed they discussed the Norman expedition to Ireland and the concerns that Kinsella had expressed.

'I hadn't thought about the expedition in those terms,' Giles told Huw. 'I never thought of it as an invasion, but now I see the possibility. At least I can understand how the Irish might think it so. But then, we were invited to come by MacMurrough,' he added, as an afterthought. 'It is troubling, though, that these people, our friends, might have their land and possessions taken.'

'They have helped us, sir, and we will do what we can to repay their help. You are doing that by making their homes secure,' Huw assured his father. 'We may not be able to influence what happens elsewhere.'

'You are ever the pragmatist and diplomat, Huw. We would all be in trouble without you.' Giles raised his cup to Huw and drank. Gwen looked up, and also drank to Huw. She had been sitting quietly at the table, listening to Giles and Huw discuss the politics of the Welsh-Norman expedition in Ireland. She had other concerns.

'I wonder about Daiwin and his friend Will,' Gwen's soft voice interrupted the others' thoughts. 'Do you think they are in Ireland?'

Daiwin had never been far from any of their thoughts, but they had spoken little about him. Huw had thought about going back to Waterford and Wexford towns to scout for information, but the de Bourg attack and the work in the village had forced his attention elsewhere.

'When the weather closes down the works here, maybe Daws and I could go to the port towns and Ferns to scout for information. Perhaps they are back, and have re-joined Sir Robert's forces. I could also get Kinsella to ask Maurice Regan to make discreet enquiries.' Huw was already planning as he spoke.

'Your friend Regan might be the best way to get news. I don't want two sons lost.' Gwen's voice quivered with emotion and both Huw and Giles looked at her with some surprise. They had been wound up in their work in the village and had not realised the anguish felt by Gwen. Huw was confident in Daiwin's ability and assumed that he would just show up one day. John Daws had been reassuring about how the events in Wales were handled and Huw hadn't felt any need for concern. He knew now his mother did not feel that way, and he began to question his own assumptions about Daiwin.

'Gwen, I'm sorry, I seem to have let Daiwin's situation slip to the back of my mind. When you and Daws and Alice arrived, I assumed that Dai would follow. We need to find out what happened.' Giles reached out to touch his wife's arm.

'Kinsella has agreed to contact Regan. He could speak to Sir Robert. But it would be better and quicker if I went myself.' Huw looked at his parents. 'I could take a couple of Kinsella's men, if he agrees. Daws should stay here, in case—'

'In case we are attacked again,' Gwen finished for him.

'Yes, mother, just in case.'

'I think Huw is right. Sir Robert will speak to him, and help if he can. He might even send some men back to Wales, if Daiwin has not arrived.' Giles nodded to Huw.

'Then go and do it, but come back quickly.' Gwen tried to hold back a sob as she spoke.

†

Three days later Huw, accompanied by two Kinsella men, arrived in Ferns. He was surprised to find that the Norman army was not there and he went straight to MacMurrough's great hall in search of Maurice Regan.

'Huw Ashe, I didn't expect to see you.' Regan was surprised when Huw was announced as his visitor. 'My lord MacMurrough and Strongbow have marched on Dublin and I expect news of their conquest shortly.'

Regan gave Huw an update of happenings since their last meeting in Waterford, as they shared wine and cheese. Huw was surprised at how quickly events happened now that Strongbow and his army had arrived. He also realised how isolated he and his family had become in their south Wexford village. *We have lost touch with our comrades and have no communication lines to find out what is happening,* he thought, resolving to find some way of regular communication. He explained to Regan the reason for his visit and his search for Daiwin.

'The garrison in Ferns is from Lord MacMurrough's soldiers, but there are a few Norman and Welsh men in the infirmary.

Some wounded, some sick,' Regan gave Huw some hope of news. 'Perhaps some of them might know of your brother.'

Huw sought out the Welsh amongst the fifty or so men in the infirmary. A number of men had serious wounds from battle, but most were sick with fever. Some were dying. He spoke to one of the monks caring for the sick and asked him to point out any Welshmen. His countrymen were housed together in an alcove and Huw recognised at least two familiar faces amongst the twenty men. He asked if anyone knew Will Hen or Daiwin Ashe.

'Huw, Huw Ashe, it's me, Tom Shenks, over here.' Shenks beckoned Huw over to his cot. 'I seen Will Hen in Waterford town, I did. He was alive and kicking after the fight.'

'Tom Shenks! How are you?' Huw smiled as he clasped the hand held out to him.

'I'm alive, Huw, alive! A bit of a leg gone missing, but they say I'll live.' Shenks pointed to his left leg underneath the covers. 'Only muscle and sinew sliced off with an axe, should still be able to draw the longbow, if I can stand straight.' Shenks grinned broadly while he held on to Huw's hand.

'Tom, do you know anything more of Will Hen and Daiwin?'

'Gone to Dublin town with the army, Huw. They're all gone to Dublin. Strongbow is here you know, with a huge army of men.' Shenks spoke rapidly, as if he didn't want to stop. 'MacMurrough gathered a huge army too, and they marched north after taking Waterford town. Left us here to get better, they did.' Shenks gestured around the infirmary. 'Some lads are not so good, Huw, not so lucky as me, I'd say.' He caught his breath as he looked around. 'I spoke to Will Hen, I did. Gave me a hand one day after the Waterford fight. They were clearing the dead and wounded. Brought me to the infirmary and gave me ale and cheese, Will did. Didn't meet Daiwin but Will told me he was there.'

'Tom, you did well to stay alive, and I thank you for telling me this. It's good to know they were safe.' Huw put his hand on his comrade's shoulder. 'Did Will speak about anything else?'

'He did say that they had been back to Wales and that some children were safe. I don't remember the children's names, Huw, sorry. They joined Strongbow's army in Milford, and they were with de Barry's troop, I think.'

'Sir Miles de Barry?' Huw asked quickly.

'Sir Miles, yes, I think it was him.'

Huw sat and talked to Shenks and the other Welshmen who were well enough to talk for an hour or so. They talked about Wales and their families and what they would do when they recovered. Before he left, Huw gave Shenks as much coin as he could spare.

'Maybe enough to get you home, Tom, if that's what you want.' Huw felt embarrassed, not knowing if Tom would be able to go home, or if he would even recover from his wound. Would the sick and wounded be allowed to go home? Who would help them? 'I will come back to call on you again, Tom. Thank you for the news about Dai and Hen – I must find them.'

'You go, Huw, go on and find them. You must, Huw. Tell them that I was asking about them and that we'll meet up again and drink ale. Tell them that.'

'I will, Tom, I'll tell them.'

†

Huw was conflicted as he walked back to Regan's quarters. He pondered over the different options. *Should I head to Dublin? If I did I would have to join up with the army again, and how would I get Dai and Hen to leave and come back with me? Would they want to leave, even if allowed? Should I return to the Kinsella village and tell my parents what I've found out? Mother will be very happy that Dai is alive and safe in Ireland. Then again, can he be safe if the army is attacking Dublin?*

He told Regan what he had found out.

'We have supply wagons travelling after the army all the time, and messengers going back and forth to Lord MacMurrough. We can easily send messages,' Regan assured him. 'We can find out about your friends, but it would not be easy to get permission for them to leave during a campaign.'

'No, indeed sir, I understand that. Getting messages to them would be a great help, and an ease to my family, thank you.'

'We must help our friends, Huw.' Regan waived his hand to dismiss Huw's thanks. 'We need to set up some more efficient communication lines between us, I think.'

Huw and Regan sat and planned how they might establish regular links between them. Regan agreed that he would be the conduit through which Huw and Giles could communicate with Sir Robert fitz Stephen. Huw told Regan of his agreement with Sir Robert.

'"Huw Ashe" is the password. Sir Robert has agreed to listen when it is used.' Huw recalled their conversation before they left Ferns.

'We will get Kinsella to put in place more regular trips from the village to Ferns. I will come up with some reason – trade in crops and mead from the monks, maybe.' Regan seemed happy to talk intrigue. 'I think it would be better if you returned to your family, Huw. From what you tell me, the village needs you more than the army. I will get messages to Sir Robert to let him know that you are safe, and I will locate your brother.'

'Thank you again, sir. I will return to the Kinsella village and wait for your messages. My mother will be happy to have news.'

Huw hesitated as he was taking his leave from Regan.

'There is something else, Huw?' Regan queried as they shook hands.

'Those men, in the infirmary, what will become of them, sir?'

'I think the time has come for you to call me Regan, or Maurice. We are friends now and equals, are we not?'

'Yes, sir— Maurice, I'm happy to be your friend.'

'The sick and wounded will be looked after by the monks and the women, as best they can. Those that recover will re-join the army, those that die will get a Christian burial,' Regan assured Huw.

'Some of them are Welsh comrades, I hadn't thought of them before. I know you will do whatever you can.' Huw gripped Regan's hand tighter. 'I hope my family can return your help and kindness in the future.'

Regan seemed pleased with Huw's fervour and their friendship.

'Go with God, Huw Ashe. We will talk again soon. Your Gaelic is now so good, you could be one of us.'

CHAPTER 15

CASTLE KINSELLA, WEXFORD
WINTER 1170

THE RAIN FINALLY STOPPED as Huw and his two companions drew nearer to the village. It was late October, and except for the sodden ground it was pleasant travelling in the afternoon sunshine. Huw had left Ferns feeling he had re-established links with the Norman forces through the offices of Maurice Regan. *We must make sure the communication lines are kept in place. We have to know what is happening in this changing situation in Ireland. We cannot become isolated again.* Huw's thoughts kept him occupied and he did not realise how far they had travelled until he began to recognise some of the landscape. He reined in his horse as they reached the top of the small hill where he had first seen the village. From a distance, the village looked very different. *A Norman fortification*, he thought, *that's what it looks like now.* The timber perimeter wall looked strong and imposing. The houses inside were hardly visible, dwarfed as they were by the wall and the tall timber building rising from the large foundation mound. There was a lot of activity on the central structure as a team of men worked on completing the roof in the bright sunshine. *Castle Kinsella*, Huw thought. *Will it be the first of many to be built in Ireland in the coming years? Will there be large stone castles, as in South Wales?*

†

Donal Kinsella quickly sought out Huw on his return. His scouts had seen small groups of men on horseback a number of times on their patrols. The men had not engaged, and rode away when they knew they had been seen.

'Were they Norman soldiers, in armour?' Huw asked.

'My lads are not sure, but the wounded de Barry was with one of the patrols. He may tell you more.'

David de Barry was almost certain that the men they saw were not Normans.

'They didn't look like knights or soldiers from what I could see, Huw, no armour or chainmail, and a Norman knight wouldn't have turned horse and raced away like that.' De Barry was firm in his opinion.

'Maybe, unless they didn't want it to be known who they were. Could they have been men on a spying mission?' Huw asked the question more to himself than de Barry.

'They did seem to be watching the pathways and checking the village. They were seen at different places overlooking the village. Should we have tried to chase them down, Huw?' de Barry asked, unsure of himself.

'No, sir, you did right. At least we now know we are being watched,' Huw assured the young knight, but he would really like to have known more about the men. *Probably spies from de Bourg*, he thought.

†

Giles and Gwen were happy with the news Huw brought about Daiwin. His mother was glad that he had not followed Dai to Dublin.

'Thank you, Huw, my mind is eased somewhat,' Gwen smiled and touched him on the shoulder. 'We would be lost without you.'

That night, when they had finished their evening meal, Huw discussed Dai's situation and the spying men with his father, who was just as happy with Huw's decision not to go to Dublin.

'You have set up a very good communication link with Regan and our Norman comrades. We will at least get to know about the main happenings with our... expedition.' Giles still did not use the word invasion. 'Do you think those men were de Bourg spies?'

'It is likely, sir, but I would like to find out for sure. Kinsella is certain they were not local kinsmen of his. They would not have run away.' Huw paused. 'I would like to take a small scouting party out before dawn on the coming days. Perhaps we can find these men again.'

'Huw, I am not your commanding officer any more. If I was, I would agree with what you say. But as your father, I want to keep you here, safe.'

'I think you know, sir, that our situation is not safe. If it was, we wouldn't be building these big walls. Everything is changing rapidly – MacMurrough is taking over Leinster; Strongbow and our Norman friends will be taking land, more people are coming over from Wales. We are under threat from de Bourg.' Huw broke off from his list to look at his father, who looked into the hearth but did not speak. 'We have to plan for our family's future, but first we must plan for our safety. The de Bourg threat is real and urgent and we have to confront it. We cannot sit and wait for them to come and kill us as they will.'

There was silence as they two of them sat there and drank their ale.

'There is no doubt that you are right, Huw.' Giles shifted in his seat and his voice quivered slightly. 'I have immersed myself in the fortification work and ignored our own long term future and safety. Let us put a plan together to flush out de Bourg and bring that threat to an end. There is no law at play here in Ireland, and no King to defer to.'

'Very good, sir. We need to be sure that these spies are from de Bourg. I will take three men on patrol in the early mornings. If we can, we will take a prisoner and find out de Bourg's plans.' Huw spoke quickly and Giles nodded. 'We will then make our plan when we have better information.'

'Huw, please be careful. We are dealing with dangerous men who will not afford us any law. Your mother need not know all the details of what we intend.' Giles touched his son on the arm. 'We will get our castle's roof finished quickly before the weather worsens.'

†

Huw and his two companions had been scouting for three mornings but had had no contact with anyone suspicious. The morning weather was cold and misty. They had almost completed a full circuit of the village, sometimes tracking close to the enclosure, at other times keeping their distance. As they were about to turn for home, one of Kinsella's men thought he saw a wisp of smoke coming from a large clump of trees in a small valley. They were out of sight of the village and Huw could not see the smoke. Perhaps the man might have been mistaken in the mist.

'We'll ride over and take a look,' Huw called quietly to the two men. 'We can head home for breakfast, then.' It was just an hour or so past dawn; it was possible that someone wanted hot food and risked starting a fire, thinking that the trees and mist would provide cover. 'Let's dismount and tie the horses. We can go in quietly on foot.' Huw signalled to his companions as they reached the edge of the tree clump.

As they crept forward through the wet trees and undergrowth, Huw got the unmistakable smell of a wood fire. *Strange that they have not posted any sentries,* Huw thought; *maybe they are all eating and not expecting visitors.* He strung his long bow just as they reached the clearing. His companions had their swords drawn and they could clearly see the small fire with smoke rising through the damp air. Two horses were tied up and chomping on grass a small distance from the fire, but there was no sign of any men. Huw put an arrow in the groove and stood still. He could hear his companions breathing heavily in the morning air. He moved forward to the edge of the clearing to get a better look, the two men following close behind. Huw had just noticed the absence of any cooking when two arrows buried into the tree close to his head. One of Kinsella's men screamed loud and dropped as a third arrow sliced through his thigh.

'Next one in the belly. Put down your weapons, we have twenty men around you!' The voice was shrill, with in a strange Gaelic accent.

Huw remained motionless, still with an arrow ready. The second Kinsella man dropped his sword and put his hands behind his head. Huw thought frantically, *Gaelic, Irish, not Norman, but who are they?* He had struggled to understand the accented words. *Can't see anyone and can't risk turning around.* He realised they had been led into a trap. *Fool,* he thought to himself, *fool for making assumptions and not being on my guard.*

'Last chance, put down the bow or die.' The voice was calmer now, but starkly clear.

Huw slackened his drawing arm and laid the bow and arrow on the wet grass. *At least live to find out who they are.*

'Now your sword and arrow bag,' the voice called again. Huw dropped his other weapons to the ground. 'Move away five paces from the weapons!' the voice demanded, as men began to appear from the undergrowth. Huw turned as he moved to one side, counting six men, all with small Irish bows and arrows pointed at them. *Maybe one or two sentries that we didn't see*, Huw thought, *that makes eight at most.*

'Who are you?' the voice asked as two of the men collected the weapons from the ground and disarmed the wounded Kinsella man.

'We are Kinsellas from the village,' Huw's companion blurted out quickly, nervously gesturing towards the village. 'We thought you were Norman attackers.'

'Norman attackers? Are they the foreigners?' The voice seemed surprised.

'Yes.' Kinsella's man glanced quickly at Huw as he spoke.

'Why do they attack the village? How many of them have come?' The man looked from Kinsella's man to Huw and back. Huw did not speak.

'We have some of them living with us and the attackers want to kill them.'

The leader of the men stood there for a moment without speaking. Then he turned to Huw. 'You, what is your name? Are you a Kinsella?' Huw stood upright and looked the man in the eye. He still did not speak. 'Answer me!' the man shouted, as he raised his bow to aim at Huw's face. 'Are you a Kinsella?'

Huw held firm and silent.

'He's not, he's one of the foreigners,' Kinsella's man answered hurriedly. 'He may not understand your talk.'

'Why are you Kinsellas giving shelter to the foreigners?' He turned back to the Kinsella.

'King Diarmaid asked the Kinsellas to shelter them. They are in danger from their own kind, I think.'

'MacMurrough? King Diarmaid MacMurrough?'

'Yes, King Diarmaid of Leinster.'

The wounded man groaned as he moved on the ground.

'We should mount and leave, Tadhg, before others come,' one of the other men said under his breath to the leader. The man called Tadhg didn't move, an arrow still pointed at Huw, seemingly working out what to do. Huw considered making a dive towards the man, assuming he was going to be killed anyway. Then, suddenly, the man lowered the bow.

'Bring their horses Gill. You two – help that man!' Tadhg gestured towards Huw and the wounded Kinsella. 'Put him on his horse. You, Kinsella, take him back to your village. He should live. You, foreigner, you will come with us,' Tadhg made rough signs to Huw to explain what he had said. When they were all mounted, he turned to Huw. 'We'll not tie your hands as we must ride quickly, but if you try to escape we will kill you: no second chances.' He mimicked shooting Huw with his bow. Huw nodded.

'Are you MacCarthys?' the Kinsella worked up the courage to ask, before they parted.

The man called Tadhg laughed.

'Yes, we are MacCarthy Mór men, come to the Kinsella land to meet your new invaders. Tell the Kinsellas that the MacCarthys are better neighbours than the foreigners ever will be.'

Huw wondered if Tadhg MacCarthy was right, as they headed west and away from Castle Kinsella on that damp October morning.

✝

They had ridden hard for over three hours before MacCarthy paused at a stream to rest and water the horses. There had been little talk as they rode, six of them together in a group, with two outlying riders scouting on the flanks. Huw noticed that the men were vigilant, constantly on the lookout and somewhat unsure of their surroundings. Tadgh MacCarthy stayed close by Huw but did not speak on the journey. On a number of occasions he sensed that MacCarthy was looking him over, but Huw refused to flinch or make any attempt to communicate. He was not sure why he had hidden his ability to speak and understand Gaelic; *maybe it will be useful to let them think I don't understand them*, he thought. He had wanted to talk to the Kinsella man before they left; he wanted him to tell his parents that he was unharmed and that he would return. He knew his parents would find out anyway, when the man returned to the village, but he would have been happier to have send a message in his own words. *Nothing I can do about it now.* He also had a dozen questions to ask MacCarthy. Why did he want him as a prisoner? Why did he let the Kinsella men go free? Why was he watching the Kinsella village, and where were they going? Maybe he would find out the answers when they got to their destination, or perhaps even sooner.

'Here, foreigner, take some stale bread and cheese.' MacCarthy handed Huw the food, looking at him intently. Huw took the food and thanked him formally in Welsh.

'What is that strange noise you're making?' MacCarthy grinned and the men sitting around laughed. Huw smiled and ate the bread and cheese quickly.

'Tadhg, how are we going to find out about the foreigners from him?' one of the MacCarthy men asked, gesturing at Huw. 'He has no idea what we're saying, and his words are useless.'

'We'll see, Bric. Maybe he understands more than we think.' Tadhg MacCarthy looked at Huw.

'Maybe one of the monks will know his way of talking,' Bric continued. 'Some of them talk other languages.'

Huw sat quietly and drank water from the stream. He wasn't sure why he kept up the pretence of not speaking Gaelic. He would like to find out more about the MacCarthys and how they became enemies of the O'Briens. They looked the same as the Kinsellas and the O'Briens; the language was the same, but the accent was different – they seemed to talk more quickly than the other Irish people he had met.

'My name is Tadhg.' MacCarthy pointed his thumb to his chest and looked at Huw. 'What is your name?' he said, pointing at Huw. Huw stared at MacCarthy. 'I'm Tadhg, that's Bric, and Gill.' MacCarthy pointed at each one in turn. 'You?'

'Huw Ashe.' Huw nodded and spoke his name loudly.

'Huw Ashe.' MacCarthy repeated the name slowly, and smiled. 'That's a start anyway. Right, we'd better get going if we want to cross the river before nightfall. Be on your guard lads, remember where we are.' MacCarthy's tone turned serious very quickly as he motioned to Huw to mount up. 'Take no risks and we'll keep our heads.' His laugh this time was taut and nervous.

Huw wondered about the river MacCarthy mentioned, assuming it was one of the rivers they had crossed near Waterford. He also wondered why MacCarthy had quickly become so edgy.

†

Over the next couple of hours Huw sensed the nervous tension begin to rise in the small group of men around him. Conversation died to a minimum, and any speech was in low whispers, as if they were afraid of being heard by some unseen enemy. Huw wished he had his longbow and sword. He felt vulnerable without his weapons. If anyone attacked them he would be defenceless, and he was sure the men would not be interested in protecting him. He had identified Gill as the man who had picked up his longbow, arrows and sword when they had been ambushed and he kept his horse behind him as they rode along. The pace had slackened as the tension rose; fearing an ambush. The land underfoot had become marshier and that slowed the pace further, as though they were getting nearer to the big river. The landscape was beginning to flatten out, but there were still some dense wooded areas and small hills. A small army could have been waiting ahead, and they would have been upon it before they even saw it. Where were the scouts? *Perhaps they are just hidden by the brow of the hill or the trees.* Maybe MacCarthy had ordered them back in to join the group for safety? MacCarthy peered intently at the small hills along either side.

Even though they seemed to be expecting it, the sudden attack took them by surprise. Huw's horse was hit twice in the first wave of arrows. One of the shafts grazed his leg as it sank into the horse's belly. He slid from the frightened animal as it panicked and bucked. Two other men and horses were down. Gill and his horse toppled sideways into a soggy ditch beside the track. Instinctively, Huw jumped into the ditch as the second volley of arrows brought down at least two more men. Gill was barely alive when Huw reached him. Two arrows had hit him in the back, with one shaft almost clean through his chest. His horse had rolled on top of him and was now lying winded at the bottom of the ditch. Gill was obviously in shock, dying. He took Gill's dagger and quickly cut his sword and arrow satchel from the horse's girths, and found his bow stave close by in the ditch – a little wet, but it should do. Huw quickly strung the bow with the spare bow cord he kept in his satchel. He crept up the side of the ditch and parted the rough prickly bushes.

MacCarthy and Bric were lying, alive, behind a dead horse on the pathway, no more than ten paces away. The arrow fire had stopped, and everything had gone quiet. Huw saw the bodies of three men further up the pathway, all with multiple arrow shafts in them.

'*Déise* animals, what are you waiting for? Come and get us!' MacCarthy roared. Two arrows thudded into the body of the dead horse in front of him. 'Cowardly bastards!' MacCarthy shifted his body position and Huw realised that he had a broken arrow shaft embedded in his thigh. He could not see if Bric was wounded.

'MacCarthy, how many of you are still alive?' Huw called as softly as he could. 'Do you have weapons?'

MacCarthy turned sideways and peered at the bushes.

'Alive, are you, Huw Ashe? I knew you could understand our language,' MacCarthy whispered almost happily. 'Where's Gill?'

'Dead. Two arrows in his back,' Huw whispered back. 'Men and horses?'

'Just me and Bric. A couple of horses ran, but the *Déise* will have them. Bric is alright, I have a shaft in the leg. Not too bad.'

'The *Déise*? What are they?' Huw asked.

'Wild savages. They're waiting to come and club us. They like cutting heads off while you're still alive,' MacCarthy replied under his breath.

'How many are there?'

'Fifteen, maybe twenty, I don't know.' MacCarthy paused. 'You should leave if you can. Head back to the Kinsella, this is not your fight.'

'Which way will they come from?' Huw asked after some moments.

'They're in the trees up on that ridge, but some will be circling around behind us, the way we came up the path. They can shoot arrows from both sides, then.' MacCarthy repeated, 'They may not know you are alive, you should get away now. You too, Bric.' MacCarthy's voice was intense as he nudged his companion.

'I'm going nowhere, Tadhg,' Bric spat out.

'I'll stay for a while too, MacCarthy. I want to meet these *Déise*. They're probably not as bad as you say. I have a bow, twelve arrows and a sword.' Huw's voice changed from slightly sarcastic to deadly serious in an instant. 'Gill's bow and shafts are here in the ditch. If Bric could make a break for the ditch, we might provoke them into attacking.'

'I'm staying with Tadhg!' Bric's voice was indignant. There was a silent pause while each man thought out a plan.

'If they attack in the open, I can take down two, maybe three, before they realise I'm here. Another man with a bow could take a few more.' Huw laid out his plan in whispered tones. 'There's a horse here in the ditch, winded but alive. One more horse, and we could run for it.'

'Stupid foreigner, you have no idea about the *Déise*.' Bric's shaky voice betrayed his fear.

'Hold, Bric, maybe there's something in what he says. You break for the ditch, they'll think you're the only one left. They might just break cover to get you. Ashe, have you Gill's bow there with you?'

'It's here, ready.'

'Good. Bric, listen now, we stay here, and we all die for sure. With you and Ashe shooting arrows, some of us might live. At least we'll kill some of the bastards.' MacCarthy reached out and touched Bric with his foot. 'Go now! Make for the ditch.'

There was another pause and a silence before Bric stirred.

'Bastards!' he shouted, as he sprung from behind the horse's body and dived through the bushes close to Huw. A number of arrows struck the ground in front of Huw. He kept his head low as more shafts whizzed through the bushes and grabbed Bric by the tunic to stop him sliding down to the bottom of the ditch. They exchanged glances but did not speak as Huw gave him Gill's bow and arrow satchel. Huw crouched onto his knees, put an arrow into the grove and put six shafts on the ground in front of him. Bric did the same.

Huw saw the three men coming up the pathway behind them with the corner of his eye, just as a loud roar came from the ridge facing them. The three men on the pathway were closing on MacCarthy and Huw took a split second to decide what to do. In an instant he stepped from the bushes on to the pathway facing the three men. The first man was down with an arrow in the chest before the other men realised what was happening. The second man was raising his bow as Huw's next arrow smashed into his face. The third man loosed an aimless bow shot and then turned and ran. Bric's arrow hit him in the lower back and brought him down.

'Right, lads, all of you, fire!' Huw screamed as loud as he could at his imaginary troops in the bushes as he turned to face the on-rushing *Déise*. Bric stood two paces from his shoulder as they loosed as many arrows as they could in quick succession. Huw counted about a dozen men screaming wildly and charging towards them. Two quickly dropped from their arrow fire. Then a third.

'Two more behind you!' MacCarthy screamed.

'I'll do them!' Bric shouted as he dropped his bow and ran back the pathway with his sword drawn. Huw kicked the bow towards MacCarthy as he let fly with another shaft. *About eight against one now*, he thought. The charging group paused as Huw's arrow took down another man. Huw threw two arrows to MacCarthy where he lay near the horse. He already had Bric's bow in his hands. *Maybe one and a half men now.*

The *Déise* seemed confused. Half of them continued to scream their battle cry and charged towards Huw and MacCarthy. The others paused, and seemed to be talking amongst themselves. The five charging men were no more than ten paces away when Huw's next shaft drove one of them backwards. MacCarthy had raised himself on to one knee and his first arrow stopped another man as it hit him in the side. Huw dropped his bow and pulled his sword and dagger. MacCarthy somehow tripped the leading man and forced an arrow into his neck as he fell. MacCarthy roared as he fell awkwardly on his wounded leg. Huw knew that he had to kill the two remaining attackers quickly, without giving the other men time to re-group and join in the attack. He stood firm as the two screaming *Déise* bore down on him. Instantly, his mind cleared as he saw how he would strike them; later, he would think that he had actually seen what was going to happen before it did.

He crouched low and smashed his sword across the front knee of the first man. The man toppled instantly, screaming as the bone in his lower leg shattered. Huw was vaguely aware of MacCarthy cutting the fallen man's throat as he and the second man circled each other. Huw stared intently at the man's eyes. Then, as the man hesitated, Huw rammed his sword into his belly. The man's head dropped and Huw stabbed deeply into his neck with his dagger. Huw let go of both sword and dagger, and had his bow in hand with an arrow in the groove, almost as the man hit the ground. The remaining four *Déise* had backed away, and now turned and ran as they saw the deadly long bow aimed at them. Huw held fire, in case he needed that arrow later.

Huw's fighting mind relaxed slightly as he saw the *Déise* disappear through the undergrowth and turned to assess their position. MacCarthy was sitting on the ground with his back against his dead horse. The arrow shaft still protruded from his thigh and he seemed barely conscious. There were three men lying on the pathway where Bric had run to engage the other *Déise*. Huw walked back to them. One of the *Déise* appeared dead; another and Bric were badly wounded with sword and stab wounds to the face and belly. Huw knelt beside Bric. His eyes were open but his breathing was short and raspy. He had a deep slash wound across his face and mouth. He tried to speak but could not. Huw reached out his hand and Bric summoned enough strength to clasp his hand with Huw's.

'You are a brave man, a credit to your people. Thank you,' Huw said softly in Gaelic as Bric died.

CHAPTER 16

EAST CORK
WINTER 1170

A DAY AFTER THE *Déise* attack, Huw and MacCarthy crossed the two big rivers as they headed west. Huw had found a second horse grazing nearby just after they left the ambush site. MacCarthy had suffered a second injury when he had tripped and killed the charging man. Huw thought that his leg or hip might be broken. Before they left, MacCarthy had insisted that Huw pull the broken arrow shaft through his thigh. He passed out with pain as this happened, and he had drifted in and out of consciousness since. Huw had got him on the horse and lashed to the horse's girths as best he could. Progress was slow, as MacCarthy swayed from side to side on the horse's back and Huw had had to ride by his side to steady him if he began to slide off. At least there had been no sign of the wild *Déise* men.

After crossing the second river, they paused to rest and eat what little food they had. Huw had checked all the dead bodies for food and weapons before leaving the ambush scene. He found small amounts of bread and cheese and he took extra swords and daggers for himself and MacCarthy, and as well as having his long bow and six arrows, he also had a smaller Irish bow and ten smaller arrows. *We're well armed*, he thought. *One and a half well-armed men crossing hostile country, trying to get to MacCarthy's kingdom.* Huw smiled to himself, realising that he didn't know where MacCarthy's kingdom was, and Tadhg MacCarthy was in no fit state to tell him.

The coldness of the river and the water that Huw forced to his lips seemed to revive MacCarthy somewhat.

'Where are we, Ashe, on the way to Kinsella's land?' Tadhg MacCarthy croaked.

'You're alive so, MacCarthy,' Huw responded as cheerfully as he could. 'No, we're heading west to your kingdom. Could you tell me where it is?'

'Ashe, I told you to go back to the Kinsellas.'

'I will, when you're safe in bed by your own fireside.'

'Too late then, you're my prisoner, and the MacCarthy savages will want to torture you.' Tadhg MacCarthy laughed and coughed violently at the same time, spitting blood. Huw gave him some more water.

'They can try, MacCarthy, they can try. But I'm armed to the teeth. I'll make sure your head goes before mine.'

'I'll keep my head, and the MacCarthys will let you keep yours. I'll see to that, if we get back to Muskerry.' MacCarthy hesitated. 'Thank you for what you did back there. You are a brave warrior, Ashe.'

'I'm sorry about your friends, and that I couldn't bury them,' Huw responded after a few moments of silence. 'We had to leave quickly.'

'They were good men and we will honour them,' MacCarthy looked away as his voice shortened. They sat there in silence for a time while the horses grazed close by.

'What is Muskerry? And how do we get there?' Huw broke the silence.

'We head a little south and then west, and keep going until we meet some friendly people,' MacCarthy pointed out the direction. 'I'm a burden to you, and we're still in danger from the *Déise*. You should leave me to go on alone, and head back east.'

'You're my prisoner now, MacCarthy. I have all the weapons and you are only good for tripping and killing innocent *Déise* people. So don't tell me what to do.'

MacCarthy laughed again through his cough as Huw helped him up off the damp ground and back onto his horse.

†

When they next stopped, Huw thought that they must have passed Waterford town to the south. MacCarthy said it was safer to keep to higher ground away from the coast. Progress was still very slow and the terrain did not help. MacCarthy had gone silent and Huw knew he must be in great pain. Sometimes he drifted into semi-consciousness and spoke under his breath. It seemed to Huw that he was talking in his sleep.

Huw helped MacCarthy from his horse and put him lying on the ground beneath two large trees. He had got fresh water from a stream and he lifted MacCarthy's head to help him drink.

'Water? Don't you have any ale?' MacCarthy's voice was weak but he managed a smile.

'I hope they have good ale in Muskerry, and hot food. Do you MacCarthy savages cook your food?'

'Sometimes, Ashe, when we have the time. When no one is attacking us,' MacCarthy responded.

Huw studied MacCarthy's face. He was pale, and he shivered for a moment before he sat up with his back to the tree trunk. His wounded leg had stiffened but the arrow wound had not become infected.

'Have you healers in Muskerry?'

MacCarthy saw Huw looking at the wounded leg. 'We do indeed. They should be able to fix this up,' he tapped his thigh with his hand. 'I don't want to be hopping around on one leg.'

'How far to Muskerry?' Huw asked.

'Maybe two days. A bit more at the pace we're going. If we could ride a bit faster—'

Huw shook his head. 'We're doing fine. Don't want you toppling off that horse and breaking the other leg.'

'Ashe, why did you help us back there? Why are you helping me? You could have gone back to the Kinsellas. Why risk your life for people you don't know?'

'MacCarthy, you ask a lot of questions. Why don't you be quiet and save your strength?' Huw answered tetchily, and then regretted his response.

It was his natural instinct to help people, and he had acted on that instinct at the ambush. But he also wanted to find out more about the MacCarthy clan. He knew, too, that they were heading west, bringing him closer to Limerick – and Bridín O'Brien. He wanted to ask MacCarthy about their conflict with the O'Briens. Would MacCarthy know the O'Brien King and his family?

They sat in silence for a time.

'How far is your land from Limerick?' Huw finally broke the silence.

'You know Limerick?' MacCarthy sounded surprised.

'I've been there. MacMurrough asked us to help Donal O'Brien against the High King.'

'You foreigners are helping O'Brien?' MacCarthy's surprise increased.

'We did, in his fight with the High King, but we returned to MacMurrough's land to fight with him,' Huw realised he was giving MacCarthy information about Norman activities, but he hoped that he might get information in return. 'How did the MacCarthys become enemies of O'Brien? Why were you scouting in Kinsella's land?'

Tadhg MacCarthy shifted in his position and coughed. Huw looked at him and saw the pain in his eyes but also maybe some unease. *He wants to find out about the Norman alliances in Ireland; that's why he took me as prisoner. Perhaps we can barter an information exchange.* Huw waited but MacCarthy did not reply.

'Very good, MacCarthy; we need not talk now, but I'm happy to tell you sometime why we came to Ireland and what I know of MacMurrough's plans. You in return could tell me about the MacCarthys and O'Briens, and the savage *Déise.*' Huw looked at MacCarthy and smiled.

'We should get going, Ashe, if you still want to come with me,' MacCarthy groaned, as he tried to raise himself from the damp ground. He could not get to his feet, and Huw had to lift him and prop him against the tree while he brought his horse.

Rain began to fall heavily as they slowly headed west.

†

It rained constantly for the next day and night. Huw tried to find some shelter when they stopped for the night, but the best he found was a small rocky cliff face with overhanging bushes close to a flooded stream. They were both very hungry now, and MacCarthy was getting weaker. The next day, Huw decided, they would go down from the hills to find a village where he might buy some food. MacCarthy was not coherent when Huw asked him if they were safe from the *Déise* and getting near MacCarthy land.

Huw slept close by MacCarthy that night. The wet ground prevented him from sleeping much. He wasn't sure if MacCarthy was asleep or unconscious; he spoke at intervals in his slumber – incoherent ravings about people and battles that

Huw could not make much sense of. At one stage, he thought he heard MacCarthy mention an O'Brien woman, but he wasn't sure. He smiled to himself when he thought about Brídín, his own O'Brien woman. *If MacCarthy has an O'Brien woman as his wife*, Huw thought, *we might become related through marriage!*

†

The rain had stopped when Huw woke at dawn. The clouds cleared overnight and it was cold, but at least it was dry. Huw was hopeful that they would get to Muskerry that day. MacCarthy was asleep and breathing heavily. Still, breathing was good. He let him sleep a little longer, while he went to wash his face and drink from the stream. No food but plenty of water. Always plenty of water in Ireland. Huw felt better this morning, more enthusiastic; maybe the fine weather was helping the mood. After waking him, he gave MacCarthy the last piece of bread and made him drink as much water as he would take. He was silent and Huw didn't speak much, knowing that it was an effort for MacCarthy to respond. His leg had stiffened badly and getting him onto his horse was more difficult. When they eventually got going, Huw headed south west, descending gradually from the hills.

†

It was mid-day and they had reached flatter ground when Huw saw smoke rising ahead beyond a line of trees and bushes. He weighed the risks and decided that they would have to take a chance, heading directly towards the smoke. MacCarthy was semi-conscious, lying forward on the horse's back, and shivering badly; there was no way he could go on. As they passed the trees, Huw saw the small village ahead with smoke rising from a number of houses. He had noticed the men watching them from the trees some time earlier. Now, a number of men rode towards them from either side, some of them with bows drawn and arrows ready in the groove. Huw nudged his horse to keep walking forward. He had the reins of MacCarthy's horse in his hands and he pulled the horse along beside him.

'This man is badly wounded, can you help him?' Huw called as the men drew up in front of him, blocking his path. The men stared at him but no one spoke.

'This is Tadhg MacCarthy, son of MacCarthy Mór, wounded in an ambush. Can you help him?' Huw spoke loudly in Gaelic, hoping that the men would understand him through his accent and that they were not *Déise*.

'Tadhg?' One of the men called, as he urged his horse forward to look at the injured man.

'Tadhg, is that you?' MacCarthy raised himself slightly on his horse so that his face could be seen. He raised his hand in greeting and tried to speak, but no words came. 'It is Tadhg!' the rider called to the other men, as he recognised MacCarthy. 'Come you, and help him!'

†

By evening, Tadhg MacCarthy had recovered his speech, and was lying in a cot by the fire when Huw was brought into the house. Huw had got plenty of hot food and ale during the day but the men had taken his weapons and watched him closely. He was allowed to sleep in one of the outhouses, but the door was barred when he tried to go out. Now, two men with drawn swords had bound his hands brought him to see MacCarthy. Huw thought that Tadhg looked pale and seemed feverish, but at least he was alive and awake.

'You bastards, untie that man!' Tadhg MacCarthy roared. His voice was weak but his anger clear. The men did nothing for an instant and MacCarthy made to get up. 'Release him now or I'll have your eyes.' His voice was deadly serious.

One of the men stepped forward and cut Huw's bonds with a dagger.

'Sorry Tadhg. Mickel said to guard him closely. We done him no harm.'

'This man killed ten *Déise* on his own and he could cut you two down in a twinkle. Bring us some ale and cheese, and get Mickel.' The men hesitated again. 'Go off now and do it!' Tadhg roared at them again.

'MacCarthy, take it easy. Ten *Déise*? It was only three or four,' Huw teased Tadhg in his best mock-serious tone, when the men had gone. 'Are you sure you should be drinking ale?'

MacCarthy laughed and coughed and beckoned Huw to sit down. 'I can drink ale all right, Ashe, thanks to you. Maybe the leg will get better, maybe not, but without you I'd have no head to drink with.' MacCarthy looked at Huw and held out his hand. Huw took it and sat close to the fire. 'I thought we were done for, back there with the *Déise*. Fool I was, to ride into their ambush. Felt it was coming, but too eager to get home. I'm sorry, Ashe, for taking you from your people, and for those fools tying you up.' MacCarthy took a breath. 'You are a true warrior. I'm glad I wasn't fighting against you.'

'You didn't do too badly yourself, for a man with one leg,' Huw smiled.

One of the guards came in bringing jugs of ale with fresh bread and cheese.

'Sorry Tadhg, but Mickel left for Muskerry to tell your father about the ambush and yourself – and him.' The man looked nervously at Huw, then back to Tadhg.

'Alright. What about the healer?'

'We sent for the monks, Tadhg, should be here tonight or the morning.'

'Good, hopefully I'll still be alive. Bring this man's weapons to him now, and put two extra men on guard.'

When the man had returned with Huw's bow and weapons, MacCarthy dismissed him for the night.

'Word travels fast here, to friends and enemies. We are not too far from *Déise* lands,' Tadhg explained to Huw. 'It'll be known quickly that I'm here and wounded. How did you know that I was the son of the MacCarthy Mór?'

'There's not much wrong with your mind, MacCarthy. I heard your men talking after you captured me,' Huw answered.

'I am son of the MacCarthy, and friends call me Tadhg. You can too, if you wish.'

'Good. Tadhg it is, so. Friends call me Huw.'

'Huw,' MacCarthy repeated. 'I'd be interested to hear about your home and your people.'

†

For a number of hours that night Huw and Tadhg talked about homes and families. Huw told him about his life in Wales and about his family. He explained what had happened between Giles and the de Bourg family and why they had come to Ireland. MacCarthy listened intently but did not question him about the Normans and their plans in Ireland. Huw knew that topic was coming, but first they needed to learn about each other – and drink more ale. For his part, Tadhg spoke openly about the MacCarthy clan, and their battles with the O'Briens and others for the land of Munster. It seemed that for now there was an uneasy peace, with the MacCarthys controlling large tracts of east Munster, and the O'Briens ruling to the north.

'The dividing line between us is not always clear, and Donal O'Brien would claim kingship over all Munster. We are happy with our own little patch,' MacCarthy smirked, 'but sometimes we have to travel abroad to see what others are up to.'

'That's why you were in Kinsella's land?' Huw ventured.

'Everyone has heard of your Norman allies coming to Leinster to fight with MacMurrough. A dangerous man with big ambitions. We need to know the lie of the land and what is intended by MacMurrough and your friends.' Tadhg MacCarthy drank deeply, watching Huw over the rim of his tankard.

Huw drank and gazed into the fire. What should he tell MacCarthy? Did he even *know* what was going to happen, really? 'I cannot be sure what will happen, but it's true that MacMurrough has ambitions to be King of all Leinster, maybe more. Strongbow, the Norman leader, has married MacMurrough's daughter and MacMurrough has named him as his successor in Leinster.'

'God above!' Tadhg sat up in his cot with a grimace, 'that's news to us. Not good! Does that mean that the Normans are here for good? Will they come to Muskerry?' He rubbed his painful leg, trying to rise without waiting for answers. 'I'll have to go and tell the MacCarthy. Blast this leg,' he groaned as he felt a sharp stab of pain.

'Tadhg, you can't go anywhere tonight, or for a day or two. The news will hold. Strongbow and MacMurrough will not be coming tomorrow. They are attacking Dublin town.' Huw spoke calmly and poured them both ale from the jug.

'Dublin town!' MacCarthy spluttered. 'They're taking Dublin town?'

Huw laughed at MacCarthy's innocent surprise. 'Dublin indeed, and my brother Dai is with them.'

'Dublin!' was all MacCarthy could say, as he downed a huge gulp of ale.

The conversation continued into the night with both men feeling better as the ale flowed. Huw slept by the fire that night. MacCarthy had fallen asleep long before Huw, and he snored and groaned from the pain in his leg during the night. Despite the noise, Huw slept soundly.

It was late morning when they awoke and MacCarthy called the guard to bring them food and fresh water for breakfast.

'Huw Ashe, you are a free man and we'll not hold you here, so you are welcome to leave when you will,' MacCarthy spoke as they finished their food. 'But I would be happy for you to stay a while. I could show you some of our country when I have recovered a little, and I would like you to meet my father.'

Huw considered before answering. 'I would wish for my family to know that I am alive and to see that they are safe.' He looked at MacCarthy, 'I could return in the springtime to meet your people and visit your lands, if your invitation holds?'

'It holds, Huw, for as long as you wish, but you cannot travel back alone through *Déise* land. If you can stay for a day or so, we can get you passage on one of our trading ships back along the coast to Kinsella land.'

Huw paused. 'A coastal trading ship, you say?'

'Safer than meeting the *Déise* men on your own. We could drop you at a Kinsella fishing village and you would be home in a day.' MacCarthy looked at Huw with some bemusement. 'You don't like ships?'

'I prefer solid ground underfoot… but perhaps you're right, and it would be quicker.'

'We'll make arrangements, so. Some of the lads here will take you. Our ships trade back and forth along the south coast. It's a good way of sending messages also. We could put a message plan in place, if we ever wanted to make contact?' MacCarthy looked to Huw for and answer.

'Very good, Tadhg. That would be valuable to us both.'

†

Huw spent the next two days enjoying the hospitality in Tadhg MacCarthy's village. News of his presence and his prowess in fighting the *Déise* spread; visitors came from other villages to look at the fighting foreigner. Everyone wanted to talk to him and hear him speak Gaelic with his Welsh accent. In turn, Huw was happy to meet more of the MacCarthy clan and to hear about their lives. *A proud fighting people*, Huw thought, *but friendly and hospitable. Not too different from South Wales.*

Tadhg MacCarthy was not able to show Huw around the village or have more long conversations with him. Once the two monks arrived, Tadhg was confined to bed. His leg wasn't broken, but a bone had been dislocated and the healers had to put it right. Tadhg was given sleeping potions for the pain and the healers thought he would recover well, maybe with a slight limp. When the man called Mickel returned, Tadhg sent him to make the arrangements for Huw's boat journey.

MacCarthy was sitting up in bed when Huw called in to say goodbye.

'I hear you are a famous MacCarthy warrior now, Huw Ashe,' Tadhg greeted him with a warm smile. 'People are talking about you all over the land.'

'Your people are very friendly and like a good story. Someone has been telling them tales. I'll run the next time I meet a *Déise* man.'

'The tales are true enough, I saw with my own eyes.' MacCarthy held out his hand. 'Mickel and the lads will look after you. Be safe, Huw.'

Huw took Tadhg MacCarthy's hand. 'Give yourself time to recover and no more scouting missions to the Kinsellas this winter. If you want to know something, send me a message.'

†

The weather was overcast but dry as Mickel and his three comrades escorted Huw to the coast. Huw thought he recognised some of the landscape from the time he spent there with his family. They rode along a huge sandy beach in the early evening before arriving at a small fishing port.

'Passage,' Mickel pointed as they saw the village beyond a headland. 'We'll spend the night at the tavern before your boat sails in the morning.'

'Very good, so,' Huw responded. He was relieved the trip would be in daylight. He had worried about being at sea during the night.

That night the four MacCarthy men settled down to drinking after their meal. Huw did not feel much like drinking, but Mickel insisted that he join them.

'Huw Ashe, tell us more about your country, and the Norman men,' Mickel called to him during a break in the men's loud conversation.

Huw repeated what he had told many times over the last few days and the men listened intently. He cut his own story short to ask, 'What about your big battle with the O'Briens. Why did that happen?'

'Battles, battles! More than one, Huw, and we won them all!' Mickel shouted, as the other men roared. 'We speared them and sent them running back west over the mountains!' The men roared again, and banged the table with their tankards. 'More ale for the MacCarthys!'

Huw wondered what he had started, but was glad that he didn't have to talk. He sat and listened as the men related drunken stories of bloody fights and battles won. The O'Briens were a ragged bunch of savages, according to this group of MacCarthys. Huw smiled to himself when he recalled the similar views he had heard about the MacCarthys during his time in Limerick.

'They're not all dirty savages. What about the O'Brien woman Tadhg brought back from Limerick?' one of the men shouted.

The men's battle cries turned to cheers at the mention of the woman.

'A fine-looking woman, and tough. Killed one of them O'Brien nobles, she did,' one of the men added. 'Will Tadhg marry her?'

They all stopped and laughed at the man who had spoken.

'Fooleen! Tadhg, marry an O'Brien?!' Someone punched the man on the shoulder as the laughter grew louder.

'To Bridín O'Brien, a fine looking woman!' The second man raised his tankard; they all stood and shouted her name and drank.

'She did everyone a favour by killing that bastard weasel, O'Muinacháin!' Mickel declared when they settled down. The MacCarthy men didn't notice the surprise on Huw's face as he sat there quietly in bemused silence.

Later when most of the men were sleeping, Huw asked Mickel about the O'Brien woman. He learned how Bridín had been captured by Tadhg and brought to Muskerry. When the MacCarthy Mór found out that she had killed O'Muinacháin, he had offered her freedom, but she chose to stay, fearing death if she returned to Limerick. She now lived freely as a lady at the MacCarthy Mór's court, until it might be safe for her to return home.

Huw listened intently, struggling to keep his excitement and emotions to himself. He did not sleep much that night. His thoughts were about Bridín and what must have happened for her to kill O'Muineacháin. He wanted to head back to Tadhg MacCarthy's village, but knew he had to go to his family. He promised himself he would return to Muskerry.

CHAPTER 17

MUSKERRY
WINTER 1170

THE BOAT JOURNEY FROM Passage to the south Wexford coast was uneventful. There was a good wind and while he felt nauseous, Huw did not get sick. His mind was occupied with thoughts of Bridín O'Brien and he spent the time planning his next trip to Muskerry. Any time he felt a bit queasy, he sat on deck and pictured Bridín.

He was bit unsteady on his feet when he finally stepped onto the small wooden quay. The boat's captain knew Kinsella's land, and gave him directions towards the village.

'We have boats big and small, up and down the coast, fishing and trading.' The captain shook his hand as Huw thanked him. 'Tadhg says we're to take messages from you and passengers when you ask, Huw Ashe.'

'Thank you, Captain. I'm sure I'll need you again.' Huw was surprised at how quickly Tadhg MacCarthy had made the arrangements.

'Any MacCarthy boat will respond to your name: Huw Ashe, the *Déise* killer!'

Huw looked a bit embarrassed as he thanked the captain again and took his leave. The weather was windy but dry and there were some hours of daylight left as he headed inland.

†

It was dark as Huw approached the village. He had taken a few wrong turns on the way, but the land nearer the village was more familiar to him. He could just see the walls about four hundred paces away and he realised there would be guards at the gate tower. He kept low to the ground as he got nearer, not wanting to take an arrow from a jittery sentry.

'Who is that now? Stop or you're dead!' The shout from the walls sent Huw diving to the ground. It took him a few moments to recognise the strange-sounding Gaelic words with the lilting accent.

'John Daws, is that you?' Huw shouted back in Welsh through the noise of the wind. 'Don't shoot me!'

'Huw Ashe! Why are you crawling about in the dirt? Come on up to the gate!'

The wooden bridge was down and the gate open when Huw got to the walls. Daws grabbed him with a huge bear hug.

'Easy, Daws, don't break my back,' Huw groaned.

'That's the second time you've been carried off since we came here. You can't look after yourself. We were all worried about you, boy.' Daws gushed out the words as he pushed Huw inside the gate. 'I'm going with you next time.'

Two Kinsella men quickly raised the bridge and bolted the gate. Huw saw a number of other men around the walls.

'What's happening, John?' Huw asked, just as Giles came running up to them.

'Huw!' Giles called and clasped Huw with another bear hug. 'Where have you been? What happened?'

Huw related the story of the capture and ambush over food and ale by the warm fire in his parents' home. The house was crowded with family and friends. Kinsella's wife and other families brought food and drink. Everyone wanted to welcome Huw. *Back from the dead*, he thought to himself, *and maybe I would be dead, but for those* Déise *attacking us!*

The village was on high alert. Daws told him that their scouting parties had encountered increasing numbers of heavily-armed men. There had been some skirmishes over the last week, but the men had always ridden away without fully engaging. Giles thought that a full scale attack on the village was imminent. They had increased the number of sentries on the walls and gate and stopped all farm work and hunting outside the walls.

'Winter weather or not, I think they are going to mount a full scale attack soon,' Giles spoke quietly to Huw when most of the Kinsella families had left. 'We've had messages from your friend Regan.' He looked at Huw.

'Daiwin?' Huw asked quickly.

'Safe and well with Will Hen, after the taking of Dublin. There may be counter assaults on the town from the High King and the Northmen. They will not give up Dublin town easily.' Giles stopped to take a drink. 'All Strongbow's forces are on high alert, including Miles de Barry's troops. Daiwin and Hen cannot leave until Dublin is safely held.'

'It's good to know they're safe.' Huw drank his ale and huddled closer to the fire. The wind had grown stronger as it howled through the village.

'There is more from Regan.' Giles lowered his voice to a whisper. Daws had returned to the gate to check the sentries, and Gwen and Alice were chatting in the kitchen. 'He sent a message that the de Bourgs have recruited a hundred men. Most are soldiers newly arrived from Wales. They have their own small army, not connected to our original Norman forces. The men are mercenaries and the de Bourgs are offering them coin and whatever else they can take.' He took another drink. 'Regan says that with MacMurrough and Strongbow on campaign in Dublin, there is no law to stop them. They plan a full assault on the village and to kill or take us all.'

They sat and drank in silence as they contemplated what Giles had said.

Huw was the first to speak. 'Sir, it is best we leave as soon as we can be ready. We are not strong enough to defend against an army of a hundred men. And if we stay, the Kinsella families will be killed alongside us.' Huw's mind was focused and clear, and he knew this was the best course of action. 'An emissary could be sent to the de Bourgs to tell them we have gone. Perhaps Regan would send the emissary, and threaten the de Bourgs with Strongbow and MacMurrough's wrath if they still attack the village.'

Giles was silent for a time as he pondered what Huw had proposed.

'It is probably the best chance to keep the Kinsellas from being attacked and slaughtered. Once again, you have seen the best course.' Giles reached across and touched his son's shoulder. 'Where will we go?' His voice trailed off, as he looked over at Gwen and Alice.

'I have made new friends in Muskerry, sir. There is an escape route already arranged and they will be glad to help us.' Huw smiled as he saw the puzzled look on his father's face. 'It will involve a short sea voyage.' Huw told Giles more about Tadhg MacCarthy and how they had become friends. 'The MacCarthys are good, fighting people and they will not take kindly to the de Bourgs or others coming to their lands. I think they will welcome us, though.'

'You are a wonder, Huw!' Giles looked at his son in amazement as he got up and grabbed him in another bear hug.

†

Huw and his parents were ready to depart the following afternoon. Some members of their group were not keen on moving.

Alice decided to remain. She had integrated well and made strong friendships amongst the young Kinsella women. She also hoped to meet Daiwin again, and felt he would come to the village when he returned from Dublin. John Daws was conflicted. He was hugely loyal to Huw, and his family and his instinct was to help protect them. But he had also developed friendships in the village and was looked up to by the young men. He liked Kinsella's oldest daughter and she seemed to like him. Daws wanted both to go and to stay, and had difficulty coming to a decision.

Donal Kinsella tried to persuade Huw to remain, feeling that they were strong enough to fight off any attack.

'We might repel them initially, but many will die, and they'll keep coming back. If we leave—and make sure they know we are leaving—they will pursue us and leave the village in peace.' Huw's logic was compelling. 'Alun and David de Barry have decided to stay. They will ride out to meet de Bourg if the village is threatened. They will ensure de Bourg knows we are gone, and they'll fight if it comes to it.'

Huw had already spoken to the de Barry brothers and they were adamant they would stay and help protect the village if needed. They would join up with Strongbow's army once the village was secure.

†

Huw found John Daws in the gate tower. The wind was still strong and it was bitterly cold, with the feel of an oncoming rain storm in the air.

'What's it like in Muskerry, Huw? Is it warmer than here?'

'Didn't know you felt the cold, John,' Huw laughed. 'Muskerry isn't that far away. It's not too different to Wexford.' The two friends sat on the floor of the small gate tower, sheltered from the wind. Huw felt Daws's turmoil. 'John, you should not feel guilty if you wish to stay with the Kinsellas, and do not fear for us. Once we get to Tadhg MacCarthy's land we will be safe. We became strong friends.' Huw paused for a moment. 'There is also another reason I want to return to Muskerry.' Huw told Daws about Bridín and how he had found out she was living with the MacCarthys.

'She killed O'Muinacháin! Slobbering pig, he was. We should have done him that night we found you.'

Huw laughed at Daws's description of O'Muinacháin. He had almost forgotten about the night he had hung upside down, waiting for his eyes to be gouged out. He shivered a little thinking about it.

The two friends sat there in the cold talking and laughing about their time in Ireland. In the springtime, it would be two years since they had first landed on the Wexford coast. When they had first arrived they had often spoke about Wales, but now their thoughts were on Ireland and the people they knew.

'Is this land our home now, Huw?' Daws asked simply, without expecting an answer.

'It is if we think it so, I suppose.' Huw was surprised at Daws' question and the emotion he felt behind it. 'Our family and friends are here.'

†

John Daws decided to stay with the Kinsellas. Huw told him about the MacCarthy boats travelling back and forth along the coast and how to use his name to send messages or escape if needed.

By early evening, everything was settled. Huw and Giles decided to stay for the night and leave early in the morning.

'Maybe the weather will be better in the morning,' Huw wished aloud.

†

It was not to be. When they set out in the morning, the weather had worsened. The rain predicted by Kinsella had arrived overnight and the winds had strengthened. Giles sat alongside Gwen in the covered cart with his horse tied to the rear, while Huw rode a fine new horse given to him by Donal Kinsella. Giles had shared what coin they had left with Daws and Alice. The Kinsellas packed the cart with dried food and ale, even though Huw protested they would not need it on the short journey. As they left, Huw felt like he was leaving part of his life behind and looking at Gwen and Giles in the cart, they looked sad. For the first time in his life he thought about his parents getting old and how hard it must be for them to be constantly under threat and moving from place to place. He resolved to find a safe place for them to settle.

†

The driving wind and rain slowed their progress greatly. The cart got stuck in the mud a number of times and Huw and Giles kept having to get behind and push to get it moving again. Their concentration on keeping the cart moving and battling the weather meant they failed to notice the three riders who had followed them after leaving the village. Otherwise, they would have seen one man leaving the group to circle back around the village, re-joining them—along with three others—some hours later. The group then split, with three riders going forward in a flanking movement until they were ahead of the cart. The other three men followed as closely as they could without showing themselves.

'Huw, why not tie your horse behind, and come into the cart for shelter?' Giles called loudly over the noise of the rain and wind.

'Safer to keep a lookout, sir,' Huw called back.

'Nobody else out in this weather,' Giles spoke to Gwen as she huddled behind him in the cart.

Huw was trying to wipe the driving rain from his eyes and face when he saw the three riders approaching them. They had emerged from a hollow in the pathway and were about two hundred paces away.

'Riders approaching ahead!' he called to his father. Giles had spotted them about the same time as Huw, and he brought the cart to a halt. The men had heavy cloaks and hoods and continued to walk their horses slowly forward, as if they hadn't seen the approaching cart.

'Can't see if they're armoured, Huw. Perhaps they're just travellers, like ourselves?' Giles posed the question hopefully.

'We can't take that risk, sir, and we can't make a run for it in this weather,' Huw spoke slowly as he peered through the rain at the advancing riders. 'Mother, please go to the back of the cart and lie face down. Now!'

Huw's voice had a sudden urgency as he dismounted and tied his horse to the cart. He had noticed one of the men's head move as though he was talking to the others. Huw saw that all three had become more rigid in the saddle, as if ready to charge. They were now no more than a hundred paces away. Huw stepped to the rear of the cart to get some shelter as he strung his long bow. The cord was wet in an instant. *Not the best but it'll have to do*, he thought. *It would be better if they get closer*. It was just then that he saw the other three men trotting towards them from the rear. He took a second or two to study the new danger. The horses were moving with some difficulty in the muddy pathway. A small advantage: none of them would be able to get up any speed to charge. He realised their plan was to get close and then attack on foot. *Maybe I can keep them at a distance for a while.*

'Three more coming from the rear!' Huw shouted to his father. 'Go to the back of the cart and call the distance to me. I'm going to slow down the front three!' He was already at the front of the cart with an arrow strung.

'Two hundred paces to the rear!' Giles called through the wind and rain as Huw loosed his first shaft. With the wind and the wet bow string it fell ten paces short.

'Fool!' Huw berated himself.

The men had seen the arrow and stopped dead in their tracks. He made the decision in an instant and raced forward towards the attackers. Startled, the men hesitated as Huw approached. He counted the paces as he ran; thirty, forty, fifty. Suddenly he stopped and planted his feet as firmly as he could in the muddy ground. One of the men shouted and charged forward. His hood blew backwards in the wind and Huw saw he had no armoured helmet. The other two men remained where they were. Huw's first arrow flew wide and whizzed past the two stationery men. The second shaft hit the charging rider in the chest, knocking him violently backwards from his horse. The horse stumbled, fell and rolled forwards towards Huw, before rising uninjured and trotting away. Huw held his ground as the two riders steadied their horses and began to ride towards him. *Get one more*, he thought, *then back to the cart.* They were closing rapidly as Huw put another arrow in the groove. He studied the charging men for a split second before deciding on the leading horse. The arrow hit the horse in the breast below the neck.

Huw stood firm as both horses continued to race towards him. They were now just twenty paces away. He had another shaft in the groove as the wounded horse came down sharply, catapulting the rider forward over its head. The fallen horse forced the third rider to pull sharply to the left to avoid going to ground. The rider lost control of the frightened animal and the horse bolted away from the pathway. The first attacker was rising from the muddy ground as Huw ran towards him with sword and dagger drawn. The man's heavy armour delayed him getting to his feet for the split second that Huw needed. His running sword blow caught the man full on the cheek. He sank to his knees as Huw drove the dagger into his exposed neck. The man groaned once as Huw pushed him face down into the mud.

'A hundred paces, Huw!' Giles shouted. He was aware that Huw had raced forward, and was not sure if he could be heard over the wind and rain. Giles felt helpless as the men approached from the rear. The muddy conditions slowed them and they paused when they saw Huw running forward. He wondered why they hesitated, then realised they had seen Huw shooting arrows to the front. They were expecting an arrow attack from the cart. Giles wished he had a long bow and knew how to use it like Huw. Giles looked down at Gwen as she lay shivering on the cart floor. He had just put his hand on her shoulder when a crossbow bolt fizzed through the canvas cart cover. Looking out the rear, Giles saw that two men had dismounted and were loading their crossbows. The third man was still approaching on horseback. Another crossbow bolt struck the side of the cart as Giles shouted the distance and grabbed his sword.

Huw heard his father call out but couldn't make out his words. Turning, after pushing the dying man into the mud, he saw Giles jump from the cart and run towards the rider on the pathway. At first he didn't see the two crossbow men as he raced back towards the cart. But then he saw a bolt ripping through the cart's canvas.

'Crossbows!' Huw muttered to himself, as he struggled

through the mud. 'Covering fire! Quickly, quickly...' He was vaguely aware of his mother getting down from the cart as he let fly an arrow at one of the crossbowmen.

Giles's surprise foot charge seemed to startle the horse and rider for a moment as they approached each other on the muddy path. He was aware of a crossbow bolt flying past him. The rider's sword caught Giles's shoulder with a slashing blow as they passed each other. Giles's sword had made contact with the horse's hind quarters, but it was Huw's arrow burying into the horse's neck that did the real damage. The wounded animal began to stagger as the rider pulled it to a halt. He dismounted quickly before the horse stumbled and fell.

William de Bourg stood for a moment to take in what was happening. He saw Huw charging towards one of the crossbow men. The man had just shot a bolt but would have no time to reload before Huw reached him. The second crossbow man was nowhere to be seen. He was aware that at least one of the three men to the front of the cart was down. When de Bourg turned to face the man who had charged towards him, he recognised Giles fitz William. His passing sword blow had opened a wound down Giles's left shoulder and arm and de Bourg could see the blood being washed by the rain down the side of Giles's tunic. De Bourg stepped forward to finish off his enemy.

Somehow, through the wind and rain, one of Huw's arrows had hit the crossbow man to the left of the road. He saw him topple as he turned his attention to the other attacker, who had stayed low and partly hidden. Dropping his bow, Huw drew his sword and raced towards him. He felt the fizz as a crossbow bolt flew by, close to his face. Huw knew there would be no time for him to reload as he was only twenty paces away. The man had just risen from his hiding place as Huw's swinging sword caught him in the side of the neck. Partially decapitated, his head rolled to one side as he dropped almost silently to his knees and then to the ground. Huw quickly turned to where his father was fighting for his life no more than forty paces away.

†

Thinking Giles was fatally wounded, de Bourg was surprised when his initial frontal attack was defended. Giles was in great pain but his sword arm was unaffected and he parried the first blows as de Bourg sought to finish him. He knew, though, that he could not survive the attack for long. His vision was cloudy, and parrying de Bourg's heavy blows was draining his strength. De Bourg hadn't said anything until now, and he paused his attack to allow Giles to hear what he said.

'First your whore, and now you, fitz William. Your bastard children will soon follow you into hell.'

Giles thought his hearing must be affected, as he couldn't understand the man's words; he saw de Bourg's mouth move but could not hear him. Black spots floated across his vision and de Bourg's face seemed to swim around his eyes. He staggered backwards and fell onto his side into the mud. His collapse took de Bourg a little by surprise and his hesitation gave Huw the time he needed to reach him before he could strike Giles again.

De Bourg regained his composure as he saw Huw for the first time. He stepped to one side, parrying the initial charging blow. Huw almost toppled over in his eagerness to get to de Bourg. Both men turned and faced each other. Huw was surprised when de Bourg took two steps backwards and lowered his sword.

'I am Sir William de Bourg, sent by King Henry to bring justice to the people who murdered my brother.' De Bourg spoke slowly and clearly in Norman-French. 'I have no quarrel with you, archer. Let me do the King's work, and you can go free. Otherwise I will kill you, too.' Huw stood and stared at de Bourg, realising he had not recognised him from their encounter at MacMurrough's court in Ferns. 'Do you understand what I say, archer?' De Bourg demanded.

'I understand you well, de Bourg. No King has sent you to kill my family. That is your own doing. You can also leave, but only to go to hell.' Huw held his voice steady even though the anger welled up inside him. He now knew that the only way to deal with the de Bourgs was to kill them.

'Ah, the bastard son.' De Bourg hid his surprise, raising his sword and stepping forward to launch a frontal attack.

The sword battle was ferocious but swift. De Bourg was heavily armoured with metal and heavy chainmail while Huw was lightly clad; de Bourg made the fatal mistake of assuming his opponent was unskilled. He launched a series of trusting and swinging sword attacks that Huw defended easily. Huw conserved his strength and waited for his moment. When de Bourg paused for breath after a lunging attack had caused one of his feet to partially stick in the thick mud, Huw stepped forward and with a swinging blow severed de Bourg's trapped leg just above the knee. De Bourg dropped his sword and clutched his leg as he fell heavily forward. With both hands Huw plunged his sword into the back of the prone man's neck. Huw held his sword firmly as the dying man writhed in the slimy mud.

†

Giles was still unconscious as Huw knelt over him. Even though the wound was deep and the shoulder probably broken, Huw thought the injury might not be fatal if it could be cleaned and infection kept away. Struggling to lift Giles, he half-carried, half-dragged him to the cart. He wished John Daws was with them; he could do with Daws's strength now. As he propped Giles against the cart wheel, Huw saw Gwen lying in the mud on the other side of the track. He wondered what she was doing, lying in the wet ground with the rain pelting down. It was only when he reached her side that he saw the crossbow bolt embedded in his mother's back. He turned her over and cleaned the mud from her face as he bent close to check if she was breathing. Huw held his mother in his arms and gently swayed from side to side, just as she had often done to him when he had hurt himself as a child.

†

Huw and Giles buried Gwen's body on a small cliff overlooking the sea. Below, they could see the fishing port where a number of ships and small boats were tied up, sheltering from the storm. Huw knew some of the boats would be from the MacCarthys of Muskerry and that they would get safe passage. The cost of their escape had been heavy: his mother dead, his father badly wounded and in need of healing if he was to survive.

'Maybe on a clear summer's day she will be able to see Wales from here.' His father's voice was weak but filled with emotion.

'Yes, sir, I'm sure she will.'

CHAPTER 18

KERRY
NOVEMBER 1170

Tadhg MacCarthy met Huw and Giles on the pathway inland.

A rider from the port had gone ahead to McCarthy's village when they arrived from Wexford. Giles had passed into unconsciousness on the voyage and Huw had thought he would die. He now lay in the cart as Huw drove through the driving rain. The weather kept their progress too slow, and Huw wished he knew more about healing and treating wounds. Giles occasionally regained consciousness for short spells; he spoke, but Huw could not make sense of what he said. Sometimes, he picked out random words and names, and groans when the cart rattled over a stony patch. Huw feared he was going to lose his father as well as his mother. He blamed himself for the decision to leave the Kinsellas without protection. Travelling alone had made them vulnerable to attack and he cursed himself for his reckless assumptions. Was he beginning to believe the invincible warrior reputation given to him by the MacCarthys? He vowed that this would not happen again. If Giles survived, Huw would protect him; he would protect Daiwin, and Giles's two young children. He wondered and worried about Daiwin. Was he still in Dublin town? Was he alive? He wondered about his younger half-brother and sister – were they safe and well?

He resolved to find them and make them part of his family. If Giles recovered, he would bring all the family together and make sure they were safe.

Huw's spirits lifted when he saw Tadhg MacCarthy, particularly when Tadhg introduced the two monks with him as healers.

'Huw, I didn't think we would meet again so soon. I'm sorry about the circumstances, and sad for your mother. I'm sure she was a great woman,' Tadhg MacCarthy sounded embarrassed as he greeted Huw in a formal manner. 'Let us pull aside to those trees for the monks to see to your father.'

'Tadhg – I am in your debt, thank you, and I'm grateful for your kind words about my mother. She was indeed a great woman.' Huw spoke warmly as he reached out to grasp MacCarthy's hand. MacCarthy seemed more at ease after Huw had spoken.

'I will always be in *your* debt, Huw Ashe, never forget that.' MacCarthy looked directly at Huw as he spoke. 'Your family is now my family, your difficulties are mine.'

Huw looked back at Tadhg MacCarthy, and nodded. Once again, he was amazed at the communication networks used by the MacCarthys; no explanations were needed from Huw, Tadhg MacCarthy seemed to know what was happening to his family almost as soon as Huw did. He was struck by the sincerity he saw in MacCarthy's face.

MacCarthy listened intently as Huw told him the details of the ambush by William de Bourg.

'One of them lived, you say?' MacCarthy immediately understood the consequences. 'They would soon know what happened and will follow your cart journey to the coast. It will be easy enough to pay for information at the village port.' Huw nodded. 'It seems you will have to stay with us for a while and come under our protection,' Tadhg smiled.

'We will be the cause of great danger to you, just like we were for the Kinsellas in Wexford.'

'We are always in danger from some attacker. We know how to survive.' Tadhg smiled again as he spoke. 'Besides, we need to find out more about your Norman people. What better way to know them than to fight them?'

Looking at MacCarthy, Huw knew he was deadly serious. He was impressed by the simple logic and acceptance in MacCarthy's words. *He believes the Normans are here to stay and needs to learn how to deal with them*, Huw thought. *Will he decide to kill us or live with us when the time comes?* For now, it was enough to know that the MacCarthys would protect them from the immediate danger of the de Bourg revenge quest.

'Thank you for offering your protection, I accept it gratefully. We can talk about it again when my father recovers.'

†

The monks spent about an hour tending to Giles under the shelter of the trees. The rain had begun to lighten when one of them approached Tadhg and Huw.

'We have cleaned the wound and set the shoulder as best we can,' the man spoke with a strange Gaelic accent that Huw had difficulty understanding. 'He has a strong fever but if he lives through the next few days, he should survive. It will hurt him to move, but you should get him to the village for warmth and comfort. We can stay and look after him for a few days.'

'Thank you, Father, you have done great work,' MacCarthy answered. 'These men are true friends of the MacCarthys, and you have done us a great service.'

'Thank you, Father, I am very grateful.' Huw held out his hand and was happy at the warmth and strength of the handshake.

'My brother and I are sorry for the loss of your mother,' the monk replied.

✝

The rain finally stopped as they started back on the journey to MacCarthy's village. The monks stayed in the cart, one of them driving the team. Huw joined Tadhg on horseback.

'How did they know about my mother?' Huw asked.

'I told them who you are and what happened,' Tadhg answered simply. 'People here want to know your story. It will add to the reputation of Huw Ashe, the *Déise* killer.' Tadhg laughed softly, and Huw could not hold back a smile. 'People know about the *Déise*, but they would be curious about why your own people are attacking you, and you killing them. I will leave that for you to explain to people, if you wish.'

They were silent for a while as they settled into the rhythm of the journey.

'I found it hard to understand the monk; he had a strange accent.' Huw looked at MacCarthy, who laughed again.

'Strange, indeed, Huw Ashe, and a good ear you are getting for our Gaelic accents. They are here on retreat from their home in Kerry.'

'What is Kerry?'

'A strange place, Huw, a strange place,' MacCarthy emphasised the 'strange' and couldn't hold in the laughter. 'To the west a bit, some of it lost out in the sea mists.' He pointed vaguely west and Huw wondered why Tadhg found the mention of the place so funny.

'I'll have to go there and see it for myself.'

Tadhg MacCarthy just laughed more in reply.

✝

Giles remained seriously ill for nearly two weeks. The two monks alternated their time with him, with one of them always remaining in the village while the other returned to the monastery. They brought new medicines and kept Giles as comfortable as possible through his pain. They always answered Huw's questions with patience and kindness. Giles regained full consciousness after a few days. His body recovered much more slowly.

'Huw, there is no reason for you to stay and sit by my bed. You should get out and scout the land with your friend Tadhg,' Giles said, somewhat impatiently, to Huw.

'It is good that you are getting better, Father. Your mind is sharp enough, anyway,' Huw responded. 'Tadhg wants me to travel with him to meet his father in Muskerry. He leaves tomorrow.'

'Go with him, there is nothing you can do here. The MacCarthys are feeding me well and the monks come running when I groan. If I mention your name, I can have anything I want.' Giles laughed at his own words but stopped quickly as the laughter brought a stabbing pain to his side.

'You need to keep quiet, sir,' Huw touched Giles's shoulder. 'I'll tell the MacCarthys not to be telling you stories and making you laugh.'

Giles lay back in his cot and smiled. He waved his hand at Huw to dismiss him.

†

'Do the MacCarthys rule over Kerry as well as these lands?' Huw broke the silence as they rode through a long, tree-lined valley, having left the village just after dawn. The wind and rain had passed and the morning was crisp and cold. The winter sun was rising behind them. MacCarthy had taken six men and two of them were scouting ahead on either side.

'What did you say?' Tadhg seemed to awake from a thoughtful slumber. He leaned to one side on the saddle, as if trying to protect his injured leg. Huw thought he still suffered pain from his wounds and wondered if they should be making a long journey on horseback. MacCarthy had dismissed Huw's concerns and insisted that they should go to meet the MacCarthy Mór.

'Kerry?' Huw reminded him.

'Some of our people live there and we have strongholds, but I'm not sure that *anyone* rules Kerry.' Tadhg replied cryptically with a smirk on his face, as Huw looked at him quizzically. 'It's a fairly wild and mountainous land. We might travel there in the springtime, if you still have an interest.'

Huw did not reply as they settled into the rhythm of the journey. He thought that Tadhg seemed very quiet and uninterested in talking, so he asked no more questions. MacCarthy had said that with good weather, a day's ride should see them to their destination. Although they passed a number of small villages in the early part of the day, Tadhg stopped only once, to talk to the local men and take the food that was offered.

As the afternoon wore on, they began to meet rising ground and the landscape became more wooded and rocky.

'We have to skirt the side of that small mountain,' Tadhg motioned to Huw, as they began to climb more steeply. 'On the other side we'll see the MacCarthy Mór's little hovel.' He gave a short laugh and Huw was glad to see that his spirits were lifting. Huw suspected that the pain from his wounds was greater than he was showing.

'Will I have to fight this MacCarthy Mór, or his champion warrior?' Huw nudged his horse closer to MacCarthy.

'If you do, I'll fight with you,' Tadhg laughed. 'My father might challenge you a bit, but not in combat. Not at first, anyway. I'll warn him about your skill with bow and sword but he'll know your reputation already.'

'I'm looking forward to meeting him.' Huw was breathing heavily as the climb intensified.

When they crested the small mountain, Tadhg gestured for them to stop.

'Mickel, call in the scouts and we'll eat,' he called to the man in front.

'He's a good man, Mickel.' Tadhg pointed towards his sergeant as he rode forward to call in the scouts, speaking quietly to Huw as they dismounted. 'He won't say it, but he's sorry how he treated you as a prisoner. A good man at your side in battle, and quick with the dagger.'

'I'll remember that if I have to fight against him, or with him.' Huw sat on a rock and drank from his water pouch. 'Are we near your home?'

'We are, indeed.' Tadhg stood and pointed down westwards into the wooded valley below. 'Muskerry to the south-west, and behind us to the south-east is the big town of Cork. If it wasn't for the evening mist rising, you could see the town and the sea beyond.' Huw peered south but couldn't make out the sea or the town. 'Cork is a big port town ruled by the Northmen. We trade with them and they allow us to use the port – sometimes,' MacCarthy added, with a smirk. 'The town is well fortified, and they are strong fighting people. Mostly we now trade and live with them.' He pointed south-west again, but Huw could see nothing except hills and trees and green pasture beyond. 'The MacCarthy Mór should be at home. Our lads will have told him we are coming. We should be there before dark, if we eat fast.'

Darkness had fallen when they arrived at the gates of the town. The scouts had ridden ahead and the gates opened as they approached.

'Tadhg! Is that you?' A sentry called from the gate tower. 'The MacCarthy is in the great hall. He wants you there now!'

'Let us take our breath,' Tadhg MacCarthy shouted back. Huw could see he was tired from the journey, as he was himself. 'I'm sorry Huw, but we had better go and meet him. We'll get you a place to sleep in my house when we can slip away.'

'I could take some food and ale before bed,' Huw laughed.

'I'm sure of it, Huw. It's me that needs rest and sleep.'

The MacCarthy Mór's great hall was noisy and packed with people when Huw and Tadhg entered through the servants' door. Tadhg insisted on going through the kitchens.

'I want to have a look around first, Huw, to see who's there,' he explained as they passed through the busy kitchen. The smell of roasting meat increased Huw's hunger.

They stood for a while at the small side door as Tadhg looked around the hall. The door was to the left and just behind the main table, where the MacCarthy and his nobles were sitting.

'I don't know what he's celebrating. There must be something big happening,' Tadhg MacCarthy whispered to Huw, before walking across to where his father sat. Huw followed at Tadhg's bidding.

'God bless the house! Father, how are you?' Tadhg called loudly, as he placed his hand firmly on the back of his father's shoulder. Startled, MacCarthy Mór rose sharply from his chair and drew his dagger as he turned round. Tadhg took a step back out of reach of the blade. The hall went silent.

Huw saw the rage on the MacCarthy's face turn to laughter as he recognised his son.

'Tadhg, bastard, blast you!' MacCarthy roared. 'I could have killed you, fool!'

'What names you use in front of all these people, Father! You admit it, so – I am a bastard!'

After a brief moment of silence, the hall erupted into loud cheering and laughter as the MacCarthys, father and son, embraced.

The MacCarthy Mór's dagger was still in his hand as he held his son with both arms. His eyes met Huw's as he released Tadhg from his huge grip.

'Father, this is Welsh Huw Ashe, single-handed killer of ten *Déise*, and our true friend. Put away your dagger, or he might run you through where you stand!' Tadhg's father hesitated, and then sheathed his dagger. 'Without him the *Déise* would have sent you my head.'

'Huw Ashe, we have heard of you. Welcome to our land!' the MacCarthy called loudly as he offered Huw his hand. When Huw took his hand, MacCarthy held both their hands high and turned to face the people in the hall.

'This is our friend, Huw Ashe of Wales, make him welcome!' he shouted loudly as the hall again erupted in cheering and banging of tables. 'Tadhg and Huw, come sit here with me. Brink more food and drink!'

†

At a side table, Bridín O'Brien did not see the two young men enter the hall through the kitchen door. She was deep in conversation with the MacCarthy ladies as they wondered about the reason for the feast. It was not a feast day, but the MacCarthy had insisted that all his nobles and their ladies should be there. Bridín and the ladies beside her had been startled when the MacCarthy had suddenly jumped from his seat with his dagger drawn. It was then that she saw Huw. If anyone had been watching, they would have seen her grip her chair tightly as her heart began to pound and her face flush a deep red. The other ladies—along with everyone else in the room—were watching the MacCarthy and his son. Bridín's eyes were fixed on Huw. She recalled a similar feast in Limerick, when she had first met him. How handsome he looked then; and still did. Her mind flooded with thoughts of Huw and with questions. Why was he here? Why was he with Tadhg MacCarthy? Was the Norman army there? Bridín listened intently as Tadhg MacCarthy introduced Huw to his father. *Will Huw see me when he looks around the hall? Will he recognise me? What will he do?*

The MacCarthy Mór insisted on Tadhg and Huw telling him the details of the *Déise* attack. He told Huw that he had not known about his son travelling to Wexford for prisoners and information on the Norman foreigners, at which Huw glanced at Tadhg, who just smirked and shrugged in return. The MacCarthy had many questions, and he clasped Huw around the shoulders as Tadhg told him about Huw's skill with the bow and sword and about the men he had killed in the attack.

'All the other lads, Gill and Bric, were lost. They fought well, Father.' Tadhg's voice waivered a little as he finished his story.

'You took an arrow to the leg?' the MacCarthy asked.

'I did. A bit of a limp, but I'll live, thanks to him.' Tadhg nodded towards Huw.

'We are indebted to you, Huw Ashe, and should you ever need our help, you have but to ask. For now, eat and drink. We must then rest, for our journey tomorrow,' the MacCarthy added, as though talking to himself.

'What journey, Father?' Tadhg was quick to ask.

'I thought you knew. We are to travel across Kerry to meet the O'Brien, bastard that he is. He has asked for a high council.' The MacCarthy paused to take a huge swallow from his tankard. 'This is a type of... last supper, before we set off!' He roared with laughter.

'A council with the O'Briens!' Tadhg sputtered with his mouth full of meat and ale. 'What do they want?'

'Land and cattle, what else? Maybe a woman or two. Who knows?' The MacCarthy's voice softened slightly. 'We can't always be at war, Tadhg. Maybe a bit of talking will be good. At least we'll find out what they're thinking and planning – that is, until the next battle. You must be ready to travel, Tadhg. Huw Ashe should come too. We'll need many brains to deal with the slippery O'Brien, and he can protect us with his long bow if they attack us.' The MacCarthy laughed as he looked towards Huw.

'I am happy to come with you, sir, if I can be of help. I have met the O'Brien King in Limerick.'

The MacCarthy looked surprised at Huw's response.

'Huw and his comrades were sent by MacMurrough to help O'Brien fight off the High King.' Tadhg explained.

'That fool O'Connor, we might have helped the O'Brien ourselves against that imposter, had they asked,' the MacCarthy said, looking Huw in the eye as he spoke. 'You have travelled much of our land, it seems, since you arrived. You will have to tell me more about these Norman men, on our travels tomorrow.' MacCarthy held out his hand and Huw clasped it strongly. 'I will be away to bed shortly, but you men stay and enjoy the feast.' With that the MacCarthy rose from the table and went to talk to some men gathered at the end of one of the long tables.

'He has to give those men his judgement on some matter: cattle, land, marriage, or something,' Tadhg explained to Huw. 'He seems to like you for some reason. It's not everyone that he takes to so easily.'

'He seems like a good and honest man, and I'm happy to have met him,' Huw answered.

'You sound like a diplomat, or a King's counsel, maybe.' Tadhg's voice was quizzical, as though a new thought had dawned on him. 'Maybe there's more to you than just a skilled assassin.'

'I sometimes talk to people, before I kill them.' They laughed together as they filled their cups with ale.

Huw was aware of the group of MacCarthy ladies sitting to their right and he wondered if Bridín was amongst them. He had not been able to look in their direction while they were in discussion with the MacCarthy Mór. Tadhg had gone to talk to someone on the other side of the hall and Huw turned to look at the ladies more closely. His eyes and Bridín's met immediately. He remembered Donal O'Brien's banquet in Limerick and the first time he had seen her. Then, she hadn't looked at him; now, her eyes and face smiled as they gazed at each other through the dim light of the MacCarthy Mór's great hall. They raised their tankards and drank deeply.

CHAPTER 19

KERRY
DECEMBER 1170

TADHG MACCARTHY WAS SLEEPING soundly when Huw entered the room and called him. It was an hour past dawn, and the main square had been alive with activity since the day broke, bright and crisp after a frosty night.

'You'll have to get up soon if you want to travel,' Huw called loudly. 'There are people and carts and horses everywhere. Didn't you hear the noise?'

'Ashe, call someone to bring food and clothes.'

Huw smiled as two young serving girls came in with plates of bread, cheese and cold meat.

'We've packed more food and clothes for your journey, sir.' One of the girls smiled at Tadhg.

'Get out while I get dressed,' Tadhg shouted, then remembered himself as the girls left. 'Thank you!'

'Your father sent me to get you, and to tell you that your friend, the Lady Bridín O'Brien, will travel with us.'

'What! He's bringing the O'Brien lady with us? Why?' Tadhg stood there half dressed.

'I asked him to.'

'Why?'

'She asked me to ask him.' Huw smirked, enjoying Tadhg's sleepy confusion.

'I don't understand.' Tadhg looked at Huw with his hands outstretched.

'Get dressed. We'll have some food, and I'll explain. You need not rush, we can follow after the main group in an hour or so. They will not be moving fast.'

†

As they sat and ate, Huw told Tadhg about how he and Bridín had met and how they were committed to each other. He did not mention that he and Bridín had spent most of the night together, talking and relating what had happened since their last meeting. When Huw finished, they sat there without speaking for a few moments.

'So, you and the Lady O'Brien will marry?' Tadhg broke the silence.

'If she'll have me, and if Donal O'Brien doesn't execute her for murdering O'Muinacháin.' Huw smiled.

'That slobbering fool! I wish I had killed him.' Tadhg laughed loudly. 'But why does she want to go back to the O'Briens? You and she could live here on MacCarthy land.'

'She's not going to surrender herself to their justice. But she wants to know what King Donal thinks and if he would give approval when we marry. She intends to ask you to find out at the council.' Huw paused to look at his friend, as Tadhg put more food on his plate. 'I also ask this of you. If you can.' They were silent for a while as they ate.

'Huw, you are my friend – I owe you my life. The Lady O'Brien is a fine woman, someone I admire. Indeed, if it wouldn't have caused a war with the O'Briens, I might have married her myself! I'll do whatever I can and I'm sure my father will too.'

'Your father has asked me to come to the council meetings, but I'm not sure, as some of the O'Brien nobles will know me.' Huw had called to see the MacCarthy Mór earlier in the morning to tell him about his association with Bridín.

'It would be good to have your diplomacy and counsel, Huw. They won't be expecting a Welsh archer, so we'll make sure you look like one of our MacCarthy bodyguards.'

'Fair enough,' Huw laughed.

†

The main group left the town about two hours after dawn. Huw, Tadhg and Bridín, with six guards, followed shortly afterwards. Huw was surprised at the size of the travelling party. There were six carts carrying food, drink and tents, with about 100 men and Tadhg told him they would gather more men on the way.

'We'll need a little back up army. You never know how these councils might go. Sometimes the talking stops and the fighting begins.'

Huw noticed that everyone was fully armed. Were they hoping for a fight? He worried about protecting Bridín and would insist that she remain to the rear when the council took place. Glancing at her he saw a determined look on her face – keeping her a safe distance away might not be easy. Bridín saw his look and smiled at him.

'What are you thinking about, sir?' she asked.

†

The previous night, Tadhg MacCarthy had left the banquet shortly after his father. Those that wanted to drink and talk had gathered in small groups, while others drifted away. When most of the ladies had gone to their beds, Bridín beckoned to Huw that she was about to leave through the servants' door.

After a short while he followed her; she took his arm just as he emerged into the darkness.

'You might get lost in the dark in a strange town,' she whispered. 'Come this way. Most people will want to sleep early tonight in preparation for the morning's travels.'

'Where are you taking me, Lady?' Huw asked. 'You know that I'm tired after my long journey.'

'Fool, I wonder how long it would have taken you to return to Limerick. You're lucky I came here to meet you.'

'I would have returned to Limerick.'

Bridín stopped suddenly beside the dark wall of a house. She pulled Huw close and kissed him. He went to speak, but she put her fingers to his lips and kissed him again. Both their hearts were pounding and Huw was sure his could be heard through the crisp silence of the night.

They spent the night in an antechamber to the single ladies' quarters in MacCarthy's household. There was a warm fire and Bridín heated some wine. They talked late into the night, relating all the events that happened since they parted in Limerick.

'O'Muincháin attacked you?' Huw was shocked and didn't know what to say.

'He was drunk, but he always had eyes for me. The King promised him a marriage from his household and O'Muincháin thought it should be me.' Bridín looked at Huw. 'I didn't mean to kill him, just to protect myself. I was in shock, and Queen Orla proved a true friend. Without her, I would not be here.' Bridín shuddered and her voice quivered.

'You did what you had to do. I wish I had been there to protect you.' Huw reached across and held her tightly in his arms.

'You are here now.' Bridín's voice began to break as they kissed. Huw tasted the salt from her tears as they slipped under the bed covers. Before they fell asleep, Huw agreed to Bridín's request to go and see the MacCarthy Mór in the morning to tell him about their connection, and ask his permission for Bridín to travel.

'He has been kind to me, and I would not wish to offend him. I almost feel I need his blessing to be with you,' Bridín explained and Huw nodded his agreement.

†

Their journey to Kerry felt like a King's parade. At every village they passed, people came out to meet the MacCarthy. If they had stopped for all the invitations, the trip would have taken weeks. Men and carts joined them as they travelled across the mountains and in to Kerry. Huw depended on Tadhg's explanations about what was happening and where they were. When they had crossed what Tadhg called the Mang River, scouts and emissaries were sent forward to find O'Brien's people and make arrangements for the council.

'It may take a day or two for them to agree the arrangements. There will be a council or two about the council first,' Tadhg explained vaguely. 'We will keep moving until there is agreement on the meeting place. Maybe near the banks of the Shannon river.'

Huw had a puzzled look on his face and MacCarthy laughed.

'The O'Briens will have a few different retreat routes planned, just in case something happens. Ships on the river might be one option.' MacCarthy seemed to enjoy Huw's confusion. 'They'll know that we have a few armies of men to fall back upon.'

'The more force both sides show, the more likely peace will prevail,' Tadhg laughed as he ended his Irish war lesson.

'But why go to all this trouble just to have talks about land? Couldn't emissaries from both sides meet and bring agreement back?' Huw asked as he tried to understand.

'Mostly that happens, but maybe every few years the Kings meet. Then there's peace for a few years, or war!'

'This time, Huw, there must be something else. We are always in dispute about land and borders. O'Brien was anxious to meet, and my father agreed. Maybe it's connected to your Norman friends?' Huw shrugged his shoulders in reply. 'We'll find out in a day or two and you'll be there to hear with your own ears.' Tadhg MacCarthy laughed as he spurred his horse forward to leave Huw and Bridín ride on alone.

†

Two days later they arrived at the banks of the Shannon river. Huw had only seen the river at Limerick. Now it was much wider as it met the open sea.

'I passed this way when I escaped from Limerick,' Bridín whispered to him as though someone was listening. 'It feels strange to be back here.'

Huw noticed the unease in her voice and reached across from his saddle to touch her arm. 'You are safe now. You will not have to run away again.' Huw's voice was reassuring. He was determined to keep Bridín safe. He remembered the MacCarthy's words at the banquet as he spoke about the council with the O'Briens. Land and borders and maybe a woman; these words had remained in Huw's head. Could the woman be Bridín? The MacCarthy had readily agreed to allow Bridín to come with them. Could it be that Bridín would be part of some bargain between the MacCarthys and O'Briens? Huw wished he had not been so eager to bring her.

†

They had stopped to eat hot food when Tadhg rode back to meet them.

'Contact has been made!' he called as he dismounted. 'Food! I'm starving.'

Huw waited impatiently while Tadhg MacCarthy ate.

'You are not usually so quiet,' Huw finally ventured as Tadhg downed a cup of ale.

'Have some ale,' Tadhg pushed a jug towards Huw. 'The O'Briens are gathered around the port further up the shore. Contact has been made, so we'll meet tomorrow morning maybe. There's no rush, so take it easy. There'll be a bit of ghost-fighting first today before the talking.'

'Ghost-fighting?'

'The O'Brien soldiers will look over our people and we'll have a look at them. A bit of riding around and spear waving.'

'Is there danger of the soldiers starting a fight?' Huw asked.

'A bit, maybe, but the counsels have agreed to meet, and that's a good sign.' Huw, looking a bit puzzled, just nodded. 'I'll be going tomorrow with Cooney, my father's counsel. The MacCarthy asks that you come with us as my personal bodyguard.' Tadhg smirked. 'It would give you a chance to listen first hand at an Irish council; what do you say?'

'Of course I'll come and protect your body. I've done it before.'

Tadhg laughed and clasped Huw around the shoulder.

'You have indeed, you have indeed,' he agreed. 'The Lady Bridín must stay here. We'll put six men as personal guards.' Tadhg lowered his voice. Bridín was sitting close by, looking out over the water. 'She is an O'Brien lady, and they will know she lives with us. We're not sure how they might see this. They may think we kidnapped her and forced her—' he broke off. 'They may want her back. They may want to execute her for killing O'Muinacháin.'

Huw nodded his understanding.

'Will your father give her back to the O'Briens, if that's what they want?' Huw asked, after some moments of silence. 'What if they want to trade land?'

'The MacCarthys do not trade land with the O'Briens,' Tadhg answered. 'We take what we can hold. But the lady herself may wish to return to her people. Maybe she would wish to right whatever wrongs happened? We would respect her wishes.'

'I will respect her wishes also, Tadhg, whatever happens.' As he spoke, Huw looked past Bridín towards the waters of the Shannon.

✝

Early next morning, Huw had changed into the clothes of a MacCarthy soldier when Tadhg called by his tent.

'With a short spear you could be taken for my brother! I must ask the MacCarthy if he has been to Wales anytime. How old are you now?' Tadhg could not hold in the laughter as he looked Huw up and down.

Bridín, too, laughed when she saw him and Huw felt foolish.

'No spear, I'm bringing my longbow staff, I don't care if they see it!' Huw huffed and walked off to mount his horse.

Tadhg and Bridín looked at each other and laughed.

'We'll mind him, Lady. You stay safe and we'll meet at evening meal,' Tadhg spoke somewhat formally to Bridín.

'You can call me Bridín now, surely, being our friend.'

'I am certainly your friend, Lady Bridín,' Tadhg smiled as they bade goodbye.

There were fifteen riders in the group, with Huw and Tadhg riding together at the rear.

'Is this Cooney your father's chief adviser?' Huw asked as they rode along close to the river bank.

'Pompous fool,' Tadhg spat out the words. 'Don't know why my father keeps him. He always seeks to better his position. I would have his head.'

'You like him, so?'

'I tolerate him because I have to. Listen closely to him at the council, and tell me if he flirts with the O'Briens. I don't trust him.'

'I'll do as you say if I have time from protecting your body.'

'I'll protect myself this time,' Tadhg laughed as they nudged their horses along.

It was not long before they saw the port with the tents of the O'Brien army all around.

'They have an army camped there!' Huw was surprised at the size of the O'Brien forces. 'They have a lot more men than you, so maybe talking is better than fighting.'

'They have a lot alright, but it's not always about numbers,' Tadhg replied. 'We've taken precautions with different groups of men spread out behind us.' He called to the men in front, 'Hold up, we'll wait here!' To Huw, 'Now we wait for their delegation.' Tadhg added quietly to Huw.

The morning was bright, but a crisp wind coming across the river added to the winter cold. Tadhg signalled for them to remain on horseback to be ready to move when the O'Brien group appeared. Cooney had edged forward maybe fifty paces with three guards around him.

'He wants to be the first to meet them,' Tadhg whispered to himself. 'I wonder who Donal O'Brien will send out? Christmas will be here shortly, Huw. Another month or so. Will you spend it with the MacCarthys?' Tadhg asked after some moments of silence. 'Did you celebrate Christmas in Wales?'

'Yes, we did indeed.' Huw was amused at Tadgh's diversion from the impending negotiations. 'It was a favourite time in my childhood, at least until I came to Ireland.' Tadhg looked at him as if to check if he was being serious. 'I would be happy to spend any time with the MacCarthys. I would also wish to find my brother Daiwin, and to see my friends in Kinsella's land.'

'Riders approaching!' Cooney's call from the front interrupted their thoughts of friends and Christmas.

When they moved forward to join Cooney, Huw saw a group of riders trotting along the costal path towards them. He counted about twenty men in the group.

'I will go forward to meet their counsel and we will agree how many are to come to the talks.' Cooney spoke formally to Tadhg.

'I'll come with you with my bodyguard and two others,' Tadhg answered. 'The O'Briens can do likewise if they wish.'

It seemed to Huw that Cooney was about to argue, but he decided against it.

'As you wish, Tadhg, but let me do the first contact and greetings.' Cooney looked for agreement and Tadhg nodded his assent.

Shortly after, the five of them walked their horses forward and as they did, five riders emerged from the O'Brien group.

The two groups were about a hundred paces apart when Huw recognised the unmistakable figure of O'Muinacháin at the head of the O'Brien group.

'Tadhg, that's O'Muinacháin!' Huw whispered the words so that only Tadhg could hear. They both stiffened in their saddles as they looked closer at the advancing riders.

'Are you sure?' Tadhg seemed as shocked as Huw. 'It does look like the slimy bastard.'

'I'm sure.' Huw had recovered from his initial shock and now he felt cold hatred and some other feeling he could not quite understand. Was that fear, he wondered?

'Hang back a little behind the guards, Huw, and hold easy. Cooney and I will move ahead.' Tadhg's voice was steely but calm. 'He won't look too closely at the bodyguards. You two, do what Huw Ashe tells you.' The other guards nodded agreement. Huw saw the tension in their faces. As Tadhg and Cooney moved forward, Huw opened the small satchel at his waist and felt for his bow cords. His bow staff was loosely tied along his horse's flank, underneath his left leg. He untied the binding holding the bow staff to make sure it was ready if needed.

Huw listened as Cooney and O'Muinacháin made their formal greetings and introductions. Tadhg was right. Nobody on the O'Brien side paid much attention to the MacCarthy guards. They had all dismounted and Huw was less than twenty paces away as the two men began to talk. Huw could hear everything, but his mind was racing. He was thinking about Bridín, about how she must have suffered, believing she had killed O'Muinacháin. She must have worried greatly about being returned to the O'Briens. How had she come to think that he was dead? He heard O'Muinacháin as he listed land and villages ruled by the O'Briens. They were willing to withdraw from these areas and cede control to the MacCarthys.

'The woman must be returned to my King.' Huw heard O'Muinacháin's raspy high pitched voice. 'She is but a whore now, after being with the MacCarthys, but my King wants her back. She is promised to me as wife, and I will have her though others would not.'

Huw stood holding his horse's rein, with the animal partly hiding him from view of the negotiating party. He slipped his bow staff from the horse's side and strung the bow. Tadhg gave a small jump as he heard the arrow fly past, close to his body. He reached for his sword as the shaft flew through O'Muinacháin's legs, ripping his cloak. O'Muinacháin staggered backwards and sank to the ground screaming and clutching his leg. There was silence for a moment as they all stood still, watching the blood trickle through O'Muinacháin's fingers. The arrow had grazed his leg below the knee.

'Treachery, treachery! Kill them, kill them!' O'Muinacháin screamed at his guards.

'Hold still, the next arrow will be through his heart!' Huw called loudly so all could hear.

Tadhg turned to see Huw with another arrow in the groove. Huw's eyes were fixed on O'Muinacháin. Tadhg wanted to laugh. After a brief pause he signalled his two guards to come forward. Like everyone else, they had stood still with disbelief at what was happening.

'Disarm those men, now!' Tadhg pointed his sword towards the O'Brien men calmly. 'We had all better do what Huw Ashe says, dangerous assassin that he is. What next, Huw Ashe of Wales? I suppose you'll have to cut his throat now,' he added, pointing at O'Muinacháin.

'Huw Ashe of Wales!' O'Muinacháin squealed as he looked up from the ground. 'What is this, MacCarthy, what have you done? War, war, this will mean war! My King will kill you all!'

'Shut up, you bastard, or I'll slit your throat myself!' Tadhg roared.

'Tadhg, we have to bring the counsel back to King Donal. We have to tell him it was the foreigner that did this, not us!' Cooney's voice was shaky.

Tadhg stepped forward and pushed the point of his sword to Cooney's neck.

'Another word, and I'll take your head.' Tadhg's voice quivered but his hand held firm. 'Huw, we should leave. The O'Brien sentries will have seen what happened. Do you want to kill O'Muinacháin?' His voice was deadly serious.

Huw was standing in the same spot, his second arrow still pointing at O'Muinacháin. He had not thought about much in the last few minutes other than killing O'Muinacháin, ever since he had heard him mention Bridín's name. Tadhg's actions had given time for his mind to clear. He now realised the position he was in and the difficulties he had created for the MacCarthys.

'I will kill him if we ever meet again, but not now.' Huw spoke loudly so that all could hear. 'Do you want him as a prisoner?'

'No use to us, Huw, no use at all. He'd just slow us down. Do you want to take your arrow back?'

O'Muinacháin stiffened on the ground.

'No, he can keep that as a Christmas gift.'

'You men, ride back to your King and tell him what happened,' Tadhg spoke to the O'Brien guards. 'You can get your weapons when you come back for the counsel. Go on now!' he roared, as the men hesitated.

†

Later that day as they headed back towards the Mang River, Tadhg joined Huw and Bridín. They had left the meeting site as quickly as they could with little time for talk or explanations. The MacCarthys left lines of rearguard soldiers at points along the way in case of a following attack by O'Brien. No attack came.

'The MacCarthy sees the funny side of it now. He didn't at first,' Tadhg's tone was slightly mocking. 'He may want to talk to you to get your advice on our war strategy. But not just now.'

Bridín smiled at Tadhg. Huw said nothing.

'The Christmas invitation is still on offer, but I may have to hide you in some village,' MacCarthy laughed. He was enjoying his own humour and Huw's discomfort.

†

A large group of MacCarthy soldiers were waiting for them when they reached the Mang River. Huw and Bridín stopped to eat on the hillside overlooking the water. They were enjoying the view of the water shimmering on the estuary when Tadhg rode up to them.

'We may have war on both sides soon,' Tadhg spoke as he dismounted. 'One of our villages was attacked. Foreigners looking for you and your father.'

'De Bourg?' Huw asked, even though he knew the answer.

'It is likely. Our people brought your father to Killarney. He is safe and well.'

'Killarney?' Huw asked.

'It's not too far. We'll take you there.'

CHAPTER 20

KILLARNEY
CHRISTMAS 1170

BRIDÍN HAD BEEN SHOCKED when Huw told her that O'Muinacháin was alive.

'I panicked when he attacked me and I didn't check if he was dead. There was blood and he collapsed, so I just ran.' Bridín shuddered as she remembered. 'Queen Orla helped me get away quickly and no one went back to check the body.'

'Cooney spoke to O'Muinacháin before he left back there.' Tadhg was listening to Bridín and Huw. 'O'Muinacháin said he nearly died from the stab wound. Donal O'Brien wanted you banished, but he offered to marry you and the King agreed.'

'It seems the O'Brien marriage agreement still holds, seeing that Huw didn't kill O'Muinacháin when he had the chance.' Tadhg was amused at his own interpretation of events. 'I thought you would finish the bastard, Huw. Why didn't you?'

'I thought I was going to kill him too. My first arrow was badly aimed.'

'Huw Ashe, the *Déise* killer, missing from ten paces? I don't believe it,' Tadhg laughed. 'You did put a hole in the bastard's cloak though. Both of you have holed him now; poor man is full of holes.'

Tadhg's infectious laugh and carefree attitude to what had happened cheered Bridín somewhat, even though she had conflicting feelings. She was glad she had not killed him but she had a sense of regret that O'Muinacháin was alive. What if he came after her and Huw with the O'Brien army? They may not always have the protection of the MacCarthys.

Huw's thoughts were also conflicted. His mind and judgement had clouded over when he had heard O'Muinacháin talk of Bridín. He had difficulty remembering the details of his actions as he had strung his bow and let the arrow fly towards O'Muinacháin. He had acted on instinct. It had been almost as if someone else was directing his thoughts and actions. He recalled similar feelings when they had been attacked by William de Bourg and during the *Déise* ambush.

'Will this be the cause of a war, Tadhg?' Huw asked the question that had begun to trouble him once realisation about his rash actions had set in. 'Attacking and wounding a King's emissary at a peaceful meeting. Surely a war-like act of aggression?'

Tadhg didn't answer for some time. 'It might, Huw Ashe, it certainly could. But I don't think it will. The O'Briens will do a bit of spear waving and will demand the Lady Bridín's return, along with your head in a bag.' He paused and smirked at Huw. 'We may have to agree, but if you were to escape, what could we do?'

'Where would we escape to?' Huw asked.

'First to Killarney, for the winter, and then maybe farther, if needed.'

'What about the O'Brien spies finding out?'

'There are always spies in this land. We have them, the O'Briens have them. Sometimes they don't get all the information and sometimes they don't live very long.'

'A very interesting land, this is.' Huw nodded his understanding to Tadhg.

'I have spoken to my father. He is not too concerned about Donal O'Brien and what happened. He had thought it strange that O'Brien should have sought a council about small matters. He is more concerned about the Norman alliance with MacMurrough and what may unfold. He thinks that O'Brien may have like concerns.' Tadhg's tone had become serious. 'We can offer our protection to you and your family, Huw. The MacCarthy may ask for your counsel and help in talking to your Norman friends, if that time comes.' Tadhg looked at Huw, posing a question.

'You shall have my help in everything except fighting against my father's people.'

'Fairer than that, we cannot ask.' MacCarthy clasped Huw around the shoulder. 'Now, let us go and find you a place in Killarney.'

†

Giles fitz William was dozing in his cot in a small room off the main hall of The MacCarthy's quarters in Killarney. He had regained his senses and was able to walk short distances but the hurried journey from Muskerry had tired him. He didn't hear the arrival of a large group of people into the hall and was taken by surprise when Huw and Bridín entered the room.

'Huw, is that you?' Giles tried to get up.

'Yes, sir, don't get up,' Huw went to his father's side and embraced him.

'This is Lady Bridín O'Brien, from Limerick.' Huw felt awkward at the formality of his words. 'This is my father, Giles fitz William,' he turned to Bridín, immediately feeling foolish for speaking Norman French to her.

'I am Bridín.' She laughed at Huw as she knelt by Giles's cot and offered him her hand.

'Bridín,' Giles repeated in his strong accent as he kissed her hand. No other words were needed as Bridín leaned over to embrace Huw's father.

†

Later that evening Huw and Giles sat by the fire as Bridín prepared food. Huw told his father about Bridín and what had happened at the O'Brien council.

'You are a lucky man Huw, to have met such a woman. Don't let yourselves be separated, no matter what.' Giles's voice was low and hoarse and his eyes welled up as he took hold of Huw's arm. 'I suffered being separated from the woman I loved for too long. Now she is gone.'

Huw had never seen his father so emotional and he could feel the tears in his own eyes. He did not speak for a while, afraid that his voice would break. They had not spoken much about his mother's death; other events had taken over. Huw wondered if their lives would always be like that in Ireland: events overtaking them, always struggling to survive, always having to move on. Maybe they would have some time to settle this winter in Killarney. He wondered about Daiwin; what had become of him, and Giles's other children?

Huw's thoughts were interrupted by Bridín bringing them cups of warm wine.

'The food is ready to eat. Roast beef and pigeon brought by Tadhg. At least, that's what he said it was. There's enough to feed ten families.' Bridín's lilting Irish voice made Huw smile. He translated for Giles, who smiled as Bridín offered her hand to help him to the table.

The three of them sat and ate without conversation. Bridín finally broke the silence.

'Huw Ashe, I would ask this myself, but I cannot speak Sir Giles's language. I want to ask your father's permission to marry you. Will you do it for me?'

Giles stopped eating and looked at Huw, waiting for the translation. Huw tried to swallow what was in his mouth, but couldn't. Bridín handed him his cup and he gulped as much wine as he could.

'Do you mean, will I marry you? Or will I ask him?' Huw finally blurted out.

'You understand what I said well enough. When you get your calmness back, ask your father – unless you don't want to marry me.' Bridín smiled at Giles and continued her table conversation. 'We cannot live together unless I am your wife or your servant. As a lady, I cannot be your servant.' Bridín waited as Huw struggled to find any words. Giles looked at Huw with a questioning expression, still waiting for the translation.

Huw took another drink of his wine and stood, facing his father.

'Sir, the lady asks your permission to marry me. I also ask your permission to marry her!'

After a moment of stunned silence, Giles began to laugh so much they thought he might collapse. Still laughing, he embraced and kissed Bridín, and then his son.

'Does that mean yes?' Bridín asked through her own laughter and tears.

'It's a yes, from us both,' Huw answered.

†

Huw discovered that the MacCarthys, just as the Kinsellas in Wexford, liked a good wedding. He wanted to be married quickly, but Tadhg insisted that any wedding in Killarney would be done properly.

'There are plenty of monks to do the ceremony, but we have to organise the festivities. That will take a week or two,' Tadhg told Huw. Bridín told him to be patient and not to argue with the hosts.

Eventually, after much planning, a date was fixed. 'A week before the Christmas feast, if that suits the lady?' Tadhg smiled, looking at Bridín.

'The lady is very happy, and she'll be there,' Bridín replied. Huw looked worried and was about to protest when he saw the look in Bridín's eyes.

'A week before Christmas it is, so,' was all he could muster.

†

A number of the MacCarthy ladies took Bridín into their quarters and Huw hardly saw her. In the days leading up to the wedding, people began to arrive in the town. Huw could not believe they were all there to celebrate the wedding. Had Tadhg invited everyone from Muskerry and Kerry? The MacCarthy Mór arrived, bringing with him his brothers and other MacCarthy nobles. All were brought and formally introduced to Huw Ashe the *Déise* killer and his father. Giles said it was as if he and Huw were holding court, with all the nobles coming to pay tribute.

'Huw, my son, these people think very highly of you. You seem to be an Irish hero, a legend.' Giles and Huw were alone late in the evening after leaving the MacCarthys feasting in the great hall.

'I think they like a reason for gathering and feasting. Any reason, even the wedding of a Welshman and a lady from their worst enemy,' Huw laughed.

'It is good to see you laugh, Huw. You have been quiet and serious these last weeks.' Giles had immersed himself in the wedding preparations, as much as his health would allow. He felt safe and happy in the company of the MacCarthys, even though he missed Gwen and wished she could have been there. 'Your mother would have been so proud.'

'Yes, sir, indeed I think she would.' Huw looked at his father. 'I would wish for Daiwin to be here, and my friends. There was no news from Wexford before you left Muskerry?'

'No, just the information we got about de Bourg and his men. They attacked a village, looking for us.' Giles's tone became serious. 'De Bourg is not for giving up, Huw. After the winter we will have to look to making ourselves more secure. When I am recovered,' he added quickly when he saw Huw's worried expression.

'The communication line is still there, between Wexford and the MacCarthys. Tadhg says so. At least Regan and Kinsella will be able to contact us,' Huw reassured himself as much as his father.

†

Huw and Bridín were married on a bright, frosty day in late December. The winter sun was low over the mountains around Killarney and the fog lifted from the big lake as the celebrations began. The town could not hold all the people who came. There were campsites on all roads leading into the town and Tadhg told Huw that the feasting and celebrations would continue until Christmas and after.

Tadhg came to congratulate Huw on his marriage. 'The MacCarthys celebrate well, and this is an event worth celebrating. I wish you and your wife a long life together. Later in the evening, you must come away for a short while. My father and I would talk with you,' he added, before going to fill his tankard.

†

Dusk was falling when Tadhg and his father approached Huw's table.

'Huw, could we take you from your wedding for a short while before darkness falls?' Tadhg asked, rather formally. 'We have some horses ready for a brief journey – the Lady Bridín Ashe might come with you.' Huw and Bridín shared a smile at the sound of her new name.

Huw shrugged his shoulders when Bridín looked at him as they mounted and trotted out of the town. The journey was short and they could still hear the noise and laughter from the wedding festivities as Tadhg pulled in and signalled for them to dismount outside a house near the shore of the big lake. The MacCarthy Mór held out his hand to Huw and they clasped hands warmly. He then went to Bridín and kissed her hand.

Tadhg smiled at the puzzled looks he saw on their faces.

'My father congratulates you on your marriage, and he and all his family are very happy for you. They ask that you will accept this small house and land as a wedding gift.' Huw looked at him in stunned silence. Bridín looked at the house and the lake beyond it. There were two horses tied at an outhouse and cattle eating dried grass all around. She counted more than twenty cattle. 'You may not like it, or wish to live here, but the cattle and animals are yours to do with as you will. There are also two small boats. Many fine fish are caught in the lake. You may take as many fish as you can eat, and hunt any animals and birds that you desire.' He painted a picture for them of what life by the lake might be like.

Bridín tried to speak, but the tears welling in her eyes and the tightness she felt in her throat prevented her. Huw was close beside and her hand found his. She squeezed Huw's hand tightly.

'The town is close and well-guarded. Anyone approaching here would have to come through the town first, or across the lake,' Tadhg continued, reminding them of the solid defences in place. 'There are routes back to Muskerry from Killarney, many of them known only to us. You are guarded by water and mountains all around.'

Huw looked at the lake and the mountains beyond. He saw the natural defences that Tadhg described. His mind was clear but he was shaken by the enormity of the gift being offered by the MacCarthys. A home and land for his family!

Tadhg had stopped speaking and the four of them stared out across the still lake as darkness began to fall. Bridín thought that she had never seen any place so beautiful.

'What is the lake called?' Huw finally broke the silence.

'The local people call it Loch Léin.' The MacCarthy spoke for the first time. 'The lake of learning. There is a holy island where the monks live.'

'Sir, the offer of this home and land by your family has left us without words.' Huw was struggling to regain his composure and his voice. 'It is generous beyond anything that I have known. If my wife is happy to live here, I am honoured to accept this wedding gift from the MacCarthy family.'

Bridín squeezed Huw's hand tight and leaned towards him, putting her head on his shoulder.

'That's settled, so.' Tadhg seemed relieved. 'We must bring you back to your wedding before people come looking for you!'

†

On that same frosty night a small group of cold and hungry men camped near the banks of the Mang River. Most of Henry de Bourg's men—disgruntled, as de Bourg had run out of money—had left his travelling band over the last few weeks, heading east towards Wexford to try to join up with the main Norman forces. De Bourg had begun to attack and rob any villages and any people who were in his path. Of the eighty men who started out with him, his party now numbered just a handful of knights and soldiers. He was desperate, but unwilling to give up his blood quest against Giles fitz William and his family. Two of his brothers were dead, and he had sworn that he would have his revenge. Earlier that day, they had captured a river boat man, and with the help of his two Irish scouts they had extracted some information from the man before he was killed. De Bourg cursed his lack of understanding of the Irish language but he had recognised 'MacCarthy' and knew that 'Killarney' must be a place.

'Tomorrow, we head for Killarney, whatever that place might be,' De Bourg said, as much to himself as to his sergeant. 'Fitz William and his bastard now seem to live with these MacCarthy people. Call over our Irish scouts.' His sergeant didn't respond. 'Call them, you fool!' Two men who came over to the campfire with some trepidation. De Bourg repeated, 'Killarney, Killarney!' He handed them a stick and pointed to a sandy patch on the ground. 'Killarney!' One of the men eventually understood, and drew a line in the ground, pointing out the direction. 'Tomorrow, we go there,' de Bourg told the men, even though he knew they did not understand.

†

Early the following afternoon, de Bourg's forward scouts reported that the town was ahead, and could be seen from the nearby wooded hill.

'Forest and lakes all around, but there's a town in the valley,' one of the soldiers called, as he approached de Bourg. 'There are lots of people camped on the approach to the town. There aren't too many pathways, mainly forest and water.'

'Let us go look from the hill,' de Bourg called to the sergeant.

When they got to the top of the hill, de Bourg reined in to gaze at the view. Through a clearing he could see the expanse of a large lake with islands in the middle and forest all around.

'What a place,' he said almost under his breath. 'What a land this is. I might nearly want to live here.' To his left, de Bourg could see columns of smoke rising from what he knew must be a large town. The town was hidden by the dense tree cover, but seemed to be close to the shore of the lake. He sat on his horse for some time considering what to do. They were all hungry, and they needed to shelter and recover from their journey across the country. He hadn't enough men now to attack even a small village and he knew he couldn't enter the town. He looked at the clear sky and across the calm waters. The day was dry and bright, but they were in the middle of winter and the weather changed quickly in this land. His mind cleared as he realised what they had to do.

'Sergeant, de Pewer, come over here!' De Bourg called the two men that he trusted most of those that were left. 'We will have to winter near here. We do not have enough men to enter the town and we cannot go back east to Wexford.' He looked at the two men. 'The journey is too dangerous in winter, and it will be known to the Irish that we are in their land.' De Pewer and the sergeant knew he was right and they nodded agreement. 'We will make for the lake shore through the forest there, away from the town.' He pointed westwards along the lake. 'We will have to build shelters, but there should be game and fish and perhaps we can find some smallholdings and take some grain. A small number of men should be able to keep watch on the town and pathways and take whatever we can from any travellers,' he added, with a smirk across his dishevelled face. Again, the two men nodded their agreement. 'I will tell the others that they can stay or go as they please. You will have to kill the Irish scouts. We don't need them now and we can't risk them talking to the MacCarthy people.'

'Yes, sir, understood,' de Pewer answered for both men.

†

The wedding celebrations merged into Christmas and some days beyond. Bridín insisted that Giles move from his quarters at the great hall and come live with them in the house by the lake. In the weeks following Christmas, a severe winter arrived in Killarney. Freezing temperatures and snow came quickly. The mountains and forests were white and the lake was so cold they thought it would freeze over. The MacCarthy people of the town made sure Huw's family were supplied with grain and meat and ale from their stores. The three of them gathered and cut as much wood as they needed for their fire.

After some weeks the snow cleared and then the storms came. Wind and bitterly cold rain kept them and everyone else inside. Despite the winter weather, Giles's health and spirits improved as his wounds healed. He and Bridín made plans for the springtime: they would plant grain, and learn to fish from the boats.

Huw found he had to translate less as Bridín began to teach Giles some Gaelic words. He was less than enthusiastic, though, when they talked about planting crops and fishing. 'I will be the forest hunter, while you do the fishing,' he volunteered. Bridín teased him about his fear of water, telling him that lake water was the best kind. He half-agreed that when the weather was better, he would go on the lake with them – but not out too far.

'We should visit the holy island,' Bridín suggested one evening as they ate their meal.

'Holy island, yes,' Giles repeated in his French accented Irish.

'Holy island – maybe,' Huw said.

Before the bad weather set in, they would sometimes meet monks from the island as they landed their boats on the shore. Huw would help them transport bags of grain from the town and load the boats before they headed back to the island.

†

Further along the lake shore, Henry de Bourg also met monks from the island when they landed close to where he and his men were camped. The monks were surprised to meet a Latin-speaking foreigner on the lake shore near Killarney. After their initial trepidation, they realised the men were starving and in danger from the approaching winter. De Bourg, for his part, was happy to meet some Irish people he could converse with, even if it was in Latin. He readily accepted the monks' invitation to spend the winter with them on the island in the lake. At least they would be fed and kept warm; they might even learn something about Killarney and Giles fitz William.

CHAPTER 21

INNISFALLEN
FEBRUARY 1171

JOHN DAWS WAS RESTLESS. The Wexford winter was severe and he had been confined to the village for long periods. Worse, Donal Kinsella had not given permission for Daws to marry his daughter Aideen.

'She's too young yet to know her mind,' Kinsella told him. 'Maybe in a year or so.'

Daws had accepted Kinsella's decision good-humouredly. But now he had little to do and found it hard to fill his days, and nights.

When Daiwin Ashe and Will Hen appeared at the village gates one morning towards the end of winter, Daws found it difficult to hide his emotions. He wanted to hug them both, but instead he pulled Daiwin off his horse and wrestled him to the ground.

'Daws, get off! I don't want to die like this,' Daiwin pushed him away. 'Survived all those battles in Dublin, and then to be squashed to death by you.'

Will Hen squealed with laughter as he jumped from his horse and slapped Daws on the back.

†

Regan's men had found Daiwin and Hen camped with de Barry's troop just outside Dublin town. There had been a number of attempts to retake the town, all beaten back by the MacMurrough-Norman alliance. Regan had been informed of the departure of Giles and Huw from the Kinsella village, and the increased threat from the de Bourg faction. He sent emissaries to the de Bourgs, warning them against attacking the village. He then arranged with the Norman commanders to allow Daiwin and Will Hen to leave the Dublin army and return to Wexford.

Alice was happy to meet Daiwin again. She had adapted well to village life in Ireland; her friendships with Kinsella's daughters and the other young women had helped her to settle better than John Daws. She and Daiwin spend a full day together talking about Wales and what had happened since they came to Ireland. They both knew that Daiwin had to leave to find his family. They discussed travelling together but decided it was safer if Alice stayed with the Kinsellas.

'I'll be here when you come back again,' Alice told him as they kissed.

'When I know where my family are and they are safe, I'll return to Wexford,' Daiwin promised. The three friends spent two nights at Kinsella's village before heading south to the coast to link up with a MacCarthy ship. Dai and Hen were impressed by Daws's new-found ability with the Gaelic language when he spoke with the ship's captain.

'I know some words, and can make up others,' Daws laughed.

†

After the wedding and Christmas celebrations, Tadhg returned to Muskerry, happy that Huw and his family would be safe for now in Killarney. He heard about the arrival of Daiwin and his companions, and made his way eastward to meet them. At first they found it difficult to communicate; John Daws had a limited Gaelic vocabulary, even though he understood much of what was said and Daiwin and Hen spoke no Gaelic at all. After a time they found that if Tadhg spoke slowly using basic words, Daws understood enough to translate into Welsh for Dai and Hen. Daws was very pleased with himself, particularly when Tadhg told him the Gaelic word for translation and called him John the Translator.

Tadhg was unsure if he should tell Daiwin about his mother's death. He knew it was not his place to do so, but it didn't feel right not telling him. Eventually, he called John Daws aside and told him what had happened, as best he could. Daws found it difficult to believe what he heard, and asked him to repeat it a number of times to make sure he understood. They agreed it was best to tell Daiwin.

Tadhg explained about the de Bourg attack, as Huw had told him. 'I am sorry for the loss of your mother. I know that Huw and Giles buried her near the Wexford coast, but I don't know where.' He struggled to find the words, and Daws in turn struggled to translate them. 'I am sorry,' Tadhg repeated as he held out his hand. Daiwin took his hand in silence.

†

Like his friend Daws in Wexford, Huw was also restless. As the weather began to soften and the daylight lingered a little longer, Bridín and Giles became engrossed in their new life by Loch Léin. They began to cultivate part of the land to prepare for planting corn and other crops. They also took to fishing on the lake from their two small boats. Some of the Killarney boat men came and showed them how to work the boats and how to find and catch the best fish. Huw helped with all the physical work but he could not find the enthusiasm that seemed to drive Bridín and Giles. Bridín loved being out on the lake or in the fields and the work helped Giles regain his strength. Giles also enthused about learning Gaelic, with Bridín as a willing teacher. They now mostly spoke Gaelic in the house.

Huw did not understand why his family's enthusiasm for learning and their new life made him feel deflated. He was not interested in farming and he didn't want to go out on the lake. He spent his time hunting and chopping firewood. He also made a large store of arrows for his longbow and even found suitable wood to make some new bows. He honed his archery skills in the forest, shooting game and rabbits.

'Come with us today, we won't go too far out,' Bridín asked him, not for the first time.

'Maybe tomorrow, love,' Huw answered. 'When all the wood is chopped.'

She laughed in return as she grabbed him around the waist.

'It is good to see you happy and smiling,' Huw kissed her. 'My father, too. Thank you for your love for him, and me.'

'It is you have made me so. I'm sorry that sometimes you seem uneasy, or sad.' Bridín held Huw closer.

'Sad, no – maybe uneasy. Sometimes, I fear this cannot last. I fear that what we have might be taken away.' Huw looked at his wife. 'You never make me sad. I wonder about Daiwin and my friends in Wexford; I wish I knew something about them.'

'Perhaps when the spring is fully here, you should go to Wexford and find out,' Bridín said what Huw had been feeling but hadn't allowed himself to consider.

'Perhaps, if my father is completely recovered,' Huw nodded.

†

On a small boat out on the lake, about halfway between Innisfallen island and the Killarney shore, Henry de Bourg fished with his companion, Ralf de Pewer. De Bourg watched the far shore closely. A religious man, he had settled well to winter life in the monastery on the island. He and his four remaining companions had been housed and fed by the monks. In return, the men worked on the farm, fished, and attended the monks' services. De Bourg actually liked the work and spiritual life on the island, and he quickly recovered his strength after their fruitless expedition of revenge. He learned from the monks about the Norman lord living on the lake shore with his son and wife. When the monks pressed him to go and meet his fellow Norman, de Bourg explained that he and Giles fitz William were friends and travelled together to Ireland, but they had quarrelled and parted ways. He asked that his presence on the island not be revealed. The monks did not question what he told them.

'I do not see our friends on the lake today,' de Bourg spoke more to himself than his companion.

'We could row over to have a closer look,' de Pewer ventured.

De Bourg thought about it for a while. 'Not today, Ralf, we'll have to bide our time with so few men.' He had considered a surprise attack during the winter, but even if successful there was no escape route. He now had just four men, only two of whom he could fully trust. He was aware from the monks that fitz William and his son had formed a strong alliance with the MacCarthy people, and the town was very close. If he was to mount an attack, he would need a sizeable army, and he would need to plan an escape route back to Wexford.

That day on the lake, Henry de Bourg realised that his revenge would have to be even longer term. Fitz William was now backed by an Irish army and the MacCarthys were formidable warriors, from what the monks told him. He knew he would have to return to Wexford—maybe even to Wales—to gather the men and resources he needed. As he fished with Ralf de Pewer on the peaceful Loch Léin, he vowed to himself that he would return to this place to take his family's revenge on fitz William.

'The bastard son and his whore too,' De Bourg finished his thoughts aloud.

†

Some weeks later, after helping two monks load provisions onto their boat, Huw invited the men to join him for a jug of ale before they rowed across to the island. It was a regular occurrence and the men agreed readily.

'Our life is back to normal again now your Norman friends have left,' the younger monk spoke after he had downed a half tankard in one gulp. 'Thirsty work.'

'Norman friends?' Huw asked, looking at both men.

'I'm sorry, Huw, they asked us not to tell anyone,' the older of the two men finally answered. 'Brother Patrick did not know. We found them starving and they stayed for the winter.'

'Who were they? Their names!' Huw demanded as he stood up from the table.

'Henry de Bourg, Ralf de Pewer and three others,' the older monk looked concerned at Huw's aggressive stance.

'De Bourg!' Huw repeated. He stood there for a moment as the two monks stared at him. 'I am sorry for my anger. They are gone, you say?' He saw fear in the younger monk's eyes.

'Yes, about a week ago. De Bourg said he had quarrelled with Sir Giles and insisted we not tell you. They were weak and hungry and we took them in. They did not cause any trouble.'

'I'm glad of that. There *is* a quarrel between our families, but not of my father's making. Did de Bourg say where he would go?'

'He mentioned returning home.'

†

'I can't believe that de Bourg was here, living so close,' Giles spoke quietly to Huw in Norman French. 'They were on the lake fishing, you say?'

'Yes, sir, the monks said they helped on their farm and fished a lot.' Huw remembered seeing boats on the lake but he had not thought anything of it. 'There are boats on the lake every day. It's a common sight.'

'They must have seen us, Bridín and I – must have been close to us, sometimes.' Giles also recalled seeing other boats.

'Why did they not attack us when they could?' Bridín joined them at the table and the language changed to Gaelic.

'They had few men and knew we would be helped by the town people. They could not have escaped, even if they had killed us.' Huw's explanation was stark, and he immediately regretted what he said when he saw Bridín shiver. 'They are gone now, and we are safe,' Huw tried to reassure his wife.

'Are we sure they have gone?' Bridín asked quietly. There was silence around the table as they thought about what Bridín had said.

'We need to make some defences and be more vigilant. It is relatively safe here, but de Bourg now knows where we live.' Giles spoke in Norman French. 'I will see to making some defensive structures.'

'The fighting instinct is taking over again, sir,' Huw smiled, as he translated the details for Bridín. 'I thought you had become a simple fisherman.'

'A fighting warrior fisherman I hope,' Giles laughed at the thought.

†

Later that night, Huw and Bridín lay quietly awake, listening to Giles snoring in the other bed chamber.

'Sleeping like a baby,' Huw spoke softly. Bridín laughed out loud. 'Quiet! You'll wake him.' Huw's mock appeal just made her laugh more.

'I felt afraid this evening when you spoke about de Bourg and how they were so close to us,' Bridín said softly once her giggling had stopped. 'It felt like evil was close and we were helpless.'

'I know, my love. I am sorry.'

'I was not just afraid for myself.'

'I know, my love.'

'I don't mean you and Giles,' Bridín said.

'No? Who then?' Huw asked as he felt himself drift off to sleep.

Bridín reached across to find Huw's hand and placed it on her stomach. 'The other person, the real baby, in there. Not Giles.' She couldn't help but let her giggles start again.

'What other person?' Huw asked.

'Our real, new, baby, in there, you fool. Wake up!' Bridín's happy giggling wouldn't stop. In the darkness of the bed chamber, Huw banged his head on the side table as he rolled out of bed in shock.

†

Giles woke next morning to the smell of fresh bread cooking in the iron pot over the wood fire. He thought it must be late, he had slept so long.

'Bridín, Huw, that smell is too much. Makes me hungry. I have much work to do today.' Giles always spoke quickly when he was excited. 'Is the weather good?' Huw and Bridín looked at him and laughed.

'What's wrong? What's happened?' Giles could not decipher the strange looks on their faces.

'We have another little person joining our family,' Bridín spoke slowly and clearly in Gaelic to help him understand. Giles looked puzzled for a moment or two.

'A baby?' he asked Huw in Norman French.

'A baby,' Huw repeated in Gaelic.

Giles didn't know what to do with himself. He hugged and kissed Bridín. He shook Huw's hand and then hugged him too.

'A baby, a baby,' he muttered in his best French-accented Gaelic.

'You are happy, then, with our news, sir?' Huw asked.

'I am indeed, happy indeed,' Giles laughed and Huw thought he saw tears in his eyes.

When the morning meal was finished the three of them sat at the table and talked about children and family. Bridín thought that the baby should be born in late summer.

'Late summer. Wonderful,' Giles repeated Bridín's Gaelic. 'Sorry, I'm still learning your words.' Their talk continued through the morning. Engrossed in conversation and happiness, they did not hear the sound of horses pulling to a halt on the pathway outside the house. It was only as the men approached the door that Huw heard footsteps and low voices and rose quickly to find his sword – it was too late to string a bow. Giles was on his feet with sword and dagger in his hands. Bridín took a food knife from the table. Huw looked at Giles and nodded in readiness.

'Huw, Huw Ashe boy, are you in there?' John Daws's lilting Welsh tones made Bridín jump.

'John Daws, is that you? Who is with you?' Huw called out in Welsh, still on alert with his sword arm stiff.

'Just me and Will Hen!' Daiwin answered back through the closed door.

'Is that fresh-baked bread I smell?' Hen called to no one in particular, with his Welsh nasal twang. Still with his sword drawn, Huw opened the door and stood looking in disbelief at the three men.

'We're starved with hunger and can't fight you now, boy,' John Daws commented.

†

There was little work done that day at the house on the lake shore. Instead, the day was spent talking, relating events, eating, and drinking. Huw and Giles were brought up to date on Strongbow and MacMurrough's campaign in Leinster. They heard with some amazement of the taking of Dublin, and the subsequent attempts by the Irish and Northmen to retake the town. Huw was happy to get news of the Kinsellas, and relieved they were secure because of Regan's intervention.

'I did not have the language to converse with Regan, but he was very helpful to us. I think he hopes you will return to Wexford,' Daiwin told Huw when they were alone. Wanting to talk about their mother, they were walking through the woods near the lake shore.

'We had talked about travelling east in the spring time. That was before I knew about the baby. He or she may change our plans,' Huw said with a smile.

'It's very peaceful here. A long way from the east coast. Do you think the Normans will come here? I know you are a bit of a Norman,' Daiwin added with a smirk.

'I don't know, Dai, but people like the MacCarthys and the O'Brien King in Limerick are wondering that also. The Irish kingdoms are wary of the Normans invading their lands.'

'There are more people coming over from Wales all the time. Ordinary people, not just Norman knights and soldiers. People are coming hoping for land and a better life.' Daiwin had heard the rumours during his time with the army, and these had been confirmed by John Daws and the Kinsellas.

'The land is good, but I'm not sure if it's our right to come here and take it,' Huw echoed discussions he had with Giles. They were more concerned about their right to be in Ireland now that they had made alliances and friendships with Irish people. 'I would like to talk to Regan to find out what MacMurrough and Strongbow plan to do, now that they have Dublin and the other port towns.'

'Whose side will we be on, Huw, now that you are friends with the MacCarthys, and living with them, and your wife a noble Irish O'Brien woman?'

'You have a way of putting things, Dai. I don't know the answer. And what about our Welsh-Norman-Irish-O'Brien child?' Huw added with a laugh.

For the next three weeks they enjoyed the early spring weather in Killarney. They cultivated land, hunted and fished in the daytime. At night they ate and drank and sometimes sang songs. They visited the town, and some of the townspeople visited them. Tadhg had left Killarney, shortly after bringing the three Welsh friends to the town.

'Family affairs and squabbles call me away, Huw. There's always fights when the weather gets better,' Tadhg had laughed as he said goodbye. 'I'll be back to meet your new family member. We celebrate children even more than weddings!'

†

The letters arrived a couple of weeks after MacCarthy left.

'Tadhg told me to get here as quick as I could, and to give these to Huw Ashe. Is that you?' the man on horseback asked.

'It is.' Huw had met the man on the road from the town, and he hurried back to the house. The letters had Giles fitz William's name on the outside.

'Robert fitz Stephen!' Giles recognised the seal on the first letter. 'I don't know the other one.'

'Open them, sir, maybe?' Huw was impatient as his father examined the seals. Bridín touched Huw's hand and smiled at him. The three of them sat around the kitchen table as Giles broke the seals carefully. Huw's patience almost left him as Giles slowly read the letters in silence.

'Sir, what news?' He couldn't wait any longer.

'MacMurrough is dead and Strongbow is declared King of Leinster. Robert fitz Stephen wants us to return to Wexford. He says that Strongbow will not side with de Bourg and will offer us protection.' There was silence for a moment as they paused to grasp the importance of the news. Huw translated Giles's words for Bridín.

'Robert has heard of your exploits and alliances, Huw. Strongbow wants you as a counsel to help form links and communicate with the Irish chieftains.' Huw looked at Giles with confusion and a little disbelief as he continued to translate for Bridín. 'The other letter is from my brother. He did not use the family seal. My children have not settled well in France, and they ask me to come for them.' Giles's voice broke and he found it difficult to complete the words. Bridín touched Giles fondly on the shoulder as she went to get a jug of wine.

'I must go to France immediately.' Giles recovered his composure as they drank their cups of wine. 'But your life is different now, Huw. You have a family. I can write to Robert to explain, if you wish. I am sorry, Bridín, for not speaking Gaelic. I don't have all the words. Huw will translate,' he added.

'These are major events and there is much to consider for everyone,' Bridín spoke when Huw had explained. 'I have a matter to mention, also. I would wish to reconcile with my O'Brien family. King Donal should know of our marriage and baby. The news may help soften hearts.'

'It is right you should reconcile with your family,' Huw nodded and looked fondly at his wife. 'Right also, Father, for you to reunite with your children. I will send a message to Tadhg. He may agree to help us once more.'

CHAPTER 22

KINGDOM OF THOMOND
SUMMER 1171

Tadhg MacCarthy sent his counsel, Cooney, as an emissary to Donal O'Brien to find out how Bridín might visit Thomond and be reconciled with the King. O'Muincháin initially prevented Cooney from gaining access to the King, so he approached Queen Orla. When Cooney gave her the news of Bridín, the Queen insisted that her husband should allow her home to have her baby. Donal Mór O'Brien feared little except his wife's wrath, and he agreed. Bridín knew on first welcome that the King was pleased with her visit. He also seemed happy to meet Huw again.

'We have heard of your exploits, Huw Ashe. You must tell me more of your Norman friends.' The King called Huw to his side at the great hall banquet table.

'Sir, I am happy to tell you all I know,' Huw replied directly to the King. He also glanced at the small portly figure of O'Muincháin by the King's side.

'Come; let us go to my court chamber,' O'Brien beckoned Huw with one hand while he held his other hand upright to stop O'Muincháin rising to follow them. O'Muincháin slumped back in his chair.

†

Huw's private meeting with the King of Thomond lasted for an hour or more. He told the King the little he knew about the Normans and their plans. It seemed that the King knew more about the Normans' exploits than he did himself.

'We were sorry to hear of the death of our father-in-law. It happened quickly,' Donal O'Brien lowered his voice as though to prevent the guards from hearing. 'Now we have this Strongbow as King of Leinster. It may bring trouble for us all; O'Connor and O'Rourke will want to wage war.' Huw was unsure what to say, so he nodded and said nothing. 'They are fools in the ways of war, Huw Ashe, fools.' The King took a long drink from his wine goblet. 'The MacCarthy, the bastard, is cleverer, a true warrior. Would that we might align together and not always be at each other's throats.' Huw looked at the King of Thomond as he drained his wine and wondered if he really wanted an alliance with the MacCarthys, or if it was idle talk. He could not be sure. 'Anyway, Huw Ashe, enough talk of war. You are welcome to my house and kingdom – even though you married an O'Brien woman without my permission.' The King raised his voice so that those listening through the open door to the great hall could hear. 'And now you will be father to an O'Brien child. Again, without my permission. But better you than my fool, O'Muinacháin,' the King whispered so only Huw could hear. 'We will accept you in our court as husband and father to an O'Brien, but you must pay recompense to my counsel O'Muinacháin for the wrong you and your wife have done him.' O'Brien raised his voice again. 'I will decide compensation. Do you agree?'

'I do so agree, sir,' Huw replied as be bowed to the King.

Bridín and most others in the great hall heard the final exchange between Huw and Donal O'Brien. She glanced at O'Muinacháin as he continued to slump over his wine. He did not look up. Bridín was given rooms in Queen Orla's quarters and restored to her position as a lady in the Queen's court.

†

Huw and Bridín agreed that when she felt safe in Limerick, he would respond to Robert fitz Stephen's summons and return to Wexford.

'I will return for the baby's arrival,' he promised. 'I'm not sure what Sir Robert has in mind and I don't know if I can be of any help to him.'

'You do not recognise your own abilities, my love. Others see them very well.' Bridín smiled at her husband. She knew that Donal O'Brien and the MacCarthys were aware of Huw's skills, not only as a warrior, but also as a negotiator and counsel. He spoke their language and understood their ways. She suspected the Norman leaders must also recognise Huw's worth. They would need skilled people like him, if they were to survive in Ireland.

In the days before he left Limerick, Huw and the King had a number of further meetings. Donal O'Brien always mentioned the MacCarthys. Even though he never asked directly for Huw's help, he indicated that he wanted an alliance and seemed to hope that Huw might pave the way. He also made it clear he would like to know more about Strongbow's intentions in Ireland.

'These are difficult times, Huw Ashe. One grows tired of fighting. If we can avoid war, it would be better for us all.' Donal O'Brien's words would remain in Huw's head.

†

'The last time I left Limerick we did not know if we would meet again. This time it should be just a month or so.' Huw spoke softly as he held Bridín on the night before his departure.

'You should only make promises you are sure of keeping,' Bridín chided him. 'Your Norman friends may need you longer.' Huw did not answer immediately. He knew Bridín was right, but he did not want to think of being separated from her for longer than a month.

'I want to be here whenever our baby decides to come, and you think that will be in August, so four months from now?'

'Yes, my love. That is what I think.'

'That should be enough time to do whatever Sir Robert wants of me. If not, I will get Tadhg MacCarthy to kidnap me again and bring me here.'

Bridín laughed at the thought. 'I might send Tadhg to get you, if you do not return on time.'

'That's settled so. We'll have to let Tadhg know our plan. He has promised to take messages for us if needed.' Huw's tone became more serious. 'You just need to send a messenger to Killarney. He will arrange delivery to the Kinsellas.'

'If we could get parchment, we could send letters,' Bridín suggested with a smile.

'But what language? I cannot write your Gaelic, so not that,' Huw laughed.

'I can show you how to make Gaelic letters when you return, but Latin could be our secret language. Only monks and a few others would understand,' Bridín continued. 'We must not write anything that a monk shouldn't read!'

'Agreed – we only use words that a monk would speak!'

They laughed together and hugged each other in silence. Bridín kissed her husband and spoke softly as she cupped his face with her hands. 'You are a wonder, Huw Ashe. You have your own personal messenger service, all across Ireland, through friends and enemies alike. People could not do in a lifetime what you have done in a year.'

†

As Huw left Limerick, Bridín felt her body tremble. She had been brave and happy for the last few days. But now as her love departed, she felt a great fear of losing him. She knew that he was just one man travelling through dangerous lands with enemies watching. What if the de Bourg people were out there, waiting? What if O'Muinacháin had Huw followed? What if he was attacked by others, as yet unknown? Bridín knew Huw was to meet with John Daws and some of MacCarthy's men in Killarney; Tadhg himself might even go with him to Wexford. But her fears took hold and she could not get them out of her mind. Even if he got to Wexford safely, what would happen to him there? Would Strongbow and Leinster be at war with all the Irish Kings? When Huw turned to wave as he passed through the gates, she barely found enough strength to stand steady and wave in return.

The days after Huw's departure were the worst. As the days became weeks, she settled into a resigned sadness. She missed Huw and often found herself smiling when she thought about something he had said or something they had done together. She also missed Giles, and wondered where he might be on his journey.

†

Giles fitz William's journey eastwards with Daiwin and Will Hen had been uneventful. Tadhg MacCarthy had had his men accompany them, and they had got passage on the established MacCarthy route along the coast. They arrived in Wexford town and were waiting for a ship going to Wales. Daiwin and Will Hen insisted on travelling with Giles to Wales and on through England to France.

'You cannot go alone, sir,' was Daiwin's simple response when Giles had protested, and Huw and everyone else had agreed with Daiwin.

They were told that a ship should berth in a day or two, and they took lodgings in a tavern near the port.

'Dai and Will, thank you for coming with me. You were right. It would be difficult to do this on my own,' Giles spoke quietly in Welsh as they settled down to their evening meal. The port was busy, with small boats coming and going throughout the day. On Tadhg's advice, Giles had changed his clothes to look a little less like a Norman lord.

'You don't want to be getting in the notice of people looking for a fight,' Tadhg had told him, knowing that a Norman knight might not be welcomed by everyone in Wexford. 'You can become a Norman again when you get to Wales and France.'

'We haven't been to England—never mind going to France—so this is an adventure for us,' Daiwin responded to Giles. Will Hen nodded his agreement as he guzzled his ale.

'We should have safe passage once we get to my brother Robert's lands. But you both know him from your rescue of Gwen and Alice' Giles suddenly remembered their expedition to Wales.

'Yes, sir, he was very kind and helpful to us.'

'A kind and generous man,' Will Hen added.

'You were both brave, and John Daws too. You did us a great service.' Giles recalled Gwen's rescue with sadness in his voice. 'You met the younger de Bourg, I believe, when you got into the castle?'

'I did, sir. I would know him again if I saw him.' Daiwin remembered the morning Vere de Bourg had challenged him to shoot his longbow across the moat.

'Hopefully you won't have to meet him again, Dai.' Giles suspected, though, that his and the de Bourg's paths—and swords—might have to cross again.

†

Henry de Bourg's journey across southern Ireland had not been easy. The Innisfallen monks had given them as much food as they could, but de Bourg and his companions had to keep away from pathways and villages, and had no guide or scouts, so they travelled much farther than needed, losing their way continually. After crossing two large rivers near Waterford town, they were attacked by a large band of men and had to flee to escape death. The five men had scattered in different directions, with only de Bourg and de Pewer managing to keep close and meet up again. De Bourg hadn't seen his sergeant or the two other men since the attack. He had intended going to Waterford town to get a ship to Wales, but the attack pushed them father east. He decided to head to Wexford port instead.

They were ragged and exhausted from their travels, but de Bourg had coin enough to pay for lodgings, and passage when the next ship left for Wales. He and de Pewer settled down to wait. On their third day in Wexford, De Bourg was at the quayside when Giles and his two companions arrived at the small port on horseback. De Bourg noticed the three riders and recognised his enemy immediately. He gripped de Pewer's arm and turned back along the quay, away from where Giles was dismounting.

'Fitz William,' de Bourg spat out. 'He too must be seeking a ship to Wales.' They watched as Giles and his companions spoke with some sailors, then followed them to their lodging tavern.

Henry de Bourg sat up late that night, sipping wine and thinking about his two dead brothers. He wondered why fitz William was returning to Wales. It must be important business with his family – why else would he risk being caught and brought to the King's court for hanging? Fitz William had all but abandoned his land and position when he went to Ireland. As he listened to Ralf de Pewer snoring loudly after many jugs of ale, de Bourg formed a plan. His revenge might be slow, but all the sweeter.

†

'Ralf, wake up! Food!' de Bourg called loudly as morning broke. He went and shook de Pewer awake when he didn't respond. As they ate their food, he asked, 'Ralf, are you awake yet?' De Pewer grunted in response. 'When the ship comes, you are to book just one berth, for yourself. Do you hear me?'

'Yes, yes, one berth. Why just me?' De Pewer's interest was aroused.

'I cannot risk fitz William recognising me. I will follow on the next ship or go back along the coast and get passage from Waterford.'

'What then, when I get to Wales?'

'I want you to follow fitz William. He will probably go to his brother's estate. It's the only place he would be safe. You wait at the nearest village tavern. When I get to Wales, I will get my brother Vere, and join you there,' de Bourg said.

'What if he should leave?'

'Follow him! Pay a messenger to go to my brother. Leave a message for me at the tavern!' De Bourg was getting impatient.

'I will need coin,' de Pewer said, as he continued to eat.

De Bourg banged a bag of coin on the table. 'There; take it, and do as I tell you! Whatever you do, stay with fitz William.'

'I won't lose him,' de Pewer growled as he stuffed the bag of coin in his satchel.

†

Fifty cattle! Caolach O'Muinacháin fumed to himself as he stuffed meat into his mouth. That was the compensation King

Donal O'Brien decreed: fifty cattle, and they hadn't even paid it themselves! O'Muinacháin knew Queen Orla had paid the reparation, not Bridín and the Welshman. Twice attacked and wounded. Twice close to death, and fifty cattle was all he got. An insult – a hundred cattle would have been an insult!

O'Muinacháin was a proud man. Born to middle-ranking parents, he had risen to be one of the most powerful men in Thomond. His family had accumulated modest wealth through their connections and trading skills. He gained an education from the monks at Ardagh monastery. His parents hoped he might follow a holy path, but religion had never interested him. Money and the power of wealth were his gods. He was now a very wealthy man in his own right.

'More wine!' he shouted as he drained his goblet. O'Muinacháin looked down the long table at his family and guests. His mother was now feeble and she cowered at the sound of his loud voice. His only brother had died as a child, and his table now consisted of cousins and other relatives, some that he did not even know. 'Why are all you people here?' he shouted. He knew well they were there to pay homage and hope that some of his wealth might find its way to them. The King had allowed O'Muinacháin return to his holdings in Ardagh – to recuperate and regain his strength, the King had told him. More likely to be kept out of the way while the Welshman curried favour and Bridín had her bastard. Bridín, Bridín: once she came into his mind, he couldn't think of anything else. Why did she not see what he could offer her? Land, wealth, position – he had everything any woman might want. But he didn't want any woman. He wanted Bridín. She was carrying a bastard child for the Welshman, but he didn't care about the child. She could have as many children as she wanted. It would be better if he was the father, but what of it? Children die all the time. People die. He wished that the Welshman would die.

Caolach O'Muineacháin staggered to his bed alone that night, drunk from too much wine and thinking of Bridín O'Brien. When he awoke just a few hours later it was still dark but his mind was clear. He didn't like the dark, or being alone. He might have brought one of the serving girls to his bed, but he had resolved that until Bridín was his, he would have no other woman. Now, wide awake in the middle of the night, he knew exactly what he must do. She would never have him while the bastard Welshman was alive. But a poor widow, with a child, would need a wealthy protector. She would see that, and would want the best for her child. The King would also reconsider, happy that his cousin would be well looked-after.

The next morning, O'Muineacháin sent a messenger to the King to tell him he was not recovering as well as he hoped, and would be away for some time. He sent another messenger eastwards to find Turlough Cooney, counsel to the MacCarthy Mór, seeking a meeting. The messenger was under strict instructions to talk only to Cooney; this was to be a private meeting between the counsels. O'Muineacháin knew that Cooney was dissatisfied with his masters, particularly young Tadhg MacCarthy. He knew he would have a willing helper to find Huw Ashe. Once found, he could buy any help he needed to make sure the Welshman never returned to Thomond again.

†

When the counsels met, O'Muineacháin was surprised at the level of venom that Cooney felt towards Tadhg MacCarthy, and his friend Huw Ashe. 'No respect. He sees me as a fool,' Cooney fumed. 'And now this Welshman. They've given him land and cattle in Killarney, and they seek his counsel.'

O'Muineacháin listened patiently as Cooney ranted. He had certainly found a willing helper, but was shocked to hear how the

Welshman had ingratiated himself amongst the MacCarthy clan. He felt something similar was happening with the Welshman and his own King. Land and cattle from the MacCarthys and a noble-born wife from the O'Briens! The Welshman had to be stopped.

'Huw Ashe has enemies though,' Cooney continued. 'There's a blood feud with Welsh Norman barons. Ashe was involved in a number of killings and the de Bourgs have sworn revenge on all his family.'

O'Muinacháin listened intently as his friend related the story of Giles fitz William and the de Bourg revenge quest. He thought that Cooney, being an experienced liar, might be adding his own details to make the story more compelling. But if there was a revenge quest, he could use it to his advantage. He needed to find out more about the foreigners. Joining forces with a Norman lord to achieve a common purpose would help him understand these people, and it could also fulfil his desire to be rid of Huw Ashe.

'How would I make contact with de Bourg?' O'Muinacháin asked, when Cooney finally paused for breath.

'The monks in Innisfallen say that he was making for Wexford and then to Wales.'

'Can you help me get to Wexford?'

'I can arrange passage through the MacCarthy lands,' Cooney responded in his pompous way. 'It may have a cost though.'

O'Muinacháin put a small bag of coin on the table. 'There's more where that came from.'

'Gold?' Cooney's eyes widened.

'That too, if it leads to the death of Huw Ashe.'

†

'O'Muinacháin from Thomond? Are you sure?' Tadhg MacCarthy asked again.

'Yes, Tadhg, the lads were positive. Headed east he did, after meeting Cooney,' Shawn the Ducker answered.

'Enna and Bawn followed?'

'They did. Enna told me to get to you as fast as I could.'

'Did O'Muinacháin have men with him?'

'Maybe ten guards, Tadhg. Cooney was heading back this way after me.'

'Good man, Shawn. Go and get some food.'

Tadhg had been wary of Turlough Cooney for a long time, and had had him watched ever since Huw and Bridín's wedding in Killarney. He wasn't quite sure what it was about Cooney that irritated him; perhaps it was how Cooney had tried to manipulate and groom him when he was younger, always trying to get Tadhg to say good things about him to his father, always trying to be his friend and advisor, trying too hard.

It was Enna who first noticed Cooney was getting ready for a trip. The MacCarthy told Tadhg that Cooney would be away for a while, dealing with family affairs. Tadhg arranged for the three lads to follow Cooney and his six guards. He sat at his table and wondered what Cooney and O'Muinacháin might be plotting. It could be that his father was arranging secret talks with Thomond, and the two counsels met under instructions from their masters. But why would O'Muinacháin venture into MacCarthy lands with such a small group of men? And why would he head east after meeting Cooney? Tadhg knew he would have to wait until his two scouts returned to find out.

†

It was two weeks later when Bawn got back. Cooney had returned a few days earlier.

'He met with a foreigner in Wexford port, Tadhg. Enna stayed to watch them.' Bawn blurted out as he dismounted. 'Bloody foreigners everywhere there.'

'Take it easy, Bawn boy, and get your breath,' Tadhg laughed at his man. 'Come on and we'll have a tankard, and you can tell me.'

Over a couple of tankards of ale, Bawn related how he had followed O'Muineacháin and his men to Wexford port. The men had visited different taverns, apparently looking for someone.

'Eanna heard them asking in a tavern for a Burk foreigner. They were looking for a Burk,' Bawn was wide-eyed with excitement to be reporting directly to Tadhg MacCarthy. 'Burk,' he repeated.

'Slow down, Bawn,' Tadhg was getting exasperated with his man, before it dawned on him who Bawn was talking about. 'Would it have been de Bourg they were looking for?'

'De Burk, yes that's it, de Burk. Enna told me to remember it.'

'Good man, Bawn,' Tadhg smiled, as he patted his man on the shoulder. When the ale had done its work and Bawn relaxed, he told Tadhg about how they had seen O'Muinacháin meeting with the foreigner, but couldn't get close enough to hear anything because of O'Muinacháin's guards. They had spoken for a long time, and O'Muinacháin had given the foreigner a large bag of coin. The next day, O'Muinacháin and the foreigner went around the taverns talking to any foreigners they could find, offering coin to any who had arms and looked like fighting men.

'Enna stayed to watch them and told me to ride as fast as I could to get you. Was Enna right, Tadhg? Did I do good?'

'You did very well, Bawn. A top rider and scout you are, for sure.'

After drinking and eating with Bawn, Tadhg sat alone into the night and reflected on what he knew. O'Muinacháin had joined forces with de Bourg, and they were recruiting soldiers. They must be going after Huw Ashe; that was the only realistic explanation. He knew O'Muinacháin was a wealthy man, and with his money they could buy whatever men and arms were needed. Huw would be in great danger. At least Giles should be safe while travelling in Wales and France; Bridín and her child also, while she was in Limerick. But then she too would be in danger, should O'Muinacháin return to Limerick.

'I think it's time for another expedition to Wexford,' Tadhg said quietly to himself.

CHAPTER 23

WEXFORD
SUMMER 1171

THE SUMMER SUN WAS high in the sky when Huw and John Daws reached Kinsella's village. Donal Kinsella broke from his busy work on the farm to make them welcome. He told Huw all he knew about events in Leinster. There was also a letter from Regan asking Huw to visit him in Ferns. Huw wondered about Regan's fate and position, now that his master Diarmaid MacMurrough was dead.

'No one knows what's going to happen. Your Strongbow is King of Leinster, but it's not clear if people will support him or fight him.' Donal Kinsella's assessment summed up what Huw had expected and his voice betrayed his concern. 'Most of the Norman forces are concentrated on Dublin, but there are new people arriving from Wales.'

'Is Strongbow in Dublin with the main force?' Huw asked.

'Some say he is headquartered at Waterford, but I'm not sure. Are you to join him?' Kinsella seemed uneasy talking about Strongbow.

Huw tried to assuage Kinsella's fears. 'I am summoned to meet Robert fitz Stephen, but first we would visit Regan at Ferns.'

'Maurice is concerned about his position, now that King Diarmaid is gone?' Kinsella posed the question that also concerned Huw.

'I'll help him in any way I can. He's a great friend to our family.'

Huw and Daws rested for the night in the village, and Donal Kinsella hosted a gathering in their honour. They rose before dawn the following day to head to Ferns.

'Alice Evans seems to have grown and changed,' John Daws picked his words carefully, as they left the village.

'Yes, she didn't mention Daiwin much,' Huw added. He suspected that was what Daws was thinking.

'No then, she seemed to be looking at that young Kinsella lad a lot.'

'No harm in that John; things change. People change, and Daiwin hasn't been around.'

'And now him gone on his travels again with Sir Giles,' Daws laughed. 'A proper travelling warrior he has become, has Dai.'

'A travelling warrior. He'd like to be called that,' Huw agreed.

†

They found Maurice Regan alone in his quarters when they reached Ferns. He seemed worried, and was relieved to see Huw.

'Huw Ashe! Much has changed since we last met. My Lord MacMurrough is dead, and now Leinster has two Kings.' Regan began to talk rapidly once his servant had brought wine and ale. 'Events change daily, people coming and going.'

Huw and Daws listened for a while as Regan continued somewhat incoherently. Daws made an excuse and went to check on their horses, leaving the other two alone. 'Two Kings you say, Maurice? I thought Strongbow was declared successor to MacMurrough,' Huw asked as Regan paused to refill their goblets from the jug.

'Lord MacMurrough's son Donal has also claimed the Kingship of Leinster under Irish law. The Irish Kings will support him. This may bring strife and war.'

'And you, Maurice, what is your position?' Huw asked.

'For now, I have no position. Young King Donal may send for me, but that hasn't happened yet. He would have his own men.' Regan paused, thinking about the importance of what he said.

'What will you do?' Huw prompted.

'My home and land is close enough to Ferns. I may return there, if I am left in peace.' There was doubt in Regan's voice as he spoke. 'But there may not be much peace for me or others.'

'Troubled times, but maybe peace will prevail.' Huw tried to find a reassuring tone.

'You have not heard much news of Leinster and your Norman friends?' Regan asked.

'Only the letter from Sir Robert fitz Stephen to my father. That is why I am here.'

'Ah, Sir Robert.' Regan took a drink of wine and looked at Huw. 'Sir Robert is held prisoner at Carrig. He was taken by the Wexford town people. Most of his knights and soldiers are fighting with Strongbow in Dublin town.'

'Fitz Stephen taken prisoner!' Huw's voice showed his surprise. 'How? Why?'

'I don't know the details, Huw, perhaps people didn't want his rule or just saw an opportunity with most Norman fighters in Dublin. Very few left to garrison Wexford or any town. Waterford was raided by men from Cork.'

'MacCarthys?' Huw asked.

'Possibly, but again I don't know the facts. The garrison came out to battle the raiding party and were defeated. A few were lucky to get back inside the town alive.'

'And Dublin, is it garrisoned and holding?' Huw's mind was working furiously to take in all that Regan told him.

'The reports are conflicting. It seems the High King O'Connor has joined forces with other Kings and there are huge armies laying siege to Dublin. There have been reports that Strongbow is defeated and has surrendered.' Regan noticed the astonished look on Huw's face. 'There is no confirmation as yet. Information changes daily,' he added. He was now the one now trying to reassure.

'Uncertainty and turmoil, as you rightly say, Maurice.'

'Uncertain times, without doubt.'

†

Huw related all he had heard to John Daws as they lay, unsleeping, in their cots. 'John, I'm uncertain what to do. Regan says it would be folly to go to Dublin, not knowing who holds the town and Strongbow possibly defeated. Two men would not make much difference.'

'Did you not come here under fitz Stephen's summons? Maybe Wexford is where we should go.' John Daws was clear. 'I could scout around; perhaps you could get to see Sir Robert?'

'You're right as usual, John.' Huw was surprised at his friend's clarity of thought. 'But maybe we'll do the scouting together. Your Gaelic comes with a strange accent.'

'You're still a Welsh farmer yourself, boy; from the valleys, you are.'

'The valleys indeed, and maybe we'll be heading back there, if what we hear is true.'

Next morning as Huw and Daws were preparing to leave, Regan arrived at their quarters with three men. The men were mounted and armed. 'Huw, you may not remember these countrymen of yours. Last time you saw them they were in the infirmary. They have lived and worked with us since.' As Regan introduced the men, Huw recalled his visit to the infirmary.

'They have agreed to help you. Five men might travel safer than two,' Regan added. Huw shook each man's hand and made sure they were there of their own accord.

'All in to help Huw Ashe,' the tallest man spoke in a soft Welsh tone. 'I'm Rhys and this is Griff and Tomwin,' he smiled as he introduced the other men. 'They're like cousins, they say.'

'I'm grateful to you, but what we're about may be dangerous, and I have little to pay you.'

'Without Lord Regan we would not be alive. That is payment enough,' Rhys answered.

'That's settled, so.' Regan called Huw aside as Daws and the other men spoke. 'I wish you well, Huw. If I am not in Ferns, Donal Kinsella will know how to contact me. This may help you get to see Sir Robert.' Regan handed Huw a bag of coin. 'King Diarmaid made me a wealthy man – cattle, land, and friends. I'll not starve,' he added, noticing Huw's reluctance to take the coin.

'Thank you, Maurice. I will return your favours someday.'

Looking back as they left Ferns, Huw wondered if he would meet Regan again.

†

Heading south along the river, it was late afternoon when they reached the beginning of the estuary. They could see Robert fitz Stephen's earth-and-timber castle at Carrig on the other side of the water. The town of Wexford was further out in the estuary, towards the sea. Regan thought that Sir Robert might be held prisoner at Carrig Castle, but he was not sure. Huw knew they would have to scout the town and castle to find out. He had some knowledge of the fortifications at Carrig from his father's description of the building. Giles had been the main designer of Sir Robert's stronghold, and Huw wished he had listened more intently when his father told him about the construction. He also wished he had his father's interest in detail. Huw smiled to himself as he thought about his father with fondness, and wondered where he might be on his travels.

'What? What did you say, Huw boy?' Daws's lilting Welsh broke Huw's thoughts.

'I was just thinking about my father.' Huw didn't realise he had spoken out loud.

'We need to find a bit of high ground to have a look at how the land lies.' Daws pointed to a hill up ahead.

An hour later, they had climbed to a vantage point that gave a clear view of the estuary. Wexford town stood away to their left, at the far side of the water's mouth.

'We're on the wrong side, Huw boy. We'll have to cross and circle around.' Daws assessed clearly what they all saw. 'There might be a boat or two, or we could go back up and find a crossing point.'

'We'll find a spot to cross without a boat,' Huw said firmly.

The sun was setting low to the west when they crossed the river and found a high wooded area where they could see the town and the castle. They were hungry after the day's journey so they ate their dried food and camped in the open for the night. In the morning they split up; Huw and Rhys headed into the town, while Daws took the other two men to scout the castle. 'Two are less likely to attract attention, and my Gaelic might be more local-sounding,' Huw smiled at Daws, who nodded.

'Right you are Huw boy,' Daws replied, mixing Gaelic with his Welsh lilt.

'Back here by sunset, or before. If one doesn't return, the others wait until morning and then come looking. Agreed?' Huw asked, and all nodded. He gave everyone some coin from Regan's bag before hiding the remainder in a thick clump of yellow bushes. 'Mark the spot and remember where the bag is hidden,' Huw added as they parted.

†

When Huw and Rhys entered the town, the place was teeming. A ship had arrived and the quay and all around were packed with people, carts and horses. Huw heard Welsh and French voices amongst the Gaelic shouts of the street traders. No one seemed to take particular notice of the two newcomers; many others in the streets were also newcomers. Huw now understood what Donal Kinsella and others had been referring to. New people were arriving on ships; local people were trading with them, selling goods, food and drink. Bargains were being made at every corner and the taverns near the quay were packed.

'We'll try some of the taverns, maybe get information from the landlords,' Huw spoke in a low tone to Rhys. 'I'll talk, and you watch my back.' They tried three taverns before Huw decided it was useless. He mentioned Robert fitz Stephen's name a number of times but just got blank stares. 'Too noisy and busy – no one wants to talk. We'll sit and have some ale. Maybe we'll see someone who looks like a soldier. Or a town official.' Huw didn't really know who to look for. They sat and talked for an hour or so, watching people coming and going. Rhys told Huw about his life in Wales and how he had been wounded at the taking of Wexford. For a while they sat and enjoyed the ale. Listening to the voices and different languages, Huw wondered if all these people were coming to settle in Ireland.

'We'll head back to the meeting place, Rhys. Maybe the others will have useful information.' They drained their ale and walked together through the open tavern door. Huw didn't see the spear coming until it hit Rhys in the chest knocking him backwards into the tavern. He heard the groan and the crash as Rhys fell. Huw's hand reached for his sword. It was then he saw the three men with spears raised and pointed at him.

'Draw the sword, and you follow him!' The strangely-accented Gaelic roar registered in Huw's brain and his hand remained still on the sword hilt. Looking behind the three spearmen he saw a tall, red-bearded man with a large battle axe held loosely in one hand.

'Good!' The man roared. 'Take his sword and dagger and tie his hands.' Two other men moved quickly and disarmed Huw. 'Bring him to the boat!'

Huw's hands were tied tightly behind his back and he was pushed towards the quay. He could feel the point of a spear at his back as they walked.

'Get in! Now!' the man roared, as Huw hesitated, looking down at the small boat bobbing beside some wooden steps. Huw stumbled down the steps, almost falling into the boat. He sat facing forward as the men rowed up the river. There were two spearmen at his back, and he could feel the spear points in his spine. The two rowers faced Huw and the red-bearded axeman stood in the bow. Huw could see the port of Wexford on his left and a small wooded headland jutting out ahead as the boat cut through the calm waters. The early afternoon sun was warm on his shoulders and he settled down for the journey. For once, he didn't mind being on the water. He was just happy to be still alive as he wondered where he was being taken.

Half an hour later as they rounded the wooded headland, fitz Stephen's fortification came into view. After a short while the boat changed direction slightly and headed for the shore. As they approached Carrig, Huw saw about six armed men waiting beside the small wooden jetty. When the boat was tied, Huw felt the sharp spears being prodded into his back.

'Out! Go on!' Red-beard shouted. Huw staggered a little as he stepped onto the shore from the jetty. It took him a moment to regain his balance. 'Up the hill, warrior. If you can,' Red-beard taunted, to peals of laughter from the guards. Once through the palisade surrounds, Huw struggled up the steep incline, his bound hands affording him no protection when he fell. After climbing a high staircase of about fifty wooden steps, he was pushed through the main door and into the big hall. From there they entered a short corridor and climbed down a steep row of twenty steps. It was dark except for a low smouldering candle on a rough table. One of the two guards at the table got up and opened the double lock on the heavy wooden door.

'So, warrior, you wanted to meet fitz Stephen. Here he is!' Red-beard laughed as Huw was pushed into the underground chamber. The light was dim and the air smelled stale. The door banged shut and Huw heard the key turn in the lock.

'Who are you, sir?' asked a familiar voice in Norman-French, as Huw's eyes tried to adjust to the dim light.

'Sir Robert! Is that you?' Huw asked, as Robert fitz Stephen stepped closer to get a better view of his visitor.

†

John Daws and his two companions watched from the cover of a large clump of trees near the shore as the boat approached Carrig jetty. They had seen the six armed men come down from the wooden castle. Daws waited patiently; he wanted to know how many men were in the garrison. When he saw Huw bound and being pushed along, he began to string his longbow. Griff reached out to hold him by the wrist. Daws wanted to kill the man where he stood but Griff held firm for a moment without speaking and Daws realised he was right. An attack now would mean certain death for Huw, and probably for himself and his companions also. He held his hand up and nodded to the two men. The three of them watched as Huw disappeared inside the tower house. Daws almost felt relief; if they were going to kill Huw, they would have done it in the boat and dumped his body in the river. They stayed there until dusk, watching as the red-bearded man and his two guards left and headed back down river in the boat.

✝

Earlier that day in Wexford town, Caolach O'Muinacháin and Henry de Bourg watched as Huw was taken prisoner. One of O'Muinacháin's spies had seen a foreigner asking for fitz Stephen, and thought he fitted the description of the man O'Muinacháin was seeking. O'Muinacháin and de Bourg were approaching along the quayside when they saw the armed group waiting outside the tavern.

'Huw Ashe, the Welsh bastard!' O'Muinacháin spat under his breath, as the spear knocked Rhys back through the door.

'Dead?' de Bourg asked.

'No, no, the other one.' They watched in silence as Huw was taken to the boat. 'Get some men and horses and follow along the shore,' O'Muinacháin whispered. 'They can't be going far in that small boat.'

✝

About five hundred paces away from John Daws, de Bourg and his companions watched under cover as Huw was taken inside the castle. He waited about an hour before sending a man back to the town to tell O'Muinacháin. As he sat in the sunshine watching the castle, de Bourg wondered if Huw Ashe would be executed and, if so, how it might be done. He would have to stay in Ireland a bit longer to find out. He hoped that Ralf de Pewer would have sense enough to contact his brother in Wales and not let Giles fitz William get away. But even if fitz William escaped again, he knew he would find him one day and kill him. He knew this, because God was on his side.

CHAPTER 24

LIMERICK
LATE SUMMER 1171

GWEN NÍ ASHE WAS born early on the morning of August 13th. She was a noisy addition to the ladies' household at Queen Orla's Limerick court. Bridín was fit and well, and she didn't linger long in bed after baby Gwen arrived. The Queen herself took personal charge of all arrangements for the new baby, and the King of Thomond, Donal O'Brien, came to pay his respects to his new cousin. He was delighted with the harvest arrival and insisted on holding a week of celebrations.

The King assured Bridín that he had sent emissaries to Leinster and they were trying to find out what had happened to her husband. Bridín had no news of Huw after his departure for Wexford. She had resigned herself that he might not return for the baby's birth, but continued to hope for some message. Now that Gwen was born, she was determined that Huw should meet his daughter. If it came to it, she would go to Wexford herself.

Bridín was surprised when the gifts began to arrive. The King promised her a house and land wherever she wanted in the Kingdom. The MacCarthy Mór sent twenty cattle, and gold brooches for the baby's clothes. Monks from Innisfallen came to bless the baby and brought barrels of mead and ale. O'Muinacháin sent a messenger with a bag of gold coin and asked if he could visit her; Bridín said no, and sent back the gold. Autumn came, but still no news of Huw. She got occasional messages from Tadhg. He had been to Wexford, but had not found Huw. His messages spoke of the turmoil and escalating conflict in Leinster. King Donal refused Bridín permission to travel to Wexford, and she resigned herself to a winter without her husband.

†

Huw lay awake and listened as fitz Stephen spoke through his snoring. He had fallen asleep again as Huw spoke to him. They conversed a lot about Wales, as it seemed to please fitz Stephen, and Huw was interested in stories about his life. He had been imprisoned for three years in Wales before being freed to lead Strongbow's Irish vanguard. His previous prison experience seemed to have prepared him for their current captivity. When Huw was first brought to Carrig, fitz Stephen had been there a number of months. His clothes were ragged; his beard and hair long and matted with dirt. Huw smiled briefly to himself, realising he must now look and smell as bad as fitz Stephen. Their ration of water did not allow them enough to wash. Fitz Stephen always slept long and well and seemed to dream a lot. Huw listened to some of his ramblings; random names and places. Occasionally, fitz Stephen moved and called out, as if rebuking someone. Huw smiled again as he recalled his father doing something similar when he was unconscious after the William de Bourg ambush.

Huw did not sleep as easily as fitz Stephen. He often lay awake at night wondering about his family. He knew it must be night, as there was no light from the candle in the corridor outside the cell door. Their only source of light was the candlelight, that crept through the bars of the tiny viewing hole and the door gaps, and the guards usually came and extinguished the candle in the evening. Huw knew when someone came into the corridor from the noise. Every second day, the guards came and brought them outside to empty the slop bucket. The short period in the fresh air was something they looked forward to. It also allowed some air to circulate through the corridor and into the cell. On these trips they were chained together by the wrists and guarded by four men; there was little chance of escape. Huw wished he had been able to send a message to Bridín before being captured – he wanted her to know he was alive. Lying there in the stale darkness, listening to Robert fitz Stephen's incoherent words, he tried to calculate how long they had been imprisoned together. It must be four months or more. Bridín would have given birth by now. Huw wondered if he had a son or a daughter, and what his child might be like.

†

Huw thought he had been asleep for a just short time when he was woken by voices in the corridor. He sat up quickly as fitz Stephen continued to snore. A small amount of light drifted in from the candle as the key turned in the lock.

'Get those chains on!' Redbeard stepped into the cell with his sword drawn. Fitz Stephen woke abruptly as two guards held him, while the others clasped the irons around Huw's wrists. When they were standing chained together, Redbeard moved closer and pushed his sword point to fitz Stephen's neck.

'You are going on a trip – your last!' Redbeard laughed, and shouted louder than he needed. 'Don't think of running or I'll take your head before your King decrees it.'

Still groggy from his deep sleep, fitz Stephen stumbled on the steps outside the main entrance and Huw had to grab tight to his arm to prevent them both falling. Huw struggled to adjust his vision to the early morning daylight as the cold wind from the sea made them both shiver.

'Huw, what do you think is happening? Where are they taking us?' Fitz Stephen whispered. 'I don't know, sir, but Redbeard mentioned the King,' Huw just had time to answer, before a guard pushed the butt of his spear into his back. Redbeard led the way as they walked briskly along the pathway down to the jetty. Huw looked across the choppy waters of the estuary and hoped the boat trip would be short. 'Back to Wexford town maybe, sir,' Huw said quietly as they sat in the stern, while the four oarsmen pulled the boat out into the current and turned downstream. Huw wondered who Redbeard had been referring to earlier: the King of Leinster? He also wondered if this trip might be his only chance of escape, and resolved to be ready for any opportunity. When they reached the quay at Wexford they were quickly transferred to a covered cart. Huw counted at least twenty mounted warriors before Redbeard shouted an order and they set off. Twenty, and the four guards with them in the cart; he knew there would be little chance of escape on their journey, wherever they were going.

†

Fitz Stephen strained his neck to look out the front of the cart, past the two drivers. Huw noticed his alertness; excitement almost. He was surprised, as fitz Stephen had dozed off to sleep for most of the journey.

'What is it, sir?' Huw asked.

'Waterford, Huw; Waterford, and it's teeming with soldiers!' Fitz Stephen half stood up from his seat to see better. The two inside guards didn't bother forcing him down. They seemed happy to have reached their destination. Huw raised his head to get a better view. There were tents and soldiers everywhere on the approach to the town. 'There are so many different banners; it's a huge army!' Huw began to feel fitz Stephen's excitement. When they crossed through the main gates the town itself was even more crowded.

'The King's banner! Henry is in Waterford!' Fitz Stephen almost shouted. The two guards laughed and prodded him to sit down.

'King Henry is here?' Huw repeated, disbelieving.

When they reached the centre of the town close to the river, they were bundled from the cart. In the brief moments before they were taken inside and down to the cells, Huw recognised the great stone hall where he had met Meiler fitz Henry and Maurice Regan after the sacking of Waterford.

'Why do you think they brought us here, sir?' Huw asked as the heavy cell door closed behind them.

'Henry being here can't be a coincidence. Maybe he has asked for me.' Fitz Stephen's words seemed to be for himself. For the first time Huw noticed fitz Stephen feeling his hair and beard and looking at the rags that hung from his body. Unlike Carrig Castle, their cell had daylight coming through a small barred window high above them; there was also a large candle on a rough table. 'Luxury indeed,' Huw muttered.

'What? Did you say something, Huw?' Fitz Stephen had begun to peel off some of the rags from his upper body. 'If I am to be brought before the King they'll have to give me proper clothes. Henry would not want beggars in his presence.'

Huw looked at fitz Stephen as he paced around the cell, talking to himself. Was he the same listless, sleepy person he had spent the last four months with at Carrig? He was glad to see glimpses of the brave Norman commander who had led Strongbow's vanguard to Ireland over two years ago.

'Do you think you will get an audience with King Henry?' Huw asked.

'I'm sure of it, Huw, I'm sure of it. There can be no other explanation. He may have my head, but I will get to talk to him and present my case.'

†

The next morning confirmed fitz Stephen's expectation. Shortly after dawn, the guards brought bread, cheese and ale. The food was followed by a large pail of water and two bundles of clothes. When fitz Stephen had washed and changed into a clean knight's tunic and boots, he beckoned to Huw.

'Wash, Huw, as best you can. I'll make sure they allow you to come with me. From the clothes, it looks like you are to be my squire!' Fitz Stephen gave a short laugh. His hair and beard were still long, but he had managed to form the hair so that it hung down his back. The wet beard was shaped into a point below his chin. Huw smiled to himself as he washed with the cold water and changed into his clean clothes.

'Now, squire Huw, we wait!' Fitz Stephen laughed as he looked Huw up and down. 'We wait to meet our King and our fate.'

†

John Daws had kept a lonely vigil for the last four months near Carrig Castle. He didn't need to be there himself every day, but knowing that Huw was inside made him want to be there. Tadhg MacCarthy had sent five men when Daws's message reached him. Tadhg came himself every couple of weeks. The Kinsellas sent three men to help when MacCarthy's emissaries contacted them.

'A strange miracle,' Tadhg told Daws. 'The Wexford Kinsellas and the Muskerry MacCarthys, cooperating to save a Welshman who invaded to take our lands!' Daws often laughed to himself when he thought about MacCarthy's words.

He had noticed the other group of men who also watched the castle. He had tried to approach them on occasion, but they always drifted away without engaging. Daws assumed that they were keeping watch for some other prisoner in the castle.

Daws was called from his sleep on the morning of Huw and fitz Stephen's departure. MacCarthy's two watchmen had observed the boat being prepared at first light.

'Someone is being taken on a trip.' Daws spoke quietly as he watched the two chained prisoners being escorted towards the jetty. He strained his eyes to make out the faces hidden behind the dirty hair and beards. The clothes of the taller man were ragged; the other man was slightly better-kept, and more upright. Daws thought that the size and shape fitted Huw. 'It must be him!' Daws grabbed the shoulder of one of his fellow watchers. They watched as the boat pulled out and turned downriver towards Wexford town.

'We'll follow along the shoreline. Send one of your scouts to tell Tadhg!' Daws signed his Gaelic words to make sure the MacCarthy men fully understood. The men nodded. As Daws and his companion set out after the boat on horseback, three other men followed in turn at a safe distance.

†

King Henry's Irish court was crowded and noisy when Huw and fitz Stephen were dragged in. Redbeard had come to the cell earlier to personally supervise as the chains were clamped to their wrists. Huw saw some familiar faces when he glanced around the great hall. Strongbow nodded to fitz Stephen; Henry de Bourg scowled and stared when Huw's eyes met his. The MacCarthy Mór grinned broadly, as he noticed the surprise on Huw's face. The King was taking wine after dealing with some earlier matter, and they were forced to wait again. They had already waited two weeks in their Waterford cell and fitz Stephen's patience had changed to anger. He had demanded to see Henry but was told the King was at Lismore and might grant an audience on his return.

'Sir Robert fitz Stephen, Sire!' the King's secretary shouted loud to be heard above the voices in court.

'Ah, Sir Robert, I trust you were not detained long, and well-treated.' The hall fell silent at the King's words. Fitz Stephen bowed low and tugged at the chains for Huw to do likewise.

'Sire, I am alive and at your service as always.' Fitz Stephen's strong voice carried across the great hall; there was a long silence as the King whispered with his secretary.

'Remove the chains from these men!' King Henry ordered. A number of people stepped forward to speak, but Henry held up his hand. 'I have heard the charges brought against you, Sir Robert. I decree that your actions were done in my name, and in my best interest. You are a free man and I will meet with you in private counsel.'

'My man here with me, Sire, has been a great servant to us.' Fitz Stephen spoke quickly as the King stood to leave.

'As with you, Sir Robert, he has no case to answer and is free to go.' King Henry nodded to Huw as he walked from the great hall.

†

Tadhg observed proceedings at the King's court from a vantage point in the great hall. He had John Daws and ten warriors stationed close to the river. He wasn't sure what his plan would be if Huw was held captive: attack King Henry's four thousand strong army with ten men? He pushed his way through the crowded hall to get to Huw before someone else captured him. He knew that de Bourg and O'Muinacháin's spies were everywhere in Waterford. MacCarthy reached Huw just in time to see him confronted by Henry de Bourg.

'You will not be free for long, Welshman,' de Bourg spoke under his breath so as not to be heard by others. Huw stood in surprised silence; the events at court had happened quickly, and he was unsure of his welcome in these surroundings.

Tadhg camouflaged his dagger as he pushed the point through de Bourg's tunic and into the skin of his lower back. 'Ah, Huw, you have met de Bourg again. We would not want to shed blood over King Henry's court, would we?' Tadhg edged closer to de Bourg as he spoke. 'We have a small army of savages outside; do not follow us.' MacCarthy grabbed Huw by the arm and led him from the hall.

†

'I must stay in Waterford with my father until it is proper to take leave of the King,' Tadhg explained to Huw. 'The MacCarthys have to make alliances with Henry; it may help prevent your Norman friends taking too much of our land.' Huw stumbled as they made their way to Daws at the river. Tadhg grabbed him by the arm to prevent him falling. 'We will discuss the politics when we meet again in a safer place. For now, we must get you to Limerick to meet your new daughter!'

'A daughter,' Huw repeated. 'A daughter!' He didn't seem able to find any other words as he clasped Tadhg's hand while his friend related the events at court to John Daws. 'My men will take you to meet a MacCarthy ship at Passage. The captain will take you west along the coast. The weather is calm, Huw, you shouldn't have too much trouble!' Tadhg knew of Huw's propensity for seasickness. He took Daws to one side before they departed. 'Huw seems weak and confused, John; you need to watch him closely. He may not have been well treated in Carrig.' Daws nodded his understanding. As they left Waterford, he noticed Huw's unsteadiness in the saddle. After initially pushing their horses to a strong gallop, he rode upsides Huw and slowed the pace.

†

Henry de Bourg spat into the river as he watched Huw and his band ride out of Waterford. He had three men ready to mount. 'Follow them but don't be seen.' He voice rasped as he spoke to the lead man. 'Send one man back when you know their direction and leave markers. I will follow on as soon as the sergeant has enough men armed and mounted.' The lead man nodded his assent. 'Don't lose them or you will lose your head!' de Bourg hissed through clenched teeth as the men left. Two hours later, de Bourg and his troop of thirty mounted soldiers galloped out of Waterford.

†

After some hours of difficult riding, Daws called a halt for food and water in a heavily-wooded valley. He thought he noticed a rider following them and he sent two men to circle back and scout. Huw seemed out of breath and was struggling to stay in the saddle before they stopped. Daws handed Huw a water pouch as they sat beneath a large tree. The weather was cold and Huw shivered as he pulled his cloak around his shoulders.

'A few more hours, and we should reach the coast. Are you feeling alright, Huw?' Daws asked as Huw sipped the water.

'Never better,' Huw lied.

Daws saw that Huw's face was flushed, and damp with sweat. 'We'll rest here for a while, boy. I've sent two of MacCarthy's lads back to scout a bit.'

'You think we're being followed?' Huw's voice was hoarse but his interest was aroused.

'Not sure; thought I saw someone. Might just be hunters.' Daws stood and looked back along the path they had travelled. They waited for half an hour by the trees. The MacCarthy men began to untie the horses.

'John, we should mount and go; the scouts will catch up.' Huw stood up from his seat beneath the tree.

Daws still stared back through the forest. 'All right, Huw boy, maybe you're right.' They heard the unmistakable sound of horses travelling at speed at the same time. 'Mount up!' he called, as he helped Huw towards his horse.

After an hour of slow riding through thick forest, the trees thinned and they reached open country. There was a low hill away to their right.

'Make for the rising ground! We'll see what's behind us!' Daws turned and called to the men.

'Hold, John!' Huw saw the riders appear on the brow of the hill as Daws turned to look back. 'Some of them have flanked us, maybe ten or twelve!'

'Don't know how many are behind us, we'll have to run.' Daws assessed their situation quickly. Huw nodded agreement. 'Keep to the tree line as close as we can!' Daws shouted, and pointed away from the riders on the hill. They galloped as fast as possible along the tree line with the hill riders keeping pace. Looking back, they saw the larger force emerge from the forest. They were riding hard in pursuit. Daws kept his horse beside Huw, knowing he was struggling to stay in the saddle. They began to meet rising ground and the pace slackened. 'Don't let the flankers get ahead of us!' Daws shouted. After a struggle, they reached a ridge at the top of the rising ground. They halted for a moment and stared down the small valley to where the forest ended near the banks of a wide river.

'A trap, but maybe also an escape!' he said quietly to Huw. 'Make for the river boys!' He slapped Huw's horse on its flanks.

'We'll hold here for a while, to see what they've got!' Daws shouted as they dismounted at the edge of the forest, close to the riverbank. They reached the river before the flanking riders, who reined in about two hundred paces away upriver. The main following force arrived and stopped along the tree line a short time later. Two riders left the main party and joined the men near the river.

'They're discussing what to do next.' Daws stood beside Huw, close to a clump of small trees. They had tied their horses about thirty paces in from the edge of the forest and posted sentries on all flanks except the riverside, so they would see anyone approaching along the river. Huw sat down and was drinking water.

'How's the fever, Huw?' Daws asked.

'Fever? What fever?' Huw spluttered the words through a dry cough.

Daws laughed. 'We'll have to get you east so as you can recover, boy. You'll need your strength to look after your new Irish princess.' Huw's cough changed to a short laugh at Daws's words. 'I think our Norman friends out there are not sure what to do next. A few of us might hold them here for a while.' Daws stared across the open ground to the two groups of men. 'It might turn out to be a bit of a siege.'

†

'Huw, help me if I get stuck with the Gaelic.' Daws had called all eight MacCarthy men together. 'Friends, we have won a little time and we have a bit of a stand-off, but not for long. I am going to hold them here with the long bow while Huw Ashe makes for the coast along the river. He has to get home to meet his new daughter.' Huw started to get up to speak but Daws put his big hand on his shoulder. 'Let me finish, I need to use all my fine Gaelic words!' He paused while Huw sat down again. 'This isn't your fight, boys, you should all go with Huw to make sure he gets to Passage and the boat. If you go quietly through the forest, our friends out there won't realise it for a while.' Daws looked around the men's faces in silence. One man stepped forward. Huw recognised him for the first time.

'I am Mickel, friend and clan to Tadhg and the MacCarthy Mór. You are wrong! This *is* our fight, and the MacCarthys will stand with you. Two men are enough to go with Huw Ashe; three men together will be quieter and quicker. Seven men here will hold them for a day.'

Huw and his two companions reached Passage after dark and boarded the MacCarthy ship. The captain waited until first light before sailing west in fair weather. Huw lay in his cot for the two days they spend at sea. His fever intensified; the seasickness weakened him further, and he drifted into unconsciousness. When he awoke, he was in a covered cart with rain pelting noisily on the canvas cover. As the cart made its way deep into Muskerry, Huw recalled his father making a similar journey; he wondered where his father was, and if he would see him again. He also thought of John Daws; what had happened after they left him and the small band of MacCarthy warriors?

Huw spent two weeks in Muskerry recovering from his fever. Tadhg arrived from Waterford with news that King Henry was departing for Dublin. 'They say he will spend the winter there and might do battle with the High King. O'Connor has not submitted!' MacCarthy seemed enthused with his stories about the English King.

'What news of John Daws, and your men?' Huw was more interested in local matters.

'No word at all Huw, I'm sorry; when we know what happened, we will get messages to you.'

†

'Christmas is not far away Huw; you'll be with your family soon.' Tadhg had travelled with Huw to Killarney and was taking his leave. 'The MacCarthy Mór is home from Waterford and I must return to him; I want to know what damage he has done!' He gave his roguish laugh as he clasped Huw's hand. 'A peaceful Christmas to you and Lady Bridín and your lady daughter!'

†

Huw turned his horse to look back at Killarney town as he climbed the wooded hill and headed towards the Mang River. In a few days, he would be in Limerick; he wondered about Bridín and their baby daughter and the colour of her hair. Later, when he held Gwen in his arms for the first time and looked at her, he saw the face of his mother.

'Do you like her name, my love?' Bridín asked.

'I like it very well.' Huw Ashe looked from up from the wide eyes of his daughter to the smiling face of his wife, and knew that this Christmas would be peaceful.

Read on for a sneak preview of the sequel 'Friends and Nomads' – coming later in 2020. Check www.bizpace.ie for updates and further previews.

FRIENDS AND NOMADS: CHAPTER 1

TORC WATERFALL, KILLARNEY AUGUST 1173

HUW ASHE ADJUSTED THE cloth straps around his shoulders as the heavy bundle on his back dragged to one side. With the weight more evenly balanced, he began to climb. He reached a small plateau and paused for a breath. He stood for a moment, listening to the noise of the water crashing down the mountain. Noticing an animal track winding up through the trees to his left, he decided to keep moving. The load on his back moved again as he began to climb the steep slope. The noise from the waterfall dulled as he climbed higher. Then, as the rough path turned sharply right, he noticed an opening through the trees to his left. He stopped and gazed with some surprise at the view which unfolded in front of him. For the first time in the two years he had spent in Killarney, he realised there were two lakes. Beyond a long piece of heavily-wooded land that divided the two bodies of water, he could see his own lake glistening in the sunshine.

'Dada!' The bundle on his back moved and spoke for the first time since they set out in the morning. 'Dada, Dada, Dada.'

'Hello, Gwen, you're awake then.' Huw turned his head slightly as he spoke softly in Gaelic to his two-year-old daughter.

'Dada, Dada, down. Nom nom.' Gwen wriggled and kicked her dangling feet against his back.

He laughed as he sat on the ground and untied the front straps that held the bundle tight to his body. 'You had a long sleep. Mama will be happy.'

'Mama, Mama, Mama,' Gwen echoed, as she ate the soft bread and berries that Bridín had prepared that morning.

'I wonder what Mama is doing now,' Huw wondered.

'Mama, Mama, Mama. Nom, nom,' Gwen answered, in between huge mouthfuls of food.

They had left their small house beside Loch Léin earlier, as the sun began to warm the day. Huw was familiar with many of the pathways around Killarney from his hunting trips. He had been at the bottom of the waterfall before but had never climbed up the mountain pathway towards the top. Now that Gwen was awake, he wouldn't get to the source of the waterfall today. He resolved to come back when she was a little bigger, and climb to the top. Bridín was spending the day in Killarney town with Maeve MacCarthy. They would be making berry jam as Maeve waited for the birth of her first child. Tadhg MacCarthy had brought his wife to live in Killarney for the later stages of her pregnancy.

'Much safer here than Muskerry,' he had told Huw. 'There's trouble and conflict everywhere in the east. It's not just the *Déise* and the other Irish kingdoms; your Norman friends seem to be fighting amongst themselves.'

Huw had listened intently as Tadhg had brought him up to date with happenings on the other side of Ireland. In the last year or so, he had grown to depend on Tadhg for news of his Norman comrades in Leinster. Tadhg had come to Killarney for a few days to visit his wife; he did not stay long, and Huw sensed his uneasiness.

'It's turmoil. Nobody seems sure of what is happening. Rumour is that Strongbow has left and gone to France to fight for your King Henry.'

'He's not my King anymore,' Huw had been quick to correct his friend, shocked at what Tadhg had told him. 'I'm a Welsh-born half-Norman, trapped here in this land trying to keep peace between you MacCarthys and the O'Briens. The MacCarthy Mór is more my King now,' he had added, with a smirk.

'Your good wife O'Brien might not agree,' Tadhg had laughed in return. 'And we haven't had a decent fight with Donal O'Brien since you half-Normans arrived in Ireland.'

'Water, Dada, water.' Gwen's tugging at his tunic brought Huw's mind back to the present. 'Water, water.'

'Let's go down to the stream and we'll get some water.' Huw lifted his daughter into his arms and headed back down the path towards the waterfall, raising his voice to be heard above the noise of the water. 'We'll go downstream a bit to find a shallow spot.' The pools at the foot of the waterfall were deep and he did not want to put Gwen down.

'Down, Dada.' Gwen squirmed and kicked him in the belly, trying her best to escape from his arms. She loved water. 'Water, water!' she shouted, kicking him harder. They stopped about two hundred paces downstream from the foot of the waterfall. The stream moved more slowly and some of the pools were shallow. Huw filled his water pouch and gave it to Gwen. She poured the water over her face and hair as she drank. 'Water, water!' she shrieked as she headed towards the stream.

Huw caught her before she jumped in. 'You can go in, Gwen, but we can't get all your clothes wet!' He took off enough clothes to leave her legs free. 'It will be cold, and you must hold my hand.'

'Water, water!' Gwen shrieked, as she kicked and splashed in the cold water.

†

The trek back home took much longer than their earlier walk to the waterfall. Gwen would not get into her back bundle; she insisted on walking. She loved walking and running as much as she loved water. Huw decided to go back through Killarney town rather than along the lake shore; maybe they would meet Bridín, and walk home with her.

'We might meet Mama in Killarney town. Wouldn't that be exciting?' Huw called after Gwen as she raced off the pathway, chasing something she had seen in the bushes.

'Bud, bud, bud!' She shouted and pointed through the trees as Huw caught up to her.

'Did you see a bird? Was it a big one?' Huw just had time to ask before she was off again, her fair curls bouncing up and down as she ran. 'It'll be dark before we get home at this pace.' He laughed as he chased after her. It was the first of many diversions they made on their way to Killarney town. Huw put all the leaves, twigs, and blue flowers that Gwen collected carefully into his pouch.

'Mama, Mama,' she shouted as she picked more blue flowers underneath a huge tree. She only collected blue flowers. Blue was her favourite colour.

'Mama will love your flowers. We must be going.'

Gwen raced away towards the next tree.

They reached Killarney town towards late afternoon and stopped at Tadhg MacCarthy's house, close to the great hall. Maeve was resting, but got up when she heard Gwen's voice. 'Bridín left earlier to get some fish from her trap in the lake. She said she'd be back this evening, when Gwen was asleep.'

'Mama, Mama, Mama.' Gwen shouted as she showed Maeve her blue flowers.

'Mama will love them, little beauty.' Maeve ran her fingers through Gwen's curls and kissed her head.

'Your time is close, Maeve?' Huw asked.

'I think it might be very soon. Tonight, maybe.' Maeve smiled. 'Can't be too soon!'

'Bridín will want to be with you. We'll go and leave you to rest.' Huw grabbed Gwen before she could protest or run away, and put her on his shoulders. She loved riding on his shoulders.

'Bye!' Gwen screeched and waved to Maeve as they left for the short walk to the lakeshore.

Bridín was not in the house when they arrived home.

'Mama must still be at the water trap, getting fish for supper. Will we go to meet her?'

'Mama, Mama, water, water, fis!' Gwen kept calling as they walked towards the lake. Their boat was still tied securely to the small wooden jetty when they reached the lakeshore. Huw looked around for any sign of Bridín.

'Where can Mama have gone?' he asked, holding Gwen's hand tightly, knowing that she would head into the water if he let her go.

'Mama, Mama, fis!' Gwen shouted.

'There's no sign of her over at the fish trap. No sign that the boat has been moved, either.' Huw spoke out loud, mainly to himself. 'Would you like to go on my shoulders again?' Huw swung Gwen over his head.

Gwen shrieked with laugher as she grabbed his hair to hold on tight. He walked along the stony lakeshore with Gwen babbling to herself, wondering if Bridín had forgotten the fish and gone looking for berries and mushrooms. She wouldn't have expected them to return home until early evening. Maybe she had gone back to Killarney town through the forest while she collected more berries for their jam making? He was about to turn and head back to the town when he saw the body in the water, wedged between the branches of a fallen tree. He turned away quickly, not wanting Gwen to see. 'Let's go to Maeve's house again!' he called to Gwen as he turned and ran back to the path that led to Killarney town.

†

Huw untied the boat and rowed the short distance to the fallen tree, chopping some of the small branches with his sword to get close to the body. He lashed the boat to a large branch and dragged it in.

'Huw Ashe! Are you alright? Who is it?' Three men had arrived on horseback and were running along the lakeshore towards him.

'Looks like a monk from the island. His throat is cut!' Huw called. 'I'll row back to the jetty and meet you there.'

When the boat was secured to the jetty, they lifted the body on to the stony shore and laid him face upwards.

'I know him,' one of the men said, as Huw wiped the dead man's face. 'He's Anselm – Brother Anselm. I've seen him many times in the town. He's one of the monks who come to trade.'

'It doesn't look like he's been in the water long. He must have been killed today,' Huw mused aloud as he tried to piece together what could have happened. 'Why would anyone kill a monk? He would have little coin, if any.'

'Your wife, any sign?' the man who knew Brother Anselm asked. Huw looked up at the man from his kneeling position, recognising him as Tadhg's cousin, and sergeant of his Killarney garrison.

'No, Conall. No sign of her. She's not here, or at the house and she's not with Maeve. There must be a connection,' Huw replied, looking down at the dead monk.

'We'll organise a search all around, Huw. Before it gets dark,' Conall offered, as he sent one of his companions to the town to get more men.

'Thank you, Conall. We should bring the body to the house.'

As Huw expected, the search found no sign of Bridín. He was relieved, hoping that it meant she was probably still alive.

'She was taken on the water. They must have come in boats.' Huw shared his thoughts as he handed Conall MacCarthy a tankard of ale. Darkness had descended, and the searchers had returned to the town. Conall had insisted on staying with Huw, placing two guards outside the house. 'I will row out to the island at first light and bring Brother Anselm.' Huw had formed an initial plan. 'The monks will be worried and they might have information on Bridín.'

'We'll get a couple of boats and come with you.'

'I must go to Maeve, and check on Gwen.' Huw went to get up.

'The little girl is happy and safe. She is with my wife, and at least three other women!' Conall smiled, as he bade Huw sit down. 'She knows them all and will be safe in the town.'

†

Ten MacCarthy men were on the lakeshore when Huw arrived just after dawn, their two boats tied beside Huw's. They had put the monk's body in one. Huw looked for Conall to thank him, but he was already organising his men to do the rowing. 'We'll row, Huw, you try to relax. We should be there by the time this fog lifts.'

Huw noticed the light fog for the first time as he stepped unsteadily into his boat. Conall and the men seemed to know of his dislike for water. Since childhood, being on water had made him feel sick, and he preferred to stay on solid ground.

The fog lifted, though, and the water was calm as they crossed; he did not get sick on this journey.

There were a number of monks waiting when they landed on Innisfallen.

'Huw Ashe! We are so sorry; did they harm your family?' Brother Patrick was the first to meet Huw.

'Who were they, Brother Patrick? What happened? Where are they now?' Huw blurted out.

'Henry de Bourg, and Norman soldiers. A few came first and took our boats. Then they brought more – maybe twenty men.'

'De Bourg! Here?' Huw stared at Brother Patrick.

'They took Brother Anselm with them when they headed for Killarney town. We could do nothing.'

'Brother Anselm is dead; I'm sorry. We brought his body.' Huw paused to allow his words to sink in. 'They took my wife, Bridín. Did they bring her here?'

'They didn't come back to the island, but we saw them on the lake yesterday. They headed towards the western shore.' Brother Patrick pointed away to the west. 'They left us without boats; we could do nothing.'

'I know, Brother, I know.'

†

'Twenty Norman soldiers! It won't be easy to travel without being seen. They should be easy to track.' Tadhg had arrived in Killarney just after the birth of his son and they were sitting together in the great hall. 'You did right not to follow them on your own. We have ten men ready to ride, more if you want them.'

'I needed to make sure Gwen was happy—' Huw's throat dried.

'My people will look after her well, she'll have ten mamas. Maeve will take her as her own when she is recovered.' Tadhg held his hand up as Huw made to speak. 'It's settled. She'll be well fattened-up when you and Bridín return.'

'Thank you, Tadhg. I didn't yet congratulate you on the birth of your son. A fine boy! You will have to mend your ways, and settle down.'

'I'll try, Huw, I'll try. If events in Ireland allow it.'

At dawn the following day they were ready to travel. Tadhg picked ten men, with his cousin Conall to lead them.

'They have two days start, but you will travel quicker. Conall and these men know the land and the people,' Tadhg assured Huw. 'And you probably know where they're heading and who they'll meet.' He raised an eyebrow.

'O'Muinacháin, somewhere north of Kerry,' Huw said what they had both been thinking. 'He has always wanted Bridín for himself.'

'Indeed. So she will be alive. It's you they want dead, and your father.' Tadhg MacCarthy held out his hand for Huw to grasp it. 'Be well and stay alive, Huw Ashe. We will need you now more than ever.'

'You too, Tadhg. If there is any news of my father...'

'We'll find you.'

Huw held and kissed Gwen before two young women came and took her by the hand to go and pick some wild blue flowers.

'Bye, Dada, Bye!' she called as he mounted and turned his horse westwards out of Killarney town.

HISTORICAL NOTE
AND CHARACTERS

IN 1169, AN EXPEDITIONARY force of between 500 and 600 men landed at Bannow Bay, County Wexford, Ireland. This was the starting point of the Norman invasion and settlement; many historians agree that the event marked the beginning of 750 years of English rule over Ireland.

The Norman leaders were barons and knights from Wales and England. The names Anglo-Norman and Cambro-Norman are sometimes used to describe them. They included people of French-Norman, Welsh, English, and Flemish backgrounds, amongst others. Many of the foot soldiers were English and Welsh archers. For clarity, I have used the term 'Norman' to describe the people who came to Ireland during the initial invasion and subsequent settlement.

There are a number of actual historical characters interwoven in the story. Some play an important role and impact on the lives of the main fictional characters. Without the assistance of Sir Robert fitz Stephen and Maurice Regan, Huw Ashe and his fictional family would have struggled to survive and evade their pursuers! The main historical figures include:

Robert fitz Stephen – Norman knight and one of the leaders of the first group of Normans to land in Ireland in 1169. He was one of the earliest to be granted land in Ireland. Fitz Stephen became lord over Wexford town and built what was probably the first Norman motte and bailey (earth and timber castle) in Ireland at Ferrycarrig, Co. Wexford.

Richard fitz Gilbert de Clare – Norman baron enlisted by Diarmaid MacMurrough, King of Leinster, to raise an army to come to Ireland and help him regain his lost kingdom. De Clare is commonly known as Strongbow. Some historians suggest the name 'Strongbow' was introduced much later and de Clare was not known by this name during the period in question; I have used the name Strongbow throughout the text.

Diarmaid MacMurrough, King of Leinster – Dispossessed of his land and kingdom in Ireland by other Irish kings, MacMurrough went to England and France seeking assistance from King Henry II of England. Tacitly, King Henry gave approval for MacMurrough to raise an army by enlisting the help of Norman barons in England and Wales. There are a number of different Irish versions and spellings of the name. I have used the spelling 'Diarmaid MacMurrough' as a simplified form. See the note 'Guide to Pronunciation of Irish/Gaelic Names'.

King Henry II of England (1133 - 1189) – Henry was the first English king to come and lay claim to Ireland. Following the early years of Strongbow's Norman invasion, King Henry landed in County Waterford in October 1171 with a large army. Historians suggest that he came to subdue Strongbow and the other invading barons and ensure their loyalty to him. During his six months in Ireland, Henry also received the sworn fealty of many Irish kings.

Maurice Regan – Secretary/counsel to Diarmaid MacMurrough.

Meiler fitz Henry – A prominent Norman knight during the invasion and later.

Donal O'Brien – King of Thomond (Northern part of present day Munster).

Orla MacMurrough – Daughter of Diarmaid MacMurrough and wife of Donal O'Brien. Again, there are a number of Irish versions of the name. I have kept to the simplified spelling of Orla.

The MacCarthy Mór – The MacCarthys were rulers in southern Munster, mainly Counties Cork and Kerry. The MacCarthy Mór is the name given to the leader of one of the main MacCarthy branches. In this story he is a fictionalised version of The MacCarthy Mór. Even though Tadhg was a common MacCarthy leader's name, his son Tadhg MacCarthy is also a fictional character.

Raymond fitz William Fitzgerald (Le Gros) – Norman knight and leader of the second Norman force to arrive in Ireland, landing at Baginbun, Co.Wexford, in May 1170.

Rory O'Connor – The Irish High King at the time of the Norman invasion. O'Connor and his allies had originally driven Diarmaid MacMurrough from his lands in Leinster and into exile in England.

OTHER AUTHORS AND RESEARCHERS

DURING THE COURSE OF my research, I learned a lot from the work of other writers and researchers. These include:

Goddard Henry Orpen: *'Ireland Under the Normans, 1169-1216.'* Published by the Clarendon Press, Oxford (1911).

Billy Colfer: *'Arrogant Trespass – Anglo-Norman Wexford 1169-1400.'* Published by Duffry Press, Wexford (2002).

Billy Colfer: *'Wexford Castles – Landscape, Context, Settlement.'* Published by Cork University Press (2013).

Conor Kostick: *'Strongbow – The Norman Invasion of Ireland.'* Published by the O'Brien Press, Dublin (2013).

Marie Therese Flanagan: *'Irish Society, Anglo-Norman Settlers, Angevin Kingship – Interactions in Ireland in the Late 12th Century.'* Published by the Clarendon Press, Oxford (1989).

Gerald O'Carroll: *'The Earls of Desmond – The Rise and Fall of a Munster Lordship.'* Published by Gerald O'Carroll, Limerick (2013).

ABOUT THE AUTHOR

GEORGE NASH IS ORIGINALLY from Tipperary and now lives on the Dingle Peninsula, County Kerry, Ireland. The name Nash is of Norman origin (de Náis in Irish). Some sources say that Nash families came to Ireland with the first Normans in 1169. George has always been fascinated with how the Welsh-Norman people integrated into Irish life.

Uneasy Quest is the first in a series set during the early Norman settlement period. The novels chronicle the lives of settler families as they struggle to integrate and make their homes in Ireland. Their life and death stories intermingle with real historical characters and events.

When not writing, George can be found on Castlegregory golf links and supporting Munster Rugby.

He can be contacted by email: george@bizpace.ie.

Printed in Poland
by Amazon Fulfillment
Poland Sp. z o.o., Wrocław

61164393R00176